W9-BEO-704

SHINING AT THE BOTTOM OF THE SEA

ALSO BY STEPHEN MARCHE

Raymond and Hannah

SHINING at the BOTTOM of the SEA

Stephen Marche

RIVERHEAD BOOKS
A MEMBER OF PENGUIN GROUP (USA) INC.
NEW YORK
2007

RIVERHEAD BOOKS
Published by the Penguin Group

Penguin Group (USA) Inc., 375 Hudson Street, New York, New York 10014, USA • Penguin Group (Canada), 90 Eglinton Avenue East, Suite 700, Toronto, Ontario M4P 2Y3, Canada (a division of Pearson Penguin Canada Inc.) • Penguin Books Ltd, 80 Strand, London WC2R 0RL, England • Penguin Ireland, 25 St Stephen's Green, Dublin 2, Ireland (a division of Penguin Books Ltd) • Penguin Group (Australia), 250 Camberwell Road, Camberwell, Victoria 3124, Australia (a division of Pearson Australia Group Pty Ltd) • Penguin Books India Pvt Ltd, 11 Community Centre, Panchsheel Park, New Delhi–110 017, India • Penguin Group (NZ), 67 Apollo Drive, Rosedale, North Shore 0745, Auckland, New Zealand (a division of Pearson New Zealand Ltd) • Penguin Books (South Africa) (Pty) Ltd, 24 Sturdee Avenue, Rosebank, Johannesburg 2196, South Africa

PENGUIN BOOKS LTD, REGISTERED OFFICES:
80 STRAND, LONDON WC2R ORL, ENGLAND

COPYRIGHT © 2007 BY STEPHEN MARCHE
All rights reserved. No part of this book may be reproduced, scanned, or distributed in any printed or electronic form without permission. Please do not participate in or encourage piracy of copyrighted materials in violation of the author's rights. Purchase only authorized editions.
Published simultaneously in Canada

Library of Congress Cataloging-in-Publication Data

Marche, Stephen.
Shining at the bottom of the sea / Stephen Marche.
p. cm.
Includes bibliographical references.
ISBN 978-1-59448-941-9
1. Experimental fiction. I. Title.
PR9199.4.M345S55 2007 2007008664
813'.6—dc22

Printed in the United States of America
1 3 5 7 9 10 8 6 4 2

BOOK DESIGN BY HENRY PHMK, ARTE DEL FUEGO

This is a work of fiction. Names, characters, places, and incidents either are the product of the author's imagination or are used fictitiously, and any resemblance to actual persons, living or dead, businesses, companies, events, or locales is entirely coincidental.

While the author has made every effort to provide accurate telephone numbers and Internet addresses at the time of publication, neither the publisher nor the author assumes any responsibility for errors, or for changes that occur after publication. Further, the publisher does not have any control over and does not assume any responsibility for author or third-party websites or their content.

To Sarah

CONTENTS

FOREWORD BY LEONARD KING 11

PREFACE BY STEPHEN MARCHE 15

THE PAMPHLETS AND EARLY FICTIONEERS

F. R. Fisher, *The Destruction of Marlyebone, the Private King* 37

Camden Mahone, *Pigeon Blackhat* 40

Julian Back, *Professor Saintfrancis and the Diamants of the End of the World* 72

Arcadio Cole, *Von Lettow-Vorbeck, Africa's White Lion* 82

George Jankin Lee, *An Interlude at the Opera* 88

UPHEAVALS AND INDEPENDENCE

Blessed Shirley, *Sufferance Row* 97

Elizabeth Rushton, *Two Stories About the Abandon Tree* 111

Augustus P. Jenkins, *The Master's Dog* 113

Cornelia Tristanos, *The Christbird* 128

Ira Rushton, *Ultimate Testament* 133

Leonard King, *To Be Read at the Hour of Independence* 136

Morley Straights, *An Old Man Mourns for His Blind Daughter* 139

Caesar Hill, *Flotsam and Jetsam* 144

EXILE AND RETURN

Charity Gurton, *Men* 155

Trinity Hopps, *Under the Skin* 159

Leonard King, *Histories of Aenea by Various Things* 166

Cato Dekkerman, *A Wedding in Restitution* 178

Marcel Henri, *The Man Friday's Review of* Robinson Crusoe 198

Octavia Kitteredge-Mann, *The End of the Beach* 202

CRITICISM

Ernest Hemingway, *Letter to John Dos Passos* 213

Sherlock Cole, *On the Motif of the Shipwreck as History* 214

Blessed Shirley, *Why It Is Imperative to Pay Close Attention to Detail* 219

Richard Williams, *Comparative Biographies of Elizabeth and Ira Rushton* 221

Arcadio Skelton, *A Note on a Code in Morley Straights* 227

Octavia Dickens, *Language in Charity Gurton's* Men and Other Stories 231

Two Reviews of A Wedding in Restitution 235

An Interview with Octavia Kitteredge-Mann 239

BIOGRAPHICAL NOTES 245

ACKNOWLEDGEMENTS 253

SHINING AT THE BOTTOM OF THE SEA

FOREWORD

Sanjanians are perhaps the most literary people on earth. Bookstalls are as common as fruit stands, the theatres around Saint Magdalene's Square dwarf the City Hall, and on Sanjair flights the stewards push small carts of books down the aisle after the beverages and pretzels. Nearly a thousand people, I remember, filled the auditorium for my first public reading after I slunk home from exile in 1994. I also remember a young woman who stood up during the question period at the end to ask, in a tone between greeting and accusation, the way a mother might speak to a mischievous child returning from a day's pranks: "Where have you been?"

She was a beautiful young woman. She had tucked a tiger lily behind her right ear for the occasion.

At the time, I muttered how I had lived in Rome and Paris, with stints in London, as if the question had been posed literally. For many years after, I wished I had replied, "I've been here all along," as I had been in spirit. Today, if that young, beautiful woman were to appear to me with that tiger lily in her hair and her lips blooming with that bold question, I would simply hand her *Shining at the Bottom of the Sea*, the book that you hold in your hands. These stories transport me into myself.

Let me explain. When I was a boy, family loyalty dictated that I help out in the inventory room during busy times at my uncle's haberdashery on the Port Hope Mall. I spent many bright childhood Saturdays in a windowless room among hatboxes. Fortunately I was not alone. A small cabinet of old pamphlets that my uncle had carried with him from our home cove kept me company. That dusty back room thronged with daring men and dangerous women, and their joys and hatreds and confusion. My favourites, I remember, were the Professor Saintfrancis stories. I adored following that crippled genius, like an intellectual toreador, skewering Portlands crime by hearsay alone.

At college, in an even darker room than the back of my uncle's shop, a friend who was later beaten to death in Simpson Street Gaol for dreaming beautiful dreams about the future of his country handed me my first Blessed Shirley story. I believed. At one reading, I believed. Not only could we face political reality through our fiction, we had to. And I remember being given a copy of "The Master's Dog" by Jenkins, copied by hand because of the ban imposed after its single print run twenty-five years earlier. We all believed then.

The struggles of my own work I must pass over. I don't remember much anyway: desks in various cities, flat surfaces between windows and beds, blind fury then at times floating free as though my thoughts were puffed full of helium. I recall crowds cheering my name in the public squares in Port Hope, and the polite applause of award ceremonies far, far from Sanjania.

Stories carried me home too, and my vanity cherishes the accidental fortune of having taught both Charity Gurton and Trinity Hopps introductory classes on Sanjanian literature. (I also taught two murderers and a Minister of Ocean Affairs.) And only five years ago, through my Sanjanian Graduate Seminar, I met Stephen Marche, our anthologist, the perfect shade of visitor to give us "the photograph from the outer," as Kitteredge-Mann puts it (or "the fresh air of the barbarian city," as I wrote in *Melody*). His choices in this anthology have surprised me in the most intimate way.

Some may ask if the world needs more Sanjanian fiction. My shelves are lined with anthologies already: *Early Sanjanian Novels*, *The Pamphlets of Sanjan Island*, *The Trumpet Supplement Fictions*, *Sanjanian Interludes*. The answer is still yes. All those other editions, including the two I myself edited, were limited by strict divisions of genre and era, while the anthology you hold in your hands opens up the varied life of the Sanjanian story as a whole, which is the best possible introduction to the tortured, complex country itself. Stories are our blood and guts. They are the most real part of us.

To the girl with the tiger lily behind her ear, I have just one more thought to add. A fictioneer whose name escapes me once wrote that the only true preface is the reader's brain. Just so. I commend this book to you who need no preface.

Leonard King
PORT HOPE UNIVERSITY

PREFACE

Should I study or should I travel? The dilemma struck me when I was living in Sanjania for the first time, taking a series of graduate courses with Leonard King at Port Hope University. I had saved a little money and wanted to use it properly, so I sought Leonard's advice. Should I pursue more academic work or head "to the boatshore"? His answer has stayed with me even though I didn't fully understand it at the time. "Opening a new book is like steering your boat into an unknown corner of the ocean," he said.

The following summer I decided on a small adventure, a circumnavigation of Sanjania. An old sailor named Easter Swift, who had circumnavigated the island seven times before, undertook the journey with me, guiding us through the devious covelets onto the immaculate beaches of their freshwater rivers. The calm of natural harbours offset the blind rage of the North Atlantic, and the proximity to the Tols, a range of inland mountains, created otherworldly climates which were sometimes paradisiacal, sometimes demoniacal, always one extreme or the other. The landscape was so gorgeous and intriguing that I even considered giving up the second year of my Fellowship in the fall.

A proverb says that a man is more at home in a Sanjanian cove than he is at home, and the strangers who put us at their tables and under their roofs proved it. In the wood house of a fishing family in Openroar Cove, North Sanjania, I found a copy of *The Masks of the Dance of the End of the World*, Leonard's second collection of essays. Its opening paragraph still haunts me:

> You are standing in a bookshop, reader. You think you are standing in a bookshop, the Lord knows where, some Godforsaken globe corner. You think so, but you are mistaken, for you are at the wheel of a great ship, and you are piloting the vessel far from the shore into the dark, secret, terrible compartments of the ocean of me.[1]

And so I abandoned travel and took up archives. Leonard claims now that he wasn't thinking of the passage the day I sought his advice, and I won't contradict him.

When I returned to the library, I was resuming a journey begun in childhood. I remember, among the collection of books in my family's basement, a fat anthology of Commonwealth literature, which I speedily devoured. Those stories opened many worlds to me, but my favourites were without question the pamphlets from the Sanjan Colony, as it was then called. Langston Hughes has written that they possess "the heady flavours of sweet mud one must eat with a silver spoon."[2] Betsy McGrath based her

1. Leonard King, *The Masks of the Dance of the End of the World* (Port Hope: Penguin Sanjania, 1963), 7.

2. Langston Hughes, *Literary Occasions* (New York: Defoe, Strabo & Carving, 1938), 275.

early poetry on the more melodramatic pirate and love stories, and remembered them in her memoirs as "the shadows of my other selves."[3] George Orwell also loved the pamphlets: "There is a kind of narrative frankness to these stories, and a secrecy too, which one finds both comforting and discomfiting. They remind me of a childhood I never had."[4] Those first glimpses of the Sanjanian story in the Commonwealth collection produced a similarly powerful reaction in me.

Perhaps that is why I find it so distressing that Sanjanian writing is virtually unknown in Europe and America and, when discussed at all, is loaded with the mystique of the country's colonial past, its tortured political history, and the shady reputation of the banking centres in its port capital. Almost universally the island's literature is portrayed as the product of vice or revolution. The first task of this anthology is to illustrate that Sanjanian writing is the product of human beings who cannot be reduced to scoundrels or ideologues. I believe that by shining an honest ray of light onto the life of the Sanjanian story in all its variety—high and low, theoretical and earthy, idealistic and cynical, old and new—the usual oversimplifications and prejudices will fall away. The distinction of this anthology is inclusivity: while I had space only for the best, most readable stories, the selection had to provide the broad view.

On those terms, I offer you this collection with confidence at least in the material. You have never read anything like it. Here indeed is a secret compartment of the sea. But first a brief overview of Sanjania's major literary developments, as the growth of fiction in Sanjania is a fascinating story in its own right. That

---

3. Elizabeth McGrath, *How the Moon Shone* (New York: Defoe, Strabo & Carving, 1946), 15.

4. George Orwell, *Selected Literary Journalism* (Abbotsford: The Colour Press, 1998), 389.

said, feel free to jump directly to the fiction if you want to read without my meddling; the stories in this collection do not require background to be understood or enjoyed.

Books have always been one of the first things visitors to Sanjania notice. *Stark's Illustrated*, the first tourist's guide to the Sanjan Colony, remarked in 1898:

> Besides theatre, there are pamphlet stories to amuse the curious visitor. If you are fishing in the coves and the weather is not all that it might be, a pamphlet is as good a way as any to while away the afternoon. Much can be learned about the country this way too; they are the simple stories of a simple people. Pirates, smugglers, soldiers and priests mingle freely in their pages. You will also find valuable moral instruction sprinkled liberally throughout Sanjanian tales. The proverbial wisdom that is so typical to the conversation in this climate is not excluded from its fiction.

The tourist's eye has not developed much in a hundred years. The entry for Port Hope in *Let's Go: Sanjania 2005* opens with

> Start your exploration of Port Hope at **Saint Magdalene's Square**, right next to the water on the city's East side. The large blue and white building to the South is **City Hall** (open Mon.–Fri. 10 am–4 pm, Sat. 10 am–1 pm). To the East, West and North are Port Hope's major showplaces, **The Leopard's Spots** (for theatre), **The Gazelle** (for opera) and **The Curtain** (for movies). A night out at the shows is an absolute must for any visitor to Sanjania but there's another reason to make sure you check out Saint Magdalene's. Seemingly endless bookstalls fill the square's edge and spill into the side streets in every direction. Bargain hunters and literature lovers cram every nook and cranny from sunrise (more or less) to sundown (more or less).

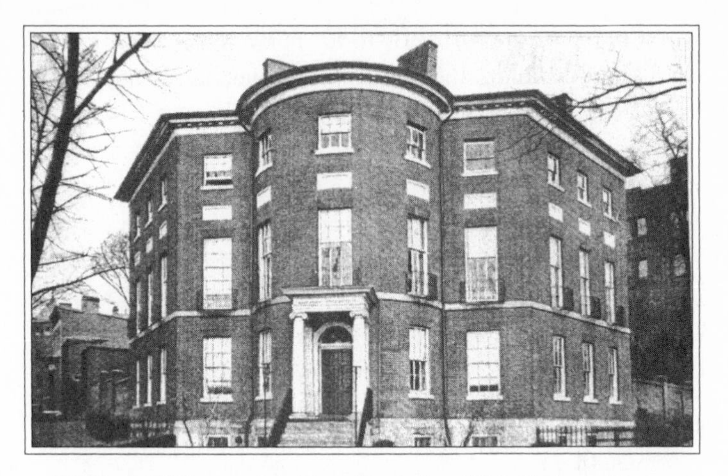

The National Library and Archives of Sanjania, which holds the world's largest collection of Sanjanian pamphlets, stands at the corner of Port Hope Mall and Thursday Street.

So it goes. Because the tourist traps in Sanjania are bookstores, tourists return to their home countries convinced of the old cliché that it is "a country like one big bookstore." They tell their friends, "The opera house is bigger than City Hall." They show off the cheap remaindered copies they bought at the Saint Magdalene's bazaar and maybe a strange pamphlet, strangely bound in white wool, with strange little stories inside. They won't be able to explain the pamphlet, what it is or where it came from, but they will know it's a find.

The tourist isn't alone in his ignorance. Like many of the murky details in Sanjania's early history, the emergence of pamphlet literature on Sanjan Island has only a partial, incomplete aetiology. The government vessels, or the geevees as they are commonly called, began circumnavigating the island on a regular basis in the 1870s. Sometime in the 1890s, the geevees began delivering close-printed, yellow-papered booklets haphazardly crammed with stories, news and illustrations and bound typically by figure eights of white wool. Lucrecio Dundad, in *A Guide to the Pamphlets*,[5] argues that Colonial Office clerks introduced these fictions and humourous anecdotes in order to encourage registration for the purposes of levying taxes, but his claim has been disputed in at least two recent articles.[6]

We do know, at least, that for roughly sixty years, the pamphleteers distributed little books filled, at first, with installments of surefire sellers like Scott, Dickens, Stevenson and Conan Doyle. Because of the irregularity of delivery no reader was guaranteed to receive the sequel, or to have the previous installment, to the story he or she was purchasing.[7] Nonetheless, pamphlet sales were outstandingly brisk, even before fictions written by Sanjanians were included in 1891.[8] In that year, Samuel Tayler placed an advertisement above the instructions for the levy on coffee after the last installment of *Nicholas Nickleby*, asking for "tales specifically from those of the Sanjan nation, to delight, to amuse and to instruct, compact enough for inclusion in a pamphlet, such as the one you now hold."

Though the advertisment ran in pamphlets sold principally to covedwellers, the few writers who responded were overwhelmingly from the city, which was already home to several vibrant theatres and possessed an equally lively church-writing tradition. Many of the first story writers were fly-by-night operators work-

---

5. Lucrecio Dundad, *A Guide to the Pamphlets* (London: The Hammond Press, 1997).

6. Aurelius Baxter, "The Valediction of Geevees: How the Good News Got from Hope to Lent," *Sanjanian Literary Renaissance* 17 (1999): 135–78, and Jonathan Heath, "A Note on Pamphlet Taxation," *Notes, Queries, and Responses* 291: 23–25.

7. For a fascinating and often hilarious look at how the villages created their own versions out of these fragmentary novels, see Goodfriday Forster, "Cove Ivanhoes," *Sanjan Writing* 4.1 (2003): 3–43.

8. Michael Airhart, "Sales Figures for Early Sanjan Houses," *Notes, Queries, and Responses* 165: 1034–53.

Government vessels, or geevees, brought to the coastal towns whatever the sea could not, literature included.

ing for fly-by-night presses. A story's length seems to have been determined by the printing space available. Issues of language also contributed to the genre's happy chaos, since each cove developed if not an individual dialect then at least a distinctive slang. Though the coves were filled with sailors, locals rarely visited each other's communities, and so regional sensibilities and characteristics developed in surprisingly short periods of time. Michael Airhart was not exaggerating much when he wrote: "Men went to sea for fish, not for other men. Communities fifteen minutes apart could not understand their neighbours."[9] The differing patois resulted in a mish-mash of writing styles as varied as the voices of "the impossible island," sometimes confusing to a general audience.

Despite these problems, Sanjanians loved their own stories

9. Michael Airhart, *Echoes in a Garden Pot: The Aetiology of C-tongues* (Port Hope: Port Hope University Press, 1989), 7.

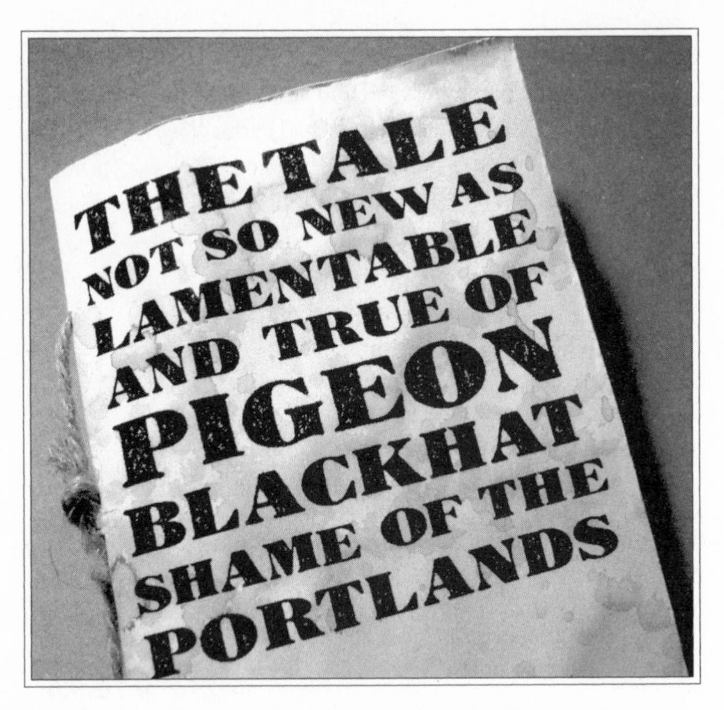

From 1901 to 1913, twenty-six editions of the Pigeon Blackhat pamphlet were printed and distributed Sanjania-wide.

and the market burgeoned.[10] Folk legends like "The Destruction of Marlyebone, the Private King" sustained the Port Hope printing houses with long runs. Slowly, niches expanded for church-writing (like "Pigeon Blackhat"), colonial propaganda, articles of scientific interest, and educational materials. An occasional piece like "Von Lettow-Vorbeck, Africa's White Lion" might explore

10. How rural Sanjanians, most living in crushing poverty, developed such a sophisticated literary market has been explored in many different contexts. See Leonard King's *Origin Is the Goal* (Port Hope: Penguin Sanjania, 2005); Antony Paulson, *Why We Read* (London: Foldham, Golding & Co., 1994); Anne Chatwin-Botton, *Ferocious Love* (Port Hope: The Blossoming Tree Press, 1982); and Cornelia Banks, *In Time All Things Are Written in the Book of Judgement* (Port Hope: The Sanjanian Publishers, 1995).

real political situations semi-fictionally, but the overwhelming hunger that the pamphlets fed and stoked was for escapist mysteries and romances. Conan Doyle had and still has a cult following in Sanjania—one still meets men named Sherlock, Arthur and Watson on the street—but the mania extended to jewel-thief stories in general. The most popular Sanjanian example of the genre was Julian Back's Professor Saintfrancis series, represented here by a late story, "Professor Saintfrancis and the Diamants of the End of the World."

The original operation, the largest and most stable of the presses, continued to belong to Samuel Tayler, who set up offices in the Portlands district. The majority of pamphlets that survive today were written between 1903 and 1922, at the height of the Tayler House period. Samuel Tayler began his professional life as an unsuccessful theatrical agent who discovered that "[he] could hire and pay [theatrical] writers without the trouble and expense of the production [of plays]."[11] His house on Brake Street, where his presses also slept, was famously open all hours, and writers in need of extra money could hand in their wares at any time. "The little house on Brake Street" is a legend of productivity. Nowhere else was so much work, of so much importance to Sanjanian letters, produced in so short a period.

No one disputes that the fictioneers earned their position in Sanjania's literary pantheon: this is work that nourishes and endures, despite hardship, isolation and terrible seas. Pamphlets are the "hard tack" of Sanjanian literature. Caesar Little even mentioned them in his speech on the occasion of Independence:

> Let us also remember that we are born with a literature, we are born like Hercules with a club in our fist, and a story in our

11. Samuel Tayler, *Tayler Papers and Documents* (Port Hope: Port Hope University Press, 1972), 54. See also the beginning to the tenth chapter of Marshall's *Wine Through a Sieve* (Port Hope: Clamour House Press, 1992).

> mouths. Yes, compatriots, even at this hour, fresh from the womb, we may go back over our memories, in those fictions and pamphlets which every father read to every son in every distant strand. The preaching of valour and compassion are our true birthright, and in this too, are we not great?[12]

Because pamphlet collections were carefully, lovingly, preserved in each cove, often to be read aloud as public entertainment, their influence survived long past the period of their dissemination, and also probably contributed somewhat to the demise of their profitability. Schools in isolated outposts to this day use their worn and dog-eared pamphlet collections. Caesar Hill, born after the war, recalled being read "The Destruction of Marlyebone" on the beach by his grandfather.

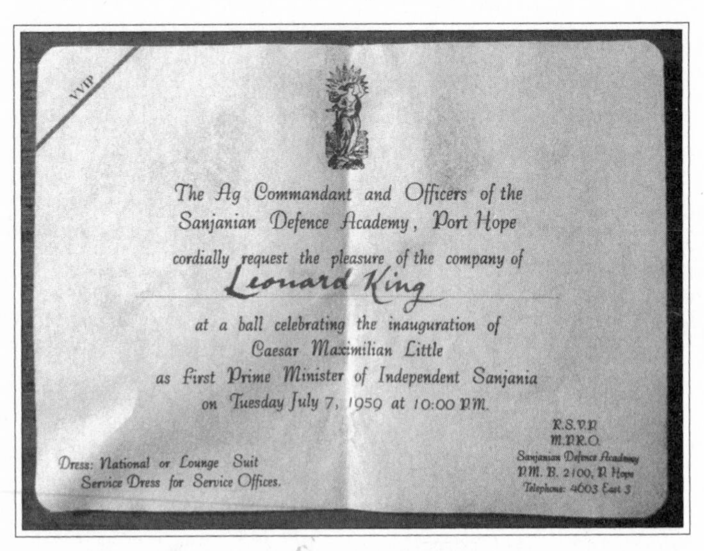

VVIP

The Ag Commandant and Officers of the
Sanjanian Defence Academy, Port Hope
cordially request the pleasure of the company of
Leonard King
at a ball celebrating the inauguration of
Caesar Maximilian Little
as First Prime Minister of Independent Sanjania
on Tuesday July 7, 1959 at 10:00 P.M.

R.S.V.P.
M.P.R.O.
Sanjanian Defence Academy
P.M.B. 2100, P. Hope
Telephone: 4603 East 3

Dress: National or Lounge Suit
Service Dress for Service Offices.

Over 10,000 copies of Leonard King's story "To Be Read at the Hour of Independence" sold on Port Hope corners during Independence Day celebrations.

---

12. Caesar Little, July 7, 1959.

It would be wrong, however, to overrate the significance of pamphlets, and fiction generally, to Sanjanian audiences. Theatre is beyond question the dominant literary form in Sanjania. Sanjanian writers have won all of their international prizes for drama, with the exception of Octavia Kitteredge-Mann's surprise victory at the Iveys for her novel *Apples and Oranges*. In the city, pamphlets were known as "getpennies," and they were sold at Saint Magdalene's Square to those who could not afford tickets to the theatre. The original pamphlet readers were Sanjanians who could not get into a play: the poor and the rural. Many of the early stories reworked dramas into pamphlet form and few writers, if any, survived solely on pamphlet writing, whereas playwrights could and did get by on stage work.

Within three decades, the Tayler writers had become victims of their own success. The market for fiction, always so steady in the coves, spread into Port Hope itself, and in 1928, *The Sanjan Trumpet*, the country's first truly national newspaper, was born out of the ashes of *The Port Hope Gazette*. Cornelia Banks, in a recent article, writes that "if the Tayler House died, there is transmigration of souls. . . . The writers, the spirit and the audience became *The Trumpet*."[13] The number of government circumnavigations of the island had increased, which made monthly delivery of a newspaper to the coves profitable for the first time.

From the beginning, *The Sanjanian Trumpet* published stories and tales, at first merely to do away with lingering competition from the pamphleteers, then to fulfill the expectations of their readers. The *Cove Supplement* always had one longer story and one shorter one. George Jankin Lee was among the best loved of the *Supplement* writers. His warm self-deprecating humour,

13. Cornelia Banks, "The Myth of Er . . . : The Transmigration of Literary Identity and the Case of the First *Trumpet* Supplements," *Sanjanian Literary Renaissance* 19 (2001): 89–109.

deep religious sensibility, and fascination with the uncanny were traits his audience loved and shared. "An Interlude at the Opera" is the quintessential example of a long *Supplement* story, full of atmosphere and luxurious setting. Religious stories were also a standby, and are represented in this collection by "The Christbird" from Cornelia Tristanos, which oddly prefigures the techniques of magic realism. The many Sanjanian collections of *Supplement* fictions are filled with such surprises. They seem, at least to this reader, like a pulp magazine peppered with the *avant garde*. Looking over this anthology, I'm shocked to find that we only have two selections from *The Trumpet*. The fact speaks eloquently to the strength of the short story during the period.

National self-awareness and pride, rising steadily since the First World War, were finding other outlets in the thirties. When Blessed Shirley founded *The Real Story*, the idea of a Sanjanian literary journal was as unprecedented as the stories in its pages, which were plain, spare descriptions of the real lives of ordinary Sanjanians. The financial support of Shirley's father, who owned two shoe stores in Port Hope, managed to keep the journal afloat for eight issues during 1931 and 1932, but finding realist writers was as much of a challenge as building an audience for the material. Even in its brief life, however, *The Real Story* stirred up important debates and brought a level of self-consciousness to literature as yet unknown on the island. The introduction of contemporary European and American literary ideas developed almost instantly into aggressive modern tales like Elizabeth Rushton's ultra-short and ultra-elegant "Two Stories About the Abandon Tree," which was published in the magazine's final issue.

Blessed Shirley is also known as the founder of the "clean school" of writing, which attempted to connect the varied cove tongues by a kind of stylistic Esperanto. His idea, demonstrated in "Sufferance Row," was to bring a simplicity of language and

The remains of the Abandon Tree still stand on the small island at the head of Marginal Cove.

sentence structure to stories which would be comprehensible to anyone in any cove. Much political writing during the upheavals, up to and including the "coded" fictions written around the time of the Independence, was modeled on Shirley's style.[14] His clearest descendants were the editors of *The Abyssinian*, founded in 1936. While primarily a political newsletter, published by the SPUA (Sanjanian Port Union Authority) to promote Socialism and to oppose the invasion of Ethiopia, the journal also published a handful of short stories, like Gus Jenkins' "The Master's Dog." *The Abyssinian* produced only a single glorious issue before its offices were shut down, and when it flashed up again, in the hands of enraged veterans during the Portlands riots of 1946, it did not publish any fiction.

For the next two decades, after the Colonial government closed almost all presses, the pro-Independence movement did use underground fiction to make political statements that plays, due to censorship, could not, but successes were few and minor.

14. For an interesting survey of the debates about Sanjanian modernism, see Cornelia Banks, *Sanjanian Literary Modernism* (Port Hope: Port Hope University Press, 1993).

The Impossible Island, in Toronto's Kensington Market, stocks over four hundred eaux-de-vie and hosts readings from Sanjanian authors every Wednesday evening.

Ira Rushton's "Ultimate Testament" is the most celebrated of the surviving pieces. Political fiction remained underground until the Hope Mall Massacre of April 23, 1956, whose forty-seven deaths of men, women and children shocked the world. The acquittal of the British officer Harlow a year later was a seismic event for Sanjanian life and literature, whetting political resolve for Independence in the general public, and subsuming all other national interests. In writing and living both, the Sanjanians were no longer content to be the Colonial underling of "Britishers." Leonard King's "To Be Read at the Hour of Independence" captures the euphoria of the dawn of self-rule; Morley Straights' terrifying "An Old Man Mourns for His Blind Daughter" doubly demonstrates the perversion of the regime which immediately followed it. Not only must the old man mourn the death of his generation's political ideals, but he must do so in circumspect allegories, so as not to ruffle the "grocer" and the "landlady."

The coded fiction of Straights still adhered to the national and political ideals of Blessed Shirley and Gus Jenkins, and could not last in the political environment of Caesar Little's government, which had learned a great deal about oppression from the British. The revolutionary censors were not easily duped, or not for long. For more than a decade following 1965 no word was heard from the island. So many, including so many excellent writers, perished in the Biddy Crackdowns. Caesar Hill called it "the Great Silence" in his book on the terror.

Into the silence flooded the voices of the Sanjanian Diaspora. Sanjanian identity in the twenty-first century is in large part an identity of exile, by way of communities in London, Brooklyn and Toronto. "Flotsam and Jetsam" by Caesar Hill, a complex and humbling work, could not be excluded from any anthology hoping to give a portrait of Sanjanity, and yet he renounced his citizenship in 1972 for political reasons. Repamphletization brought the old Sanjanian practice to a world stage: stories travel hand to hand, not by a geevee circumnavigating the coves, but by manuscripts moving from bar to bar and from classroom to classroom. The Sanjanian Diaspora has produced some of the island's richest literary expressions. Octavia Kitteredge-Mann comes to mind first because she grows better-known, it seems, by the hour, but she is far from alone. Marcel Henri is of Sanjanian descent but has never lived in Sanjania, in fact has never visited the island, and yet "The Man Friday's Review of *Robinson Crusoe*" is in its own way a story perfectly representative of the Sanjanian character and its distinctive voice. Cato "Sandy" Dekkerman, with "A Wedding in Restitution," has brought Sanjanian character to the world twice—first with the story, then with the film.

Many writers returned from exile with the amnesty of 1992, the opening of the port in that year, and the simultaneous declaration of a free press. Leonard King, Charity Gurton, and Trinity Hopps were among that group and they are all included here. Gurton and Hopps present something of a literary Janus: "Men" looks back to the cove languages which are always at the root of Sanjanian fiction; "Under the Skin" looks forward to the new forms and new voices developing out of the tradition. These styles range from the essayistic "Histories of Aenea" to the hypnotic poetry of "The End of the Beach."

As for the future, there is more potential than ever. I have my own theories about its direction and destiny, but I will let Octavia Kitteredge-Mann have the last word. She recently gave a statement of her vision in an interview with *Japan Folders*:

> JF: Where does a frontier start?
> OKM: I find it interesting that you should choose that word. "Frontier." Because there are no frontiers anymore. Nobody believes in outer space. There is no frontier in America anymore, either, which is interesting. Sanjania was once on the frontier. I will say one thing, there is one feature of the island, everyone stays on the borders, on the sea. Very few people live in the mountains in the centre. And so the mountains are the frontier.
> JF: So the frontier is interior?
> OKM: Exactly.
> JF: And this is a feature of Sanjanian literature?
> OKM: I think perhaps it is not only Sanjania that has the limit inside. I think it is also perhaps Japan. I think it is also any decent novel or story. The interior is infinite, you know. The frontier, we have seen, it ends. Where is the centre? Where is the core? That will go on forever.
> JF: Do you feel this applies to you personally as well?
> OKM: I am my own country.[15]

15. "Interview with Octavia Kitteredge-Mann," *Japan Folders*, Winter 2003: 135–40.

Birds are a common theme on Sanjanian postage.

Before I go, I ought to confess my failures as an anthologist, since my sins (mostly of omission) are many and great. Carving a single volume from a literature as diverse as Sanjania's was dizzying in its difficulty, and while I tried to make myself as open as possible, the decisions were ultimately personal. I suppose any anthology reveals more about its editor than its subject. A book of the authors I excluded, I know, would make as interesting and representative an anthology as this one. I could have chosen, for example, the British writers living in the Sanjan Colony during the eighteenth and nineteenth centuries. They mainly wrote poetry, but some of it was long narrative poetry, like William Marsh's "Fort Saint John" with its famous opening quatrain:

> Where the clouds over the deeps aroam
> Beyond the wafts o' th'ocean foam
> And choirs of mermaids do make moan
> In Fort Saint John I am alone.

The petroglyphs on Mount Ruby in Sanjania's interior are the only surviving artifacts of the island's indigenous population.

I did not include them because, to me, these are not Sanjanian writers, but British writers living in Sanjania, and third-rate British writers at that. Living on the island is not enough of a qualification—otherwise I would have included the Mount Ruby petroglyphs.[16]

Beyond the obvious challenges facing the editor of any anthology—what to include and why—there was a specific question I had to consider in the preparation of this book, which is principally aimed at non-native readers: How much contextualization of Sanjanian life and culture should be provided? My own predis-

16. Sherlock Cole in his *Introduction to Sanjanian Literature* from 1963 demonstrates convincingly that the petroglyphs in the Mount Ruby cave do form a continuous narrative, either about a hunt or the performance of an initiation ritual involving animal masks. Other than a few arrowheads, these petroglyphs are the only evidence we have of Sanjania's original inhabitants. The records of the Spanish raiders show that, between 1520 and 1532, the entire population, 17,521 men, women and children, were taken from Saint John Island as slaves. All perished in the New World mines in what must be the most complete genocide in history. Not one word of their language, not even their name for themselves, survives.

position was to provide none at all, but a few of my colleagues at the National Library, in particular the always rigorous and practical Mary Wellings, offered compelling reasons to include detailed annotations.

The example that came up most often in our discussions was the spilling greeting, a Sanjanian custom performed as a gesture of hospitality. When two or more persons share an alcoholic beverage, tea or coffee, it is considered polite to spill a drop or two onto the ground—or, in a host's home, onto a plate, where it can be quickly wiped up. Records of this practice have been documented well back into the nineteenth century, and the majority of scholars attribute it to an imitation of ship launches during the Victorian period, when Sanjan's shipbuilding industry was at its height. It is true that a reader without direct knowledge of Sanjanian life would be unaware of the tradition, and hence misunderstand several key moments in the collection's stories. Nonetheless, to include such an explanation begs the question of how many explanations to give—a basic account of the gesture's current significance, a summary of its history, or my own interpretation? Even Leonard King's casual reference to the Sanjan swallow in "To Be Read at the Hour of Independence" needs a description of the flightless bird itself, its near-extinction after the settlement of the island and the recent attempts at reintroduction. In the end, I thought it better to let the reader figure these things out for him- or herself. The fiction here should above all be read as fiction, and not as anthropological data. Joy is the point. If the reader is looking for knowledge of Sanjania from an historical perspective, I can recommend *A Survey of Sanjanian History* by Sarah Belmuto, and *Sanjanian Life and Manners* by Michael Barnes-Jones, or the more recent *When the World's on Fire*, edited by Trin Hopps. For the interested reader, Goodfriday Forster, Mary Wellings and I have also compiled a small collection of criticism, found in an appendix at the back of the book, as an introduction to the varied interpretations surrounding these stories.

On the maps of the world, the Island of Sanjania is little more than an invisible dot in the middle of the North Atlantic, almost in danger of becoming a phantom island like mythical Frisland, the Isle of Demons, or Buss. Treat this anthology then, not as a complete atlas to one island's literature, but as a first glance over its magnificent landscape, before maps, before surveys, before names have been given to places. My hope is to bring its wonderful stories to the eyes of a world that barely knows it exists. I too, like Fisher, the first writer of this collection, wish "to be a wind on the wild waters so that they know it breathed," but above all I want to share with other readers these stories that have given me so much pleasure. Enough of me. Enjoy.

Stephen Marche
NATIONAL LIBRARY AND
ARCHIVES OF SANJANIA

THE PAMPHLETS

AND

EARLY FICTIONEERS

THE DESTRUCTION OF MARLYEBONE, THE PRIVATE KING

F. R. Fisher

NO DATES

For the sake of readability and accessibility, the spelling and in some cases the syntax of this story have been normalized.—S.M.

Wherever they may be, and wherever they may be from, all men do relish a hanging. The Drama of Law, with its Crime and its Punish and its splendid gibbet Finish, musters healthy crowds alltimes, but when Marlyebone hung, no bell clung, no bottle glugged on the greengrass, no flowerpath strewed to the noose. No crowd, not a body, overwatched the Destruction of that Private King. Here's why so.

In his eighteenth year, Marlyebone oxchopped and mangled the other wolfheads Goodfriday Martins, Samuel Baker Deloney, Abraham Crisp and Lover Gomes, and claimed the overward. In his nineteenth year, the Crown pursued him. Crownagent Keagan Poulter took a bulletsmash in the face and could not be regaliated. Agent Will Champion's moniker fibbed everafter his failure. Robert Strunk sunk. In Marlyebone's twentieth year, his Scourge Sally Parkman, a Woman Crownagent, grabbed the pirate fleet, and yawled it against the waves of Portuguese Cove, and Marlyebone scuppered with his sister Virginia and his goodfriend Moses Tumbledown overhill byland toward his homecove Restitution, flittering.

In that Fatal Fight, Tumbledown had connived to scape the ravages of their Vessel's Capsize but Marlyebone was grazed over the bellyfront, and a Crown ball caromed his sister Virginia above the hip. She was truly near dead, so Tumbledown and Marlyebone hamperlegged Virginia between them. Gutshocked, windundered, brinesoaked, our three stopped in the Forestblankets to staunch wounds panting and shivering in the starlessness, and that's where they talked one to another.

Tumbledown, first, to Marlyebone. "Sally Parkman owns this Wildness."

"The nearest haven?" Marlyebone, patting his still-bleeding flank with tohand Slushmoss.

"Waiting Cove. Command me."

"Oath me no oaths," Marlyebone, "but go to it and wait."

Moses Tumbledown was so monikered because Marlyebone had rescued him from flotsam on open sea, shipwrecked, so Tumbledown left brother and sister in a Silence dark and daft to him, Godlike.

Marlyebone turned to his Wound, turned to his sister who moaned in the Dark beyond Words. In her todeath eyes which seemed to scrape the coraline Mysteries, Marlyebone, softly, simply, "Virginia, our Fates are grappled together and I will never leave you but Sally Parkman slides by morning so if you want me to live, don't die tomorrow, die tonight."

Thus Sally Parkman shackled and darbied the Private King next dew. The scenario is tattooed on many sailor backs, but it has as many meanings as muscles roiling under it. Sally Parkman rises to clap wires on the wrists of the pirate. Only sailors with Shipwrecks and Lostloves behind them may have that scenario inked on their fleshes, a wellknown. Here was a man who once dragged a mutineer under keel, until skin flayed from the poor man's roundbits, the faintest whisper of a crosspurpose to him on the sea and the whisperer was soon whispering through a cutthroat, but Marlyebone waited by Virginia's side, still-and-always, until his lockup, and they massacred his crew, all but Tumbledown, and they chummed his sister's afterdeath, for spite.

Avoid the Finger of Oblivion, that's half the bigness, two-thirds of the surface of the earth Oceanshrouded, the horror of it. Maybe there's another truth to the Shipwreck of Marlyebone too.

I mean rough men tell rough tales. Church and Crown sleep well in our Coves, if they do toss-me turn-me in strange dreams also. Seamen and schoolboys gathering around spilled liquor or liquorice laugh at the Marlyebone murders and lawflights, finestanders as they are.

Ask any covefellow to tell the true end to that atrocious man. He will account that the Trial lasted one Clockround solo, that the criminal Private King was summary hanged on the twentieth anniversary of the day of his birth, refused the chance for Famous Last Words. Not one from Waiting Cove came out to his Crown-murder by hanging, and reports do tell that even the figuremen turned their heads away when that body, so fraught with Hope and Corruptness, undertrapped the whole world.

Not a body overwatched the Destruction of the Private King, I've said why so.

PIGEON BLACKHAT

Camden Mahone

1881 – 1963

As with "The Destruction of Marlyebone," spelling has been normalized. See the biographical note for a brief description of the "scandal of identity" (Trampasano's phrase) surrounding Mahone's work. —S.M.

You have already heard my story through another's mouth I imagine, for there is no covetown without its crashedwoman, and mine is a tale not so new as lamentable and true. The freshness resides in its purpose and conclusion, which I hope to make the common ending, for Jesus Christ has spoken that

Salvation is open to all

and my story is proof.

As a young one, I never knew the city but by report. The village of Lydiat on the Western coast of Sanjan Island gave me life, a cove so removed from the urbane commerce of the nation that a mere two or three in a decade might hazard the journey to Port Hope, lengthy by sea and mazy overland through the tolly rock centre of the country. The buildings in Lydiat, which might more readily be called stackings, were a quiet strewn of casual flotsam along the shore. My mother was the proprietress of the inn, though it is the merest charity to call it so. I mean that we possessed a yard filled with crates of various sizes, which our custom, principally the government vessel men, would sit upon when required to eat what foodstuffs we prepared for them. Out of lazy ease, the establishment took the family name, "Blackhats." My mother must have christened me, but the name was swiftly lost: they called me Pigeon because I was always delivering messages from one goodwife to another.

I should tell you about my parents, who were no better and no worse than others. My uncle Charity had the kind, seawearied expression of the fish sailor; his eyes shone like a glisten of sharp pearls. He was of that kind of man who speaks with seamen roughly and hangs tenderly to any woman's whim. My mother enjoyed nothing but booklets, brandy and beach conversations, her face nicely fattened from sugar and her eyes finely brightened by tealeaf. She rarely spoke a hard word to anyone, and never to herself. In our cove, and for all I can say in the outlying districts as well, her vanity was a watchword. She was most careful about her hair and her jewelry, always brushing the one and polishing the other, and the pleasures of her life were principally superficial, her cruelties accidental, her satisfactions brief. As for my Christian education, my uncle Charity found it too expensive to espouse "that silly claptrap Godspeak," as he termed it, and my mother did not spend money unless it was compensated by sailors' attentions. They saved money on tithes and I was the one to pay.

The child who has never been to a strange town
says its mother cooks best.

But let me pass briefly over my childhood, which is not to the point. Let me pass on to my fourteenth year.

It is difficult to say when the first step of my destruction was taken, for every time I pause at one moment, another earlier clambers to the front. Let me then slip over myself, and say that I was always vain, but my fourteenth year gave occasion to that vanity when I turned viewlysome. While I was ripening in all places and all senses, none of the sailors were satisfied unless I was resting my hips against their table to balance the tray. None wanted to bite into the beef saltporridge and stew unless I put down the plate. With a look I could make the youngest or oldest squirm like bait shrimp.

"What lips!" one said.

"What hips!" said another.

"What can the rest be like!" All the men hung their heads in wonderment, for certainly, I knew what I was doing with my other vaingames. My good uncle warned me: "You must heed such rough men, Pigeon, for they are not looking at you, but at your things! Careful now!"

"Uncle, I am just playing!"

"Fish think they are playing with hooks, until they are caught, chopped and basted!" His words were sincere, but they brought only a fuller laughter to my mouth, for it was all a vaingame to me.

Beside, he, hypocrite, was in the main a disturber of the cove womanhood. "Well, you are still a fine figure of a fisherman!" I retorted to uncle Charity, who smiled. So I have known since I was merely fourteen that men take odd pride in their fortitude for vice.

My mother also half-tried to avert me from dangerous paths. "Don't run into those sailors, kiddie!" she said. "Sailor's arms are their true nets, I know it better than you can know."

"Bitten by a snake, and afraid of the rope!"

I said, for she was known to be mankeen, but I said it solely inwards, to myself, for she could slap a fury when the mind overran her. I replied outwards to mother by showering the table with the silvers and coppers which the sailors had left me for gratuities. As the coins jingled and rolled to a stop, into her face flitted an overhappy glint, as much to say it was reply enough. So it was with me that vanity was at first happy to course on its own power, without the need to open the topsail.

Crooked wood makes crooked ashes,

and in the spring of my sixteenth year, as a band of fishermen had blown off course and onto our piece of island, I found my ill match in a seemingly superficial amoret.

"That Pigeon girl is more welcome than a black diamond in hogfilth," opined one of a crew after I had served them their drinks.

The captain stopped him with a sip of brandy and a weighted word. "A fingernail of gold for her."

"She a whore?" divers asked him, expecting his usual randy reply, for it was a common joke that captain made about all women, aspersing the best with the brush of the worst, and he was ready to vent no doubt, but the youngest of the crew, whose name was Goodman Harvey, the name slips a sigh under my tongue even now, had dropped in love with me at the merest glance.

"Captain!" he interrupted. "Not this one!"

"Why not this one?" asked the Captain, firming his drink down.

"She's she, sir captain!" said Goodman Harvey, living up to his name then, brave good man.

The truth, and I will give you only the truth, as Jesus Christ would wish it, the truth is that I did not notice the missing sailor when I returned with food platters, so slyly did they undo the poor fellow in the dark. But the next morning lay a half-chawed fellow on our portion of beach, with his crew already departed. Fate was always malleting poor Goodman on the forehead and he did his best through the stuns of his time on earth. His mangled words whispered through cracked bloody lips when I found the boy: "Love of you," were his mere three words. Remembering the words, my heart is too freighted with the winds of nostalgia to give breath to speech, so let me only say . . . But the cask of feeling is plugged with its own outpouring: I loved him too! In an instant. What sixteen-year-old maiden could find such a shipwrack and not! My heart was not my own, my thoughts were for nothing but Goodman, and my vanity was sent tingling forever forward from the moment he spoke. Jesus, forgive my weak heart!

Mother and uncle knew too well how a young sailor and voluptuous daughter under one roof might teach each other that pleasantly impossible mathematics whereby one plus one adds up to three or four. My tears pled for the wounded sailor boy, my tears were countered a dozen ways. I think wheedling little availed, but he nonetheless joined us; there was nowhere else to put the boy. It could not be gainsaid that the sick man required a woman's fingers to stitch up his unravelment, so mother and uncle eventually did concede Goody, as I soon called the lad, into the house to recuperate.

Mother's eye constantly on us in a ramshackle habitation which held no secrets for or from anyone did not end our business together. "How did you like the look . . . of your fishstew tonight?" I might ask him carrying out his dirty bowl, and he might say, "It was all a man could find on the ground." And we had many more tricks.

Water always finds its way.

Mother kept her ears high the while, but she could not hear my clever glances. "The soup was perfectly delicious in every detail," Goodman might say with his eyes drifting across me instead of his fingers.

"It cannot possibly taste as eloquently as the food you have eaten elsewhere?"

"I have eaten in Port Hope and eaten in other coves too," he admitted without being troubled by the fact of sugared perdition too much, "but the food was nothing like what I see here."

"You mean tasted," I said, but left quick after, since even mother could stitch up those torn threads. I had crossed a line, though, I must say, if she had lain one down, I never received my invitation to the ceremonials.

A week or so passing, Goody said, "Pigeon, there appears to be a debate in this cove on travel to Port Hope. I have spent the long forenoon with your uncle on the question of my return, whether by waftage or overland. Which do you favour?"

The fellow was asking whether I would elope with him. Remember I was only a young girl, serious love matters seemed only a cheery vaingame to me, and I was sunfaced to involve myself. After a moment's thought, I declared: "Some of the older, wiser men claim that overland is best." My age asks my youth for the secrets of its boldness. Witness how I gave away life and wellness as if they were novelty shells at a barker tent. It follows that I would fleck my soul away like a reamed lemon pip as you will see.

Thus, strand by strand, Goodman and I knitted together an escape. We departed at once. In the open sky, the moon guided us almost as well as the sun, and all nature was quiet, but still how grim! How terrible! I kissed my mother farewell without touching her lips, worrying when a tear rolled down my cheek onto hers that that faint collision might wake her. Unhappy felicity! She brushed it away and did not wake. Praying and weeping outside the door of my uncle's house, I could not risk raising the alarm by going to thank him; I hope and pray that he never confuses my fugitive escapade with ingratitude, but it is too much! It is too much to hope! Only the expectation of Port Hope mollified the agony of leaving my family in Lydiat. The love for homecove is fierce, but the new odour of love for Goodman smothered it:

A house may hold a hundred men, but the heart
of a woman has room for only one.

We tripped lightly and quickly up the path into the hills, he wiped away my tears, he kept me close to his side, the night pressed in as the hills hovered in the distance, there was the danger, we plunged bravely into the Tols, he stopped me from looking back, and there was no more. I never saw Lydiat again. I never shall.

As we crept away, I asked Goody, where was our route? Through the centre of the island he said. Was there a trail? He did not know. Did he know how far was the journey to Port Hope? No. Had he traveled into the Tols before? He had not. Since he could give no more varying answer, I stopped questioning him, and, after this brief introduction to his conversation out of surveillance, we marched and dreamt through the wild night and our own dark, guided only by the asterisms, which Goody I think was only pretending to know.

Night and dark passed into day. Light showed us that the brambled path through the centre of the island was arduous and perilous, the Tols still snowboned. Indeed, I could have found time to rest all day among the bracken to explore the fresh tools we had discovered to serve vanity, the answers to vanity's questions only provoking more curiosity in the questioners. Out of his sickbed, Goodman stood a Sanjanian sailor, with the inner and outer strength for a mountain journey and the back for a night on planks or stones. In short, here was a man, I thought, and no more hopeful honeymoon could there have been. Little cause for hope had I known the future he was carrying me to! Indeed, it seems to me that there is a lesson about sin and vanity in this passage of my life, which Jesus would wish me to open up and pass around. When I left Lydiat, little could I have guessed what lay stored for me, but the meadows smelled sweetly, with hilly air and flowers and snow dust caps, pure, lovely, clean, and with a caring man to carry me across them. Coursing on this path, in the briefest span of time, it may have been a week, we arrived tagrag and illicit in the stinking fleshtrap Port Hope City. To moralize:

Under clear water, stones.
Under green grasses, ordure.

I must speak of that city now without the wisdom of my experience, merely as the place first arrived to my eye, and here is the difficulty. Understand that I had never in my time witnessed any larger piece of the human community than the anthill Lydiat. Knowing no other highway than the trail through the bushes and Tols, fresh from solitude, I arrived in Port Hope, which is both shame and wonder of its virtuous, both ease and terror of its vicious, the maze of all, the heart of our glorious country, seat of our nation, transfer city of the Empire. How marvelous and terrible to my little self! But

Even the minnow learns to swim in the ocean.

Goody led me from the suburbs to the portlands, where he claimed some acquaintanceship, and in that little walk I imagine that I saw more faces than I had seen in all the other strolls I ever had strolled before.

Money was the first thought amazement let me think. Goodman had been offered no compensatory wages to accompany his beating, but I had managed to scrape a little of my own from the inn's gratuities. Our "grand" sum hardly figured to a seamer's sufficiency. As I saw from his befuddled manners and querulous hesitations around strangers, Goody did not have the reflection of a flicker of the faintest clue, a born baggabone. In fairness, the boy set himself directly to the matter, and if you had seen the maddening confusion radiant from Goodman's face as he wrestled our poverty with his spirit, you too would have forgiven him. We sat down in an easy bar, while he wrestled, head in hands, with how to make money. Sometimes, from the look of despair in his eyes, it seemed as if money had the best of him, and then at others, from the manly determination there, he seemed to have wrested the upper hand. Then his face cleared like dust breezing off a whitewashed wall. I thought, the man has pinned money! "Sit down here, darling," he said in his lovingest voice, his hand outstretched for the remnants of our fortune. "Sit down here and I'll go find us some money, and swiftly!" He dissipated into the steam of the neighbourhood, leaving me desolate and penniless on a wooden bench in an inn with no friend, no protection and no passage for time but to watch empty-fisted the sale of steam beer and muttonchops, my eyes, for fear, fastened on an unswept floor littered with seashells. I wondered six hundred thousand times if he would ever return.

But the man did return, tears salting his foolish cheeks. "Forgive me, Pigeon, forgive me!"

The poor bulverhead had lost all of our scrapings, our last tease of fleece, playing "four, five and nine" at a brandytakers. Listen to me, young ladies, it is better to pledge yourself to a stone than a rattleboner, for with a gambler, there is always the worry of how to get money. How to get money, whispered my man's moist eyes, and money, the busy innkeepers, and our hungry bellies muttered money. The elements out of doors and the dangerous streets, the threat of rain in the sky above, they whispered "how will you get money?" That first night, Goodman found me a piece of clean ground among the crates and stretched a shredded sail to cover us, and told me such lies, to which my vanity responded so easily, that I found it almost a pleasantish dwelling. "Look at this dome of gilded diamants, darling," he said pointing to a flap of burl, "and this magnificent mosaic like a Sultan's dream of a floor," pointing to the flagstones. Vanity made our rough bags luxuriant pillows, his words softer than goosedown to me. Even the rats he confectioned to charming footmen and companions. Vanity is vanity. But also, poverty is poverty, and when we awoke the following morning, sunshine fell on cold and dirt, and the cold and dirt were asking us how we expected to get money.

No sunset or fresh Easter paint had as much glint as a grimy shilling to us ever after. The city was aflood with doltish, empty-headed, empty-handed clusterfists like us, and a few coppers were worth more to most than a day hauling cargo. Goody never made any money, and his dockwork was rare, and whatever scraps of cash scattered into his grasp from the table of the port, he instantly gambled at "crossroads" or "four, five and nine" or any surefirer method of donating our little securities to roguers by way of bristledice. No quantity of tears or scolds could inch him from the course, my befuddled half-husband. Goody had no brains for cash, and so, God in his mercy ensured that he never had any! What little money I was labouring for in a variety of inns paid for a moiety of nourishment, the rest he gambled off. Always the word money in our thoughts, never the Godly, and always how to acquire it, spend it, find it, lose it, gain it; never how to give it. Money is the city to new eyes: over every haughty rich lady, every pustulous beggar, the dour, suspicious workers and the spendthrift fantasticks, money holds perpetual dominion, no matter what flag is fluttering over the monuments.

Still, each day brought its loaf, and shuttleheaded Goody and I stitched up our pocket of a life after his tosses of bitchbones tore it open and spilled out our little prosperity. I will pass lightly over the knockdowns that could not keep me from standing, to describe instead the helping hand that pushed me down. Such "help" arrived as I was dealing steam beer in an inn of my employment, come in the shape of a gentle and corpulent customer, well dressed in a suit of fine cotton, with flaring bushes of brows and an oiled mustache, and all the accoutrements of wealth, progress and stability, a whangee, a gilded pocket watch, bowler hat and spats; his sweaty palms grabbed stuff like a thresher, beer after desolated beer, plate upon plate stacked like tosspennies beside him. He seemed to lack only the ordinary indifference to innmaids, finding simular compassion staring into my tired eyes as he sucked a marrowbone.

"Dear my good heart, miss," he said, "what sorrows can follow such a pretty maid as yourself into such a festive place as this?"

I told the gentle fellow that, thanks for his kindness, but my sorrows were not great and not unusual.

"My dear, tell me all."

I thanked him, and explained that my difficulties were with money, which was how I could say they were neither great nor unusual.

"Better to say they are not troubles at all. This materialistic spirit will undo our young nation. Difficulties with money! Money troubles, indeed! Well, I mean if money is the trouble, it can't be trouble, as they say. Come now." The gentleman finessed the dishrag from my hand and hung it neatly over the back of a near chair. "Offence to heaven that a figure like your own should so begrudge the image of God its requisites," he said, muting my protests, and whisking me away to the tailorshop on the Port Hope Mall. I had never so much as dared to wander a vicarious eye through the neighbourhood of that haberdasher, but all of a trice, the gentleman was hurrying me through the foyer past a half-dozen grimacing ladies and servile footmen. In the costume chamber itself, the sneers at my stained grubby dress were adzed away by the sharp hand of my patron. The man purchased for me a violent dress all in scarlet, carnadine as sin, which my vain heart loved. "Call me Mr. Money, and I'm worth as much to you," he said impishly, when I asked his name as he dragged my poor happy self into the millinery, where a new black hat was hammered to match my red dress and my old name. I cherished, in my still innocent coastal heart, the image of Goody's face alight at my metamorphosis when I would walk into the inn with my red dress and my black hat. How ridiculous vanity can make us!

An almond for a parrot!

"In such a dress and such a hat," said Mr. Money, as if thumbing my thoughts, "one must off and be seen."

Off to the dining restaurant I went with the dapperwit, and oysters, wines and whitebread with sausages were squeezed down into us by cheery waiters, and to put it simply, we weren't eating fishstew and claw. I blame my own heart, but consider the mitigation that from my first footfall into Port Hope, the hour of this fanciful dinner was the first when money ceased whispering in my ear. Blanks-and-prizes was a luxury to me before then, and with money's silence, all my worries faded like dawn into day, until, as coffee steamed to our table after the pudding and biscuits, a foggy veil lifted from me, and I recalled my shipwrecked sailor Goodman, to whom I had plighted at least a kind of sacred troth. Gathering my scant things, all purchased with the true from my new friend, I begged his pardon for my departure.

"Oh my dearest me in a hat with a lump!" he said slapping his forehead. "I forgot myself that I promised you assistance! Come with me, child. Follow!"

Swiftly arranging the payment for our meal, Mr. Money whirled me from the white table napkins and fresh linenstands of the hotel esplanade up the gilded trim stairways of the hotel proper. How innocent and vain was I both, that I followed him without the murmur of a rumour of a question to his hotel room, which was the largest suite of rooms for a single person that I have ever witnessed to this day. I thought he might unfold himself into several persons who might then wander into several rooms. Instead, he took from the billfold on his nightstand two pound notes which I most gratefully pocketed. Innocent maidens heed the sequel to stranger generosity! Then he tried to pocket me!

"Pray gentle sir what are you at there?" I asked, spilling the money to the earth in my fright.

To which question, Mr. Money cut a snide grin, and said with a differing voice than the restauranter or milliner heard: "Whoredom is a state of affairs where a reckoning must be had before the menu is even half-presented, but you must admit, as a woman of custom, that I have paid amply to see what wares I have purchased!"

"You have not purchased a thing to my recollection!" I said.

"Accept my unpolished misery and disillusionment, but I did think this was your generosity speaking before!"

"My generosity was speaking," he said with false wit, "but I have tired of its conversation!"

"Listen to it again, sir!" I said.

Then his rage truly furied. "How can you pay back? And with what?" he boomed. "Pray, most infinitely gentle lady, do you think these dirty bills are what I paid with? What about oysters and black hats and red dresses? Do you figure, foolish woman, that these luxuries come without price? Fine, whore! Pay me back my dress in kind!"

With his eyes turned away from his threshing palms, since a sinner cannot stare at his sin for too long, he prepared to tear off my coverings right there and then. My innocence had not stunted my cleverness. "Fine sir, gather up my money, pay me, and I will render what you desire."

After a flicker of doubt, snapped up short, he simpered shadily, and replied, stooping, "I knew you would be tractable."

As the man was kneeling to address the crumpled bills which were to pay for his crumpled action, I bowled him over, before he could recover, fleeing out the oak door and down the gilded stair. Such is the terrible vanity and wickedness of Port Hope City that my half-torn dress and terrified eye were less wonder to the maids, hotelkeepers, doormen and street dawdlers than my proper but plain grey gown had been before. My bescumbered kind of comet had plunged through their ken more than once in a lifespan. Blindly I ran straight to Goody's sailor arms, and whether he was more surprised by my breathless voice or the torn scarlet dress and black hat, I would not say. My story troubled him, but while fretting about my proximity to the Enemy, his vision, I noticed, wavered most when I spoke of the two pound notes left behind. The precipice of my virtue hurt his pride and he could never stand to see me weeping, but he regretted the money I dare say nonetheless.

Not that he had so far as a fortnight for regret, since one strange sorrow told the wind that we made bountiful hosts, and soon other, stranger sorrows flocked around the bark like petrels. To poor Goody, and I did adore the foolish sod, the ultimate fortune and misfortune befell, death took him. A cargo of coffee tipped over its holding bar, and crushed him underneath, so that for next to a month I could not so much as sip brew. For myself, I was seventeen years of age, and a widow under the judging sun without the honourable shade of the title or the time for great grief. Poor Goody had his body laid down in a common grave in those suburbs near the end of the beach, and the cost of the spadework chewed up the remaining paucity I possessed. I hope and I pray that the Lord will be finicky when he divvies up the bodies in that foul pit on the Final Judgement, the poor corpses are so casually strewn together. I hope no poor fool find his self crutched in unknown bones. With the absence of Goodman Harvey's company, it seemed that the demons struggled among each other to see who would have the first piece of me. Poverty argued his right firmly, but Despair claimed privilege of age. Loneliness and Womanly Weakness each had their demands, but Debt also, like any creditor, bullied sharply for a piece. Vanity lay back laughing at all the suitors, for she knew that the first lien on my soul was to her. But of all these, there were no demons more terrible than Mr. and Mrs. Beacham, into whose ashen circle I now descended.

Let me refresh the story for you. In our routine of sojourns around the inns and hostels of the portlands, Goody and I were always fleeing from one household to another, for arrears and general lack of fistcash, which is the fundamental crime in Port

Hope City, for all the rest can have forgiveness bought. Thus we had progressed, or digressed I should say, from bad places, which we could not afford, to the worst places, which we could no better afford. At the moment of Goody's death, we happened to be in residence at the Beachams', and the Beachams were intractable: they had seen too many runaways and Abraham-men to be deceived by our attempted flights, and they held on no less tenaciously when I was a widow. But I must describe them in further detail, since they were the surroundings and substance of my life for many years of struggle, and to bear witness to those years you must be able to see them as through an unglazed window.

The Beacham house prospered because in it, vice was admired, righteousness was despised, charity was laughed at, and might and opportunity embraced above all things. Mr. Beacham was always Mr. Beacham to me, his forename I never knew. The man could easily have offered himself to a freak parade, since a more malformed colossus never troubled this island. He proved that a man is just a stone with a little more. Heads taller than ordinary men, he overlooked his wife standing when he himself was sitting. With contempt for honest energy and the good use of his strength, Mr. Beacham filled his vessels with a prodigy of nasty habits, drink and dark tobacco, the two requiring fresh influences of hard cash daily, for which need, instead of labouring, he would lazily strike his wife or any other weak, defenceless woman until the items were provided. Peachy was the idleton's wife, no more diversivolent or superficial creature have I ever known. She was the creeping moss to her husband's rock. When poor Goody and I first tumbled into their corner of hell, no housewife could have been more agreeable and hospitable. Over the course of our residence, which it must be admitted was not absent of absent payments, Mrs. Beacham's manner towards us had proportionally altered, until hostility and cruelty were the watchwords of her presence. Her clothing seemed to alter from taffeta to raggings, as if mimicking her deportment to Goody's poor self and mine. Her tongue was cowish, smooth one way, rough the other. The moment Goodman died, Mrs. Beacham's manner burnished up its old taffeta, cleaned its smiling teeth with a brush, and opened its former hospitality for custom. She was no mere liar, but a conscientious deceiver; she was bait and lime to all good things, not merely an ordinary fraud. Mrs. Beacham made money by any method to hand in order to buy drink and tobacco for Mr. Beacham; then Mr. Beacham would cease from cuffing her about; such was the cloacal economy of their household.

Into such a diabolical machinery, it was my lot to catch a hem. Mrs. Beacham's baited hand upon the death of my half-husband embraced me before pinching the quick. Giving enough to accompany me to his funeral, without raising a shilling to find his body a better rest, Mrs. Beacham solaced me in the first blush of my mourning, when even guised sympathy was sufficient.

"My dear," said Mrs. Beacham, after the first half-week had passed. "My dear, if I may, have you planned your futures near and distant any? Chucked a thought down that alley?"

In place of answer, I betrayed, by the anxious paroxysms of my face, the entire sum of my worries to her clever eyes, which were perpetually guarding my merest eyebrow flicker.

"Do not trouble your skull with your largish debt to me, my child, since my thoughts are for your welfare sure. But are you, could you be, will you consider about considering returning to your homecove?"

Fair question, you may be asking it yourself. In place of yes or no, the answer is "vanity." How often had I slyly daydreamingly mesmerized myself with the imago of my old happy, happy home, far from the beer and chopshops of my sad employments. How often had I remembered the long sandy bank behind the cove head, and the cheerful return of the men from their fishing duties, and the women—oh such happy women in their fidelity—running out to meet the sailors. Happy, happy days! I longed for a taste of its fares, a glimpse of its faces, but my nostalgia would never suffer the shame of a return. Besides, I lacked the money and a solo woman could never attempt such perils. There was a little wolfish puckering at the corners of Mrs. Beacham's mouth when I so told her.

"Pray, how do you foresee a living then?" she enquired flatly.

I burst into tears, for I had no answer, not even vanity, and no notion where, when or how one might flourish alone and friendless in the City. The devil in Peachy Beacham knew to grab at me and how; the love in her eyes was the love a farmer possesses for his fattest goose around Christmastide. One week later, at dusk, as she and I were preparing the tables for the other guests, she suddenly dropped a bowl of flour, which shattered on the ground, choking me and shocking me, since Mrs. Beacham never dropped a penny loosely. The lost copper accruing might amount to one less fist in the gullet from her tyrannic husband.

"Whatever could be wrong, Mrs. Beacham?" I enquired.

"Forgive my clumsy throwaway, Pigeon darling, but the spirit offered me a solution to your peril, and it is so brilliant and glittering and it arrived so nickily that I dropped the bowl and shattered the thing." Her mask, for it was not a human face, displayed the keenest possible excitement, to whet my curious girl's heart.

"Tell me, tell me please, Mrs. Beacham," I begged.

"No," she said, with a false moment's false reflection, "no, I will keep it a surprise, for a lark, but this very night I promise you will know the way."

That very night, my life of crime began. Mrs. Beacham led me by the arm from the scullery to the upstairs closet, in which she bolted and locked the scant and few precious things that weren't tobacco and brandy. Therein was the red dress and the black hat that the nameless man had purchased for me, Goody having pawned them to the Beachams in lieu of rent before dying. Mrs. Beacham, her face lemonsqueezed with a blank stare meaning nothing, clothed me and painted me while I to no end pestered her. "You will take dinner with an old friend," was all she would explain, and when I demanded how dinner could make me a penny, and insisted in tears that I did not possess any friends, she replied that it was a certainty that money would crue from the meal, and to be thankful. When I had been tucked, crimped and styled enough for her judgement, as a cook tastes a dish before envoying it over the floor, she led me by the hand into the private dining room of the inn, set plainly and sumptuously in what I knew from washing day was the finest whitest linen and best silver the establishment could offer.

"And what shall I do now? I asked.

"Sit down, darling darling," replied Mrs. Beacham.

"And how will sitting down earn me a penny?" I further demanded.

"What you sit upon will earn you bread and salt now," she said. As I innocently scrutinized the seat of the chair, she let free a devilish laugh, but her revealing mistake was then permissible, there being no further need for dissimulation. Mr. Money waltzed in, politely and victoriously bowed, and, with a nod of his gentle head, took place in the seat opposite, reaching for the silver as he lighted.

There may be among you readers who will judge me ill for not escaping the dagger point that twisted and cored my soul. I ask you, was I to run to the streets of the portlands, for worse treatment? Or suicide? May Jesus Christ in His holy revolving circles of Mercy forgive me that I turned whore, but let your mortal judgement be conditioned by Port Hope City, my youth and my later repentance. I leave this record so that other women will scan the ground as they go and will not be snared by the devil's wires or smeared with the lime of Mrs. Beachams. Mr. Money, of whose name I still have no knowledge, gave a portion of the fee to Mrs. Beacham who gave a portion to me, and the largest piece of the earnings fed brandy and tobacco to the lumpish thug by our fire, so he would, for a stretch, not beat our poor tired womanflesh.

I will not add to the stench of details ascribed to wicked portlands life through common blabs by portraying my "education." Mr. Money played with me until the gutter of his soul demanded fresh filth, at which turn he disposed of me and Mrs. Beacham with a gratuity. This gratuity was partly in pounds and partly to offer the name of Pigeon Blackhat to the thick stew of bedswervers he kept as familiars. Having considered that fount of my misery for many years now, the way a lion in the zoo must think of the cage which trapped it, I have come to believe that the larger slice of Mr. Money's pleasure was not in the simular act of love, but in the broader ruination of women. His desire was first to make a whore, then to have a whore, and I pray that Lucifer assigns a distinct and lively devil for the particularity of each vice. Mr. Money's friends became my friends, and soon the Beacham house was abuzzing with my old friends. Such old friends bring more old friends, like flies, and new and newer showers of money poured onto Mrs. Beacham's euphoric head. On me, poured the fear, cruelty and loathing properly belonging to a whore.

The world is her husband,
and her husband is never home.

Frankly, I dankly enjoyed hooking men on a claw of perdition, crablike. The warning of my watch is for innocent men as much for women. When whores are laughing, they are viewing in "the mind's eye" the men of their crime scorching in the pit like a sulphur match endlessly sparkling. Jesus forgive us all. Other scarlet moments of my education were tobacco smoking and brandy drinking, both of which I received with almost as much passion and gusto as the gargoyle at the fireplace. Also, part of my custom grew into the habit of paying me plum.[1] At first try, I found the drug emptying my heart of its sorrows like casting a chamberpot into the street out a window, which I lusted for. Money no longer whispered as it had in the days of my vanity; hardened vice instead bellowed money, and just as constantly as in my days of poverty. While there was no luxury I did not love and indulge frequently, I was no less the kept thing of Mrs. Beacham as her mottled cat, and a prisoner worse of my own vice.

Your wealth is your destruction.

My soul followed one vice with another, like links in a crown of lead chains I wore.

I hated women more than men. Contempt for fellow creatures, a state which whoredom makes as surely as baking makes bread, stained my whole soul with a swiftness you would barely countenance. Oh yes, my loathing for my own sex was absolute perfection! How terrible that it found occasion for expression! One dawn, as the last of my charges disappeared into the world of light, Mrs. Beacham spoke in a new vein to me. "My dear darling, that last man was a handsome roguer, didn't you see?" A smile

1. Opium, or any opiate product. Sanjan, as one of the larger ports in the North Atlantic, and relatively isolated, saw virtually all the traffic in opium and hashish which circumnavigated the Cape of Good Hope.

mudslided her face, a smile far worse threat to me than a scowl, I reckoned by then. I replied that I distinctly believed the gentleman to be a rogue, at any rate.

"I suppose there is truth in what you apply, my darling dear, and not the handsomest of the fleet, to put it in a kind way, but he gave handsomely, don't you see?" Onto the dirty table by the hearth, she slapped the scant bills which served as my portion of what I had earned, giggling at her own joke. Then a look of sudden surprise animated her wicked jowly visage, as if carried by a thought. I knew it meant the introduction of a careful scheme she had long weighed.

"My sweetest, how unfair is it that you pay such a rent as in this house," she said. Had you been in the room as those words developed from that mouth, you could have plucked a hair off my head, and my whole body would have unraveled.

She continued talking into my awed, disbelieving and arrested silence. "I mean, we might find a partner as helpmeet of sorts, to share the burden of the custom, and divide the charges in two."

At a blink I saw what her gambit meant. Such are empires, that a queen of whores, with one subject, wants expansion of her petty borders. Mrs. Beacham wanted to turn her sweetest fly into a fellow spider!

I was still a woman with a woman's heart, but my hate for my own sex had blossomed, as I said, and I thought little of anything other than money. I loathed wives, whom I devilishly took to be yokefellows, whores chained to a single unvarying customer; I despised maidens as ignorant children unworthy of their adult bodies; streetwalkers were less than mud under beasts to me. Since I had become a kept woman, the kept woman was the ideal to me. Only in rare flashes would reason strike through, and in that case I had a trusty defence from reason, in a pipe of tobacco mixed with plum. The devil wants company, they say, and more than the hard cash was that hunger, I think now, so fully did I lack and want a companion to my whoredom. Pain creases my face that I am blinded, considering the jolly girl, who joined the house unsullied by any taint of unnaturalness or vice, and whom I happily threw into Mrs. Beacham's crucible. Tears mingle with the ink, and I must question to what end the Lord suffered to extend my life so to foul and blot such a happy pasture in the prairie of human creation. Jesus forgive me for this and all other evils.

Maggie was a mild, pretty girl, with her hair pulled back modestly and the pinkish rough hands of a seamstress. Her eyes never looked up but they would gapesnatch in awe or fear of one or another perfectly ordinary turn. Even the paperthins flustering down the mountainsides at springtime brought her fright, as if she expected reproaches on her work and a slap from the butterflies. She would see, with us, many extraordinary turns of evil. Mrs. Beacham hired the girl, at first to serve the noxious antechamber where Mr. Beacham silently guarded himself by the fire, with bowl and pipe in hand, and where my old friends refreshed and attended my better leisure; you see, I would always insist that they buy me a form of indulgence, a drink or a cigar, even if I did not desire the pleasure, so as to line the pockets of Mrs. Beacham another way with their pounds. As servant, Maggie could view unimpeded the viceways of lust, perjury and blasphemy. By the strong device of habit, her virtue was ever so slowly loosened and undone, and also Mrs. Beacham crept into the poor girl's pockets and soul by holding back the rent prices and costs of food, and I quickly taught Maggie trimtram luxuries like tobacco, so that for every two hours of work she careened an hour's wage into debt. After a season, the poor child was firmly in the bawd's grip and how Peachy could squeeze and pinch and tear! Soon the cue was spoken for my role in the melo Mrs. Beacham had commissioned under the title The Perdition of Marguerite. I was to play the "kind sister."

"Don't cry, my most darling Marguerite," I said aside after one of Peachy's furies, for the poor mite took the mistress's tongue-lashings worse than the fist-and-nail beatings. "Come and sit with your old friend Pigeon."

"O thank you, best of the best Pigeon, you have always been the kindest woman!" The poor maiden was weeping softly through her country talk, so that I pitied her, and, pitying, hated.

"Tell me your troubles then," I said devilishly, "spill them on a poor fellow girl's lap."

"What troubles? I have no troubles!" she rung out in a desperate voice. "Except I owe forty, eight and six to the witch Peacham! Every night all night for two weeks I have stayed up wondering if it is not best to go and chuck my nearcorpse into the Hope river!"

"Child, don't talk such hypocrisy," I said severely.

"Begged water does not come to a boil."

With my sudden sternness, her innocent cheeks grew weeping-ripe. "Oh mistress Blackhat, not you too!" she cried out. "Not you too will turn away from my poor despised body!"

"Abandon you, never, look, I will give you a ten-pound note." And here I really did so give her, baiting the hook with bacony fingertips. "See it? I can give that to you like a bauble, my dearest. A full fourth of your debt, and you want to see how I made it? From a gesture. Nothing more grand or difficult than that, my darling darling. Less troubling than threading a needle as you found it." I stroked Marguerite's hair, and continued mouthing for a half hour or so, but I could have spared my breath, for Maggie's face brightened at the first glint of despicable hope. The money bait, which Mrs. Beacham had given me for the purpose of deceit, took and snatched her. Mrs. Beacham and I auctioned her virginity for a highprize that very night. I took my piece of the loin, with my portion of the sin, and so Marguerite and I began the best of friendships, sharing men and tobacco and streethawked pamphlets together:

"Two birds in the cage must sing in harmony,"

she liked to say, laughing lostly. But in some piece of my shattered heart, I hated her more than all the wives and virgins combined, for I could see, in her as in a glass, the closest reflection of my perfidy.

Do not ask me to recall the horrors and crimes of so many years. You know wickedness? I was more wicked. In will more evil, in evil more natural, in nature more corrupt, in corruption more willing. Marguerite was the first of the false brides we auctioned like sheep, but far from the last or most eminent, since the pounds from that sale were only a tease to Mrs. Beacham and myself. Better luck, the husband Mr. Beacham died, right in his fireside chair, with a pipe still fuming. Clothed in mystery to me is God's blessing upon the man to give him a fairdeath, but so little did any person care for him that we considered throwing his corpse into a nearby slough heap, until we thought of the police. Then we considered selling the gigantic freak to a show, except none were passing in town to buy. In the end, we had the city's cheapest coldcook douse him in lime and chuck the body in a suburb grave pit. Many tears for many ugly men have been shed over that bit of ground, including my own for Goody, but not a salt drop spilled for Beacham's bones, unless someone happened to be eating pistachios and spat.

After a few bouts, the house was shown clearly that I could

pummel Mrs. Beacham as well as her man did, and I was the whoreward, the true dunghill queen, portioning her a fragment of the nightly catch for her services as bawd and potboiler. She brewed the witchiest potions for thoroughcleaning the double-ribbed, worse than murder. Duping and seducing many a poor, stupid and eyeable girl, for which Peachy had an exact eye worth her fee, we grew our brothel and it flourished faster than hell or bamboo. For many years, I ran the doomed ship of damned sailor-ines, and like any captain knew the warp of its every timber: I can unpack memorially every room of that fish shop like a doll house: the youngest girls ginglegangled at the portal for bait, the innmaids and new whores in the foyer drinking, smoking and chatting with the custom, all watched over steadily by the Beacham, the second floor hallway lined with the vicious chambers; the kitchen for trade in plum, theft and dirtier huggermugger crime. By such economy, the household prospered with the intricacies of machines and devices. In that time, no sailor on Sanjan Island did not know of the Beacham house and Pigeon Blackhat, I say it to my shame. Money flowed like filthy spring sewers.

The world is like a dancing girl,
it shakes itself to everyone
for a little while.

But listen, virgins and young men, to the end of my whoredom!

One evening, in walked a white-haired man for service, and I was a whore, I served. The old sheep are as good as the young, so long as they shed fleece. I had familiarity with many men in the portlands, so the slight recollection which ran through me at our encounter never troubled me. At his turn, he procured cigars in the antechamber, which I lit for us off a tobacco leaf.

"Where do you come from, girlie, if I may be bold?" he asked. I had long before learned that generous gratuities never suited news of a shared homecove, so my practice was always to repose that question on the asker. This particular old fellow seemed, as they mostly did, gratified at my curiosity.

He said, "A small cove, but a precious one no less, fairness. By name Lydiat. On the farthest edge of the coasts, I'm sure you could never have journeyed to it."

My laughter rang out despite me, but stuck in my gullet when I recognized him. His eyes glistened like sharp pearls. My uncle Charity! Smothering a horrified howl with a silken smile, I slunk, with an excuse I hardly recall, to my private chamber. After a good quarter-pie of clock, he sent Mrs. Beacham to call me down, but the bawd discovered a slobbering pool of weakness and womanly tears, and was truly astonished, for I had by then become hardened even to the most abject indelicacies and cruel violences. To witness Pigeon Blackhat shivering from fright boggled her, I spoke no word to the reason, and she left the room, disturbed herself, to pay for my uncle's cigars and find him another tool for the evening. My weeping shudders on the bed were not merely for the sin I had stood on the brink of committing, and which I cannot name, but also for its indictment of my life entire. Jesus sent Charity to me, just as now I send this pamphlet to you, a soulwarning.

Despite that warning from the mercies above, I kept whoring the portlands, loud and still, flowing into wealth beyond all the money in my homecove, and sent more men to peril through the bonarobas in my fishroom than can be numbered by any other than the Judge. I will spare you those stories. I have done with them now, now I must turn to happier matters and give testimony to the power and glory of Jesus Christ and his servants in the Holy Church. I offer up the salvation of my soul in praise of Him.

In the inverted life of whoredom, morning stands as evening. We call our dinner a dewbit. The light peeks from the tops of houses, the bloodstain on the stone is first noticed, the sparrows squabble in the gutter, our last customers stumble to disease their trusting wives, while we sweep the floor and our memories and prepare for rest. One morning, at the end of the working day then, at Mrs. Beacham's house, a man, closer to an angel, and not fallen at that, cracked open the door of the Beacham den. He was no sailor I could see, that was plain from his hands, which were soft, and his gait, which was light, but a natural peace radiated from his visage as from a cathedral statue. He gazed with loathing at the gross room and my common body, and asked, after seeing I was the only attendant present, "May I enquire if you have seen my brother, Luther Pendright?"

"Yes, he is upstair," I said. "Take your leisure here and wait."

The man did, in fact, seat himself at the offered table, like Christ himself did once as our pious will recall, and I brought him coffee, which he thanked me for. Then he asked if Luther was a frequent visitor to our den.

"To tell the truth, I am an old friend of Luther's. I am the old friend of many who pass through Mrs. Beacham's, and for a price I do not see why I cannot be as old a friend of yours as I am of Luther's," I said slyly.

He sniffed at the brew without tasting it, and peered with folded strong arms around the establishment, his silent sneer answer enough.

"Drink from wherever you like sir," I said with a flash of anger at his refusal.

"Many drink from the common well.
It does not wreck the water."

He answered me quietly subdued, but his voice was nonetheless a whirlwind of words. "Indeed, there are many who drink here, since the tongue deceives us with sweetness. A whore is sugar sprinkled over swamp water, a little shining paste smeared on the mud. A whore does not know who steps in her, since like a swamp, the water soaks in and the pression is lost immediately, and no one can tell who before them sunk beneath the mud. They call a whore a port for good reason, since the white man and the Chinaman also find shelter in her, depending on the tempest of accident. For my part, Pigeon Blackhat, I would rather be tied to a corpse than lay with a whore since a corpse is chewed only by worms and crows, but a whore is eaten up by all diseases and chewed up and spat out by all the birds of the sky and the vermin of the ground. No, I will wait for Luther in some cleaner sewer." Finished, he left. My face heated with guilty blood, my eyes were cloudy with tears. Shame was melting the icy core inside my heart, my hands trembled, I knew I was repenting. Some among you may say that Pigeon Blackhat is a whore, forever and beyond repentance, but I say that no one is beyond repentance. Some may say that my heart was too hardened to be so easily cracked, but the seraphim's tongue was a sword of flame, and the embers pierced my heart to the root. Who had been an innocent maiden? Pigeon Blackhat. Who had been unknown to the world? Pigeon Blackhat. Who was lost in the city? Pigeon Blackhat. Who became the most infamous whore in the portlands? Pigeon Blackhat. Who owned the most renowned fish shop? Pigeon Blackhat. Who did Jesus Christ shine his mercy into most freely? Pigeon Blackhat. At my epiphany all divisions were clear: that foul vice, that clean virtue, that vicious foulness, that virtuous cleanliness. Between them, the divider, stood the strange visitor. What agony of expectation as I waited for Luther to descend the flight so I could enquire the name of his brother. Calvin was my saviour's name. Their holy mother had known to give heroes' names to her sons.

Wrathful fire burned me that day. Hell was harrowed on that day as surely as it will be on the day of the Resurrection, for His Love descended and engulfed my whole being with the true spirit of holy repentance. I knew, as if by instinct, that my sole hope was to throw myself at the feet of a priest to beg indulgence in Jesus' mercy. And so the dens and denizens of that corner of the portlands were witness to the peculiar sight of Pigeon Blackhat, infamous whore, chasing the streets begging directions to a church. There were many mocking devils; but one necessary angel pointed the Way. Stepping into the Anchordown chapel, my heart sang a hymn of joy for my future and an elegy of regret for my past, and both wanted to find expression in the confessional booth.

I spared that cached witnessing priest no lascivious detail of my crimes, showing no tenderness to myself or the listener in my account of the horror I had spread like false coin throughout the commonwealth. My heart ached with relief at the open view of my wound. Behind the curtain, the priest gave plain advice and the most sanguine hopes for my soul: Jesus Christ learned patience, and did not hesitate to carry in his entourage even the most depraved sinners. He was truly the Againbuyer. I might yet leaven my degradation with consistent good works, but for salvation I would have to abandon vice that very minute. I did not need so to contemplate, because the memory of my vice was so noxious to me, I wanted nothing more than to abandon it. The priest behind the curtain told me that, despite the shame of it, I would have to earn my repentance by working in the same neighbourhood in which I had wreaked so much damage to the innocent and guilty alike. The surgeon cut with his sharpest blade there, for I longed to escape the portlands more than ever before, yet the reason was clear to me, that I must rebuild the ruin I had knocked over. I must plant the seed in the very place where the wildflower I had crushed underfoot had once flourished. And after I had so determined to work beside the priest in aid of the salvation of its innocent and guilty alike, the soft pleasure of mending stole over my whole person and I felt well.

I have more wonders of my blessedness to relate than that! Who pulled the curtain of the booth back but Calvin, the brothel visitor! My angel was my stellifying priest! And he has continued to be my guide in the recovery of virtue ever since.

So I have written my narrative. Reader, read it. Recover the grain from the bran of my tale, to care for your soul and to keep close to the Path.

Watch the plain, not the subtle traps.

So I say, put your hand in Jesus Christ's and let Him guide every step. For I have heard some say that whoredom is inevitable, and common, and perspectual across time, and so should be looked at with a leisurely eye, but the line is absurd, since once all these same verities could have been uttered once upon a time of the cannibals, and we do not tolerate them. Why not the same disgust for whores? As for money, I have been poor, yet I have been fulfilled. I have needed, yet I have not wanted. Indeed, from that day forward, I have lived always pursuing the salvation of lost women and their damned prizes. Mrs. Beacham's revulsion and that of her keeps was my lot firstly at returning to the old haunt, and more than a few blunted broomsticks beat my poor headpan when the queens of whoredom figured at last that there was little chance of a return to my former self. The servant of the

Lord must take the abuse of the world. It only wounded my poor soul to see Marguerite, the lost soul I had lost, spit on my hems. To the memory of her irrecoverable innocence I dedicate myself. For her sake, and the sake of endangered maidens all over this glorious island, I have written this pamphlet, to remind all that the mercy of Jesus Christ is infinite and His church imitates His mercy, in truth and goodness.

Salvation is open to all.

To give proof, let me end my story with the greatest wonder and felicity in all my encounters with Port Hope City. Preacher Calvin Pendright of Anchordown chapel has found mercy enough to make as his fellow servant in the church, the wife of his own body, that once most brazen of whores, Pigeon Blackhat myself!

PROFESSOR SAINTFRANCIS AND THE DIAMANTS OF THE END OF THE WORLD

Julian Back

1863? – 1921

The call came at the very backsunded end of the darkening, a clusterfist roughcutting my lintel and my future sleep, while I was just settling down for that truecomforting one last one at the old chafery. I must admit the old winkers grow beleaded latehours-wise, and I had no yen for a cold zlear down portlandsway for another child-of-the-people murder or break-and-enter. Crown-agent I am and duty is duty and all, but I left the fist pounding that eve, that is till I heard Clarker's voice behind it.

"Inspector Langer, sir," he yared from backoak.

I yared back, "Find Stevens, or Morley, or Blankett."

"No, no, sir. Langer tonight, sir. S.R."

"Special request? Dash it." Special request meant a mustdo, and the evening's prospect appalled me.

"I will whisper, sir, that it's up Hopemallsways," and my trusty whipsman then named a woman I won't. She had curtsied before

His Majesty on the Visit, I recalled. There are forty kinds of madness and only one kind of common sense, and one of my forty is richfolks. I come over all woodenheaded with the quality. Suffice it that the Lady's moniker had my bowl down, my head up and my cloak dashed before Clarker could bang again, and in a winksworth, on a night just fashioned for a quiet cantel with pipe and blaze, we were cringlecrangling through Port Hope streets on my way to Lady G—'s Manse on the Catchlands, the highest heredity of the boldest lady on the Colony.

So nickly did Clarker cut the carriage that the midlit Manse levied like a sunkship before us in no time. At the door a flossy, clearly freaked, greeted me and undashed me. A solemn butler carried me up a grand case and through many dark twistways into Lady G—'s sally, the most bantamworked sally I ever stood straight in, and there upped Lady G— herself, the most anointed lonelywoman I ever struck, ginglegangled and goldhedged every which way. To the eye, a goodgerlack seemed to do her femaleness some good, but those are not my onions. A dernful priest was perched on her settee, I caught, once I'd smeared the dazzle from my peeps.

"Inspector Langer, I declare." Her voice, like cabbage fume, was warm but cruelwise. Her breeding, I posed, kept her so morningsealike.

"Yes, My Lady, I am the Inspector."

"My jewels." She said it as if marking poor servantry at table.

"Not the Diamants?"

"Yes, this evening, my most precious gems, I think it fair to say the richest gems on this island entire, the Diamants of the End of the World, were filched from under my very greyhairs, and under this exact roof. Some master dodank no doubt."

"Did you catch any sound, my Lady?"

"Father Alexander and I"—a dovewing of her hand noticed the priest at her side, who sat dumb and glum to the wordpassing between us—"were enjoining a game of whist the whole evening post supper, when, in a trifle, a massive kerbanging, a real fussocking gabber, disturbed our play. One assumed it was the flossy dolloping the glitter, so one let it pass. When I went bedwise, to my shock and horror up the safe is rocked."

"And what time?"

"Our game quite possessed us, but within the pair or triplet of hours between supper and sleep."

"Father Alexander," I questioned, "the time stuck to you?"

The priest mewed like a sad veal, so distrait was he, but I could see he meant nay. Unlike him, Lady G— was cold to the bone throughout the loss of the jewels but blood will open the door for itself, as they say, and cash opens doors too. By the roomwork I reckoned the diamant loss would not leave her chomping hazzled loaves tomorrow supper.

"And neither caught a disturbance?"

"Neither of us saw aught but trumps and not trumps."

"I see," I said, accolding my mismazement.

Her eyeflicks pinced to catch me so lostabout with her luxuriants missing.

"I am gladdened that you see, Inspector. I would be further gladdened if you would recover the jewels."

"Yes, My Lady. May I see the safe?"

She skiffed a palm to the side of her salle and returned to javver with the priest about certain expectations one might have concerning Colony Police. I clutched a candelabra, a ropey white-gold affair of the gorgeousest leafspun, and crept cornerwise with my illuminant brand. The cantel wall of the sally was utterly aslapdash and caroused. A rendering of the Sinking of the *Titanic* grieved on the ground. The safe door flopped on a mangled hinge. I enclosed toward the gape.

What I caught next near to backfloored me.

When I upheld the lightstick to the safe and inpeeked, the Diamants merried and brighted there.

Let me depict them as they flashed up at me. At the heart of the Diamants of the End of the World crouched a ruby the size of my spoonthumb joint, thieved from one incarnadine idol in one Imperial culvert or another, and tuliped in widening and widening rings of brown and orange and green and blue and black diamants, all argentined and baccated with pearls. Against the candleglare, it was like nothing other than the eye of God. It seemed to watch me. It seemed to know me. It seemed to love me and judge me. And I was afraid.

My crownservice has hamsamly swung so easily. I merely picked up the Diamants and demonstrated them to Lady G——. The Lady was flustergated for half a moment, then she blinked, then crashheaped at the foot of the settee, with no Father Alexander handersome to catch her. The Father must have holyghosted the while between my cherishing the Diamants and gussocking down to the Lady's aid. The flossy brought strongwaters from the next room while I leaned Lady G— against the settee and started fanning.

When Lady G— rebrandished, her anger was more fullflushed than before.

"Out, out, out!" she yalloped, punching the diamants from my grip.

"My Lady, what is so wrong?"

"Out, out, out, out!" And out she tore from the sally herself.

Thusly I found myself solo in a Catchlands Manse, utterly nashgrammared, with no one to curlpoint about no crime, and not the steam of an idea how it had all crashed over me. What could I do? The butler was guiding me eyeways from the sally, to where the flossy stood with my coat. I had to leave. I would catch no curiosalve with Lady Lonelywoman in her dogflaws, I reckoned. Besides, no crime means no crownagent, it's an axiom.

"Solve it yet, Inspector?" Old Clarker crackled as I stomped down the flags.

"I don't know."

"How can you not know?"

"I don't know that either."

"Too fathomy for me, sir," said Clarker, gnidging the horse-startler. Too fathomy for me too, I wondered as we overclattered down from the Mall into the clummersome city. Although the self-recovering jewels may have been no crime, it was a darkdeed surely and in need of a good thrashout with Professor Saint-francis. That night I dreamt of the end of the world turning in glory, celestialike, and mine were uncouth, leavening visions of great and small mysteries.

The next day, the thought of the Diamants were still flustergusting about me when I cut my coat corners to the little house of Professor Saintfrancis. All of my sofar successes, the Mystery of the Three Daffodils, the Recovery of the Governor's Daughter and the Heart of Oak Ruby Affair had all been pathed with the Professor's hardaid and strongmain, though the reports in the rags and then the people's tonguerags portioned the fame to me. The truth is that his upperstory is a glorified palace to my quaint, though comfortful, corner.

I showed to his petite suburban dwelling at the end of Richmond Road a little past elevensies and in the midst of a winter mistclear found him astare from the gingerbread boxwindow into his rose garden. I do not know, what with his strange whiteeye, whether he caught the blossoms or even caught the fog belaundering heavenwards rumple by rumple. Although with Professor Saintfrancis, the blinder he falls, the farther his seeing strides, as he demonstrated right then and there.

"My dear Inspector Langer, a rough night for you I see, but a rough night fashions a milder manner."

"Come now, Professor, how could you know I was up in the nightsbelly?" He could not even see me, I believed.

"You glent by at eleven and a third. Otherwise you arrive restfreshed in the early a.m., or postmeridian after a good dewlabour. There could be no other explanation."

"Fantastic, sir."

"Oh, the merest blobscotch. Enter, pray."

We arumpered ourselves by his chafery, and his girl Jenny shimmied over tea and biscuitry. His wrizzled visage queried and fatched as I recalled him the darkdeed, that was yet no crime, as I have abovescribbled it, but in that griffgraff manner he needed, grashing out times and precisions in the least gracile way. He heard it sailorfaced, even the breathcatch of the Diamants safe in the safe, and Lady G—— floorbannered, and when I finished with the secondhandwoman going high in the instep the moment after she was hull up, and then hettling me doorwards, the Professor nodded.

"Understandable."

"How I long for your keenness. Upon my word, I cannot say whether we should even be hazarding the matter of these jewels, without points to anyone or to anywhere."

The Professor splitfaced. "I have always believed that to serve your Crown best, it is best to serve your curiosity."

I did not follow and said that I thought I would be strumming the guitar by taking time to unhash the gritbits of the case.

"Oh, spend no more than the postmeridian, Inspector. Find Lady G——'s seamer, her footman, and this Father Alexander, and your duty resolves itself. You must do it. Think, should it become modish to rustle you from your private chafery at all hours? I should say not.

"And remember," he added, puzzling me. "The thief always catches himself."

More accombered than earlier I left him, but the Professor had never glued my duty to the witchetpost before, I reckoned.

Lady G——'s seamer was the grandest poppy in Rumourstown, what with her flighty shop plum on the cantel and twelve girls knotting paper cherryblossoms onto a lengthy backdrape the colour of a blueberry's inside.

"A wondrous woman, the true quality," she responded to my mark of Lady G——, overflushed to gibber about her famousest luxuriast.

"She gussies up a good deal then?"

"Lady G—— has the most lithesome form on the colony and her havers are reproachless."

"Oh, for sure, I see."

"And her credit, I need not note, is sans reproach." Not keening to my hamsam tone about the Holy Widow, she then arrowed me doorwards but I remarked innerly that the question of credit had not flittered by my lips.

The Lady's footman too was silentward, not from hiddenness but from stupidness. The fellow was about as thick a block of pork as didn't oink and root pen.

"When did Lady G—— call you?" I started.

"She called me up, yes."

"But when?"

"Right after."

"After what?"

"After the safe dove in." I could catch my spadework was slicing clay with the man.

"What did she want?"

"She called for Inspector Langer."

"For me?"

"You're Inspector Langer?"

"Yes."

"She called for you then."

That was all the figure I could carve out of his woodenheadedness.

I was to have worse luck in my duties around the fantastic Diamants yet, for when I searched for Father Alexander, the priest had already scuppered, from the Catchland Manse, and the Cathedral holdpot, and the isle entire. Bundled into the *Restorer*, that day's dewship, he would aground next at Southampton. No diocesan would hazard why neither, and myself I could not net the threadbarest reason a holy fellow would flitter from no crime. I was stonied.

The whisty needledame, the dunderhead footman and the spectral priest—a seamrent sum. I knew my little all was an orphansmouth when I turned to Professor Saintfrancis, to catch what he could ply from it. I recalled near evetide. His Jenny had prepped us a good swallowsworth of hocks and yellows for supper, and he eared with relish my hedleymedley of neants.

"Well done indeed, Inspector," he said when I closelipped.

"How's that?"

"I believe you remarked the raffish sight of a silver candelabra up at the Manse, and a picture of the *Titanic* Downgoing."

I could not catch how that mattered.

"The only curlpoint now is which one you will bid for."

Professor Saintfrancis slivered me another ham from the hock with not another word, and I admit I thought the disease had at last saffled his stem, so I taved my tongue and et an egg. The Professor jollily let my sure foot rest on the falsepeninsula.

My doubt in the Professor inevitably seawashed. In a fortnight, at the Michaelmas sessions, I happened across the auction of all Lady G—'s earthlies, for she had fled the colony to the ruination of a six of chapmen and half Rumourstown. To my good fortune, I snatched up both the candelabra and the *Titanic* picture, and at hayprices, but I longed more deeply for some clearweather into the soupmist of the Diamants of the End of the World.

"Steal from a thief make God Almighty laugh," said the Professor when I visited the end of Richmond Road with my auction trophies for some revelation.

"How could you have known that the Lady's chattels would soon be vendage, Professor?"

"Logic."

"Oh, logic, sure, but explain this evident logic to me, Professor. I've stood in the drizzle long enough."

"You have waited true, though anyone knows you have been repaid for your hardlement by a lovely candelabra and a standout depiction. However, I will tell you what I know.

"The seamer's testimony, as you accounted it, demonstrated that our Lady was in the grift, since only a chapwoman owed hugeous debts would praise a client's credit so plainfaced. That debtage is common with the quality, more so in the colony. The footman next confirmed that the Lady mouthed your name. I remarked upon it with your first tale, that she monikered you the postmoment of the crime. Why would such a lady know of a lowly Inspector like yourself? One cannot watch the thief in one's own house."

"I don't follow."

"She was researching inspectory and hence prepping the thieving herself. Mortgagers cannot reclaim stolen articles for debt and insurers must againbuy. And then the flyaway Father, he undashed my last doubts."

"How so?"

"I am only a blindman but here's what I catch. Lady G— prays to the Father to steal the World's End, to save her from ruination. The Father's heart opens, and he hingesmashes the safe for the Lady, prongs the Diamants. The bauble itself, however, and I have this from your excellent and vivid accounting, Inspector, acts whistily as a kind of preachment. The Alpha and the Omega haunt the priest's mindseye while he handles the mere thing, and the eighth commandment foghorns to him. Under the downpour of his conscience, he returns the diamantry and flitters. He who learns to steal must learn to run."

"Incredible," I murmured.

"Not so when you do not forget the power of the beautiful and the unlikely."

"I meant that you are incredible, Professor."

"Me? I am a nobbly old nowheresman with groatsworth of breathing days left, and an endless redlane down my crookback. The true shame," he said, somberizing, "is that the auctioneers will brake up that glorious gigglegaggle whose riches seemed, unlike all others, to better men."

The Professor's face turned stony with the thought and no more mystery to solve. I could tell his greatmind wanted to stew solo awhile. I left the silverroped candelabra for him. The Sinking of the *Titanic* hangs on my best wall.

VON LETTOW-VORBECK, AFRICA'S WHITE LION

Arcadio Cole
1891 – 1926

So they've packed their kits full of wallop
   To carry 'em ocean far
And battle looks just like a wind-up toy
   To the boys of the KSR.

Their sweethearts are thronging the throughways
   Each wishing upon a star
That they'll soon taste the joys of returning,
   The boys of the KSR.

—MRS. LETITIA SMYTHE-BRYANT

A lion devoured my pal Praisegod half a season into our East Africa campaign. There never was a better fellow than Praisegod. He did his bit. So when I heard a man claiming soon after that the Hun general Von Lettow-Vorbeck was training lions for the German army, I went a bit crackers and took a poke at the tale-teller. It was only Mr. Singh, an old sweat and a kind sort who had helped out greenhorns like myself often enough. He was very good about the whole thing when I came to my senses.

"Sanjanian," he said to me, "I know you are smarting on account of your comrade but I tell you Von Lettow-Vorbeck owns this land like a demon. Tomorrow I will tell you the story of the Tanga battles and you will apologize to me. I will accept your apology."

I wanted to apologize right there. I was through. We were all pretty well through by then. The King's Sanjanian Rifles had been a late arrival to the small East Africa corner of the Great War. The Nigerians in the West African Fighting Force were the only soldiers to follow. By the time we arrived the Britishers and Imperialists had more or less packed up their hand when it came to the Germans. Our camp was tossed salad. The KSR were stretching already thin tinned beef and dop, which was the name the men gave to the force's bad brandy. Right off I had been taken over all queer by the fever and by the time I took up my bed a stranger could not have told where the Indians stopped and we began. Most of my Sanjanian brothers spent their time just warming the clock.

A good story is gravy to bored men so when Mr. Singh came the next day to tell me about the battle of Tanga a good crowd had circled round. He spoke as if it were just the two of us.

"Sir," he began, "I serve the empire with daring and flair. I will serve it until my death. Before this current and ridiculous state of shilly-shallyment our generals in their wisdom chose a straight thrust at the German territories through the city of Tanga. We are an old detachment but had never before had the privilege of a battle for the King. Stationed in Zanzibar, a most healthful and welcoming country, we were eager to set sail for the fighting.

"Permit me to set the scene, from the perspective of the Indian rifles, sir. At first sight Tanga appeared deserted. Our orders were to disembark several miles to the East of the city. Never have I known heat so thick in the air. We had to chop down fresh coconuts for thirst as our supply of water was huffed up so quickly.

"On we frogged it, obedient to orders we did not comprehend. For hours we hacked through dogged bush, blindly muddling our way. We muddled into death, for Von Lettow-Vorbeck foresaw all our movements into Tanga and gunned us down the moment we hove into sight. An Askari we captured later told me that the streets of Tanga were so littered with the bodies of our dead that they had to stack them like cordwood.

"Why were we not covered, you may be asking. The covering artillery had been taken, I would then answer. Unfortunate, you may say, but it was unnatural, I may say. For they were not taken by a troop of soldiers or men or even women. To put a tin hat on it, sir, huge hives of honeybees beset our covering troops. Ask any fellow here. Von Lettow-Vorbeck trained the bees to attack the hill."

The audience was silent as the tomb at this point. Their attention focused like a magnifying glass when the bees were bandied about.

"Let me tell you, Sanjan, Herr Von Lettow-Vorbeck is no man but an avatar. During the bluster of all this battle the Lion danced over the field on his bicycle and laughed at the five bullet holes he found after. I do not know about your country, sir, but in my village when ten men go to kill one man they kill him. Now we are ten men in Chase-me-Charlies for this one man. This one man comes to kill ten of us."

I was all apologies when he finished of course. I could understand why he might think Von Lettow-Vorbeck capable of training lions, which any circus can do, when he had been training bees. Mr. Singh understood that the camp was so restless that sometimes we young fellows would fuss. Infernal death kept chipping away and the dop which arrived in kerosene cans was the only real comfort. There was bound to be a bit of argy-bargy.

The longer we waited in that forsaken camp the deeper into the bog we slipped. The general feeling about Vorbie and his *Schutztruppe* was admiration not hatred. Our men could barely tolerate to sleep in the heat. Von Lettow's happily galloped through it. His chaps were men who laughed at drinking their own bodily waters.

We complained when the dop grew low. When one of theirs grew sick they left him to die as a matter of course. Of all the corpses of Askari and white men we found mauled to death by wild beasts not one had a rifle in his hands. They did not grant the poor chaps even the luxury of a gun. It was little wonder then that we had more respect for our enemies than ourselves.

For my part, I was coming to know the medical corps all too well. Every time I awoke from the fever someone else I knew like a brother had stopped his packet. Reginald Draper, our CO, who had seen us all the way from Port Hope, took the wrong end of one of their infernal ambuscades. The KSR no longer had a leader so the brass hats incorporated us into the West Africa Fighting Force, the "bed-and-bath-brigade."

Chasing Vorbie was like trying to catch a fish barefisted. We were ever so much bigger than the quarry but he was in his natural state and slithered easily out of our clumsy plunges. The Britisher plan was to corner the Hun against the Portuguese border. Vorbie didn't care. He had no time for anything but his own getaways. His soldiers' loyalty was the toughest bit of gristle. A captured Askari would shout despite his wounds, "I am a German soldier."

Von Lettow-Vorbeck would release captured men after they had sworn to their God or gods never to take arms against the *Schutztruppe* again. Most Imperial soldiers were only too keen to take such a vow. All of them were far too devout to consider breaking it after the fact.

He smashed every bridge on every river. Each smashed bridge meant he would catch it a bit longer. He could survive until the Rovuma, we whispered to each other. Then he would go trumpet cleaning like the rest of us.

The rains of that chase are what craw my brain most. They overflowed the rivers to the same effect as smashed bridges.

Even the arrival of supply dop was enough to puggle and queer us but we kept marching and we drove Vorbie ever closer to the Rovuma. Our troubles would end at the Rovuma where the Portos were all in a line. His renegade band could never smash through an entire nation's fresh troops, we thought. History will tell that Von Lettow did exactly that. He destroyed the Tonies in one swift kick and went running again. I had the good fortune to reencounter my companion Mr. Singh once more after the crossing of the Rovuma. We had time for a sip of tea together.

"This war will never end," he told me.

All wars end, I said.

"Consider the matter, Sanjan. Von Lettow's surrender is a ludicrous notion. Neither can the empire abandon the hunt. If he can pass the Rovuma he can carry us in a basket to the Nile Delta. If he can, he will."

I had no answer to that.

Never did I see Mr. Singh again. I can only hope that that paragon of the Empire is now telling the story of the bees to his grandchildren in his strange home country. I never saw him again because one day later we won the war.

I felt like a man in a night terror who wakes up surprised to be alive. Vorbie only discovered his defeat two weeks later by capturing a news transport, that's how untouchable he was.

My one encounter with the White Lion took place after he had downed arms. I caught him from behind a fence at the camp north of Kasama where my troop had bivvied. You can wager I took a good long look. His host was a brass hat in the Britisher ranks and well-provisioned. He poured Von Lettow a glass of French wine. Von Lettow examined it as if it were the rarest of jewels. From the first quaff the purest enjoyment permeated his whole smacker. A spoonful of the plum jam brighted him as well as if an angel had entered through his mouth. He must have eaten little more than young coconuts for over a year. He glutted on the news as well though it must have been mourning news to him. He had not read so much as a scrap of paper for several years.

The Nigerian friend beside me muttered at this unrivalled scene that he was "just a man." It struck me too.

He was the worthiest opponent one could name. I buried Praisegod along with two dozen others of the finest fruits of Sanjanian manhood. I buried them and I wept for them but there was no shame to their blood being spilt in that vast, wonderful land. They did their bit. It is rather an honour to the rest of us that a portion of our nation remains in Africa.

AN INTERLUDE AT THE OPERA

George Jankin Lee
1896 – 1936

My ring . . . the ring . . .
He took it from me . . . but cannot . . .
Take back his image . . .
The impression is here . . . in the heart.
Nor you, the pledge of eternal love,
O flower . . . I haven't lost you . . .
Again I kiss you . . . but . . .
You are withered.
Ah! I never thought to see you
Perished so soon, O flower,
You passed like our love,
That lasted only a day!

—*LA SONNAMBULA*

For a decade now, our little *partie carrée* has been meeting at The Gazelle every fortnight of the operatic season, and since the company can be relied upon, the occasion is always pleasant, no matter the quality of the performance. We are not quite the butcher, the baker and the candlestick maker, but different portions of good fortune have been allotted to each, so the conversations at our evenings always possess a pleasing variety as well. The civil servant among us has risen steadily through the Colonial bureaucracy. Our jeweler procures larger consignments and undertakes more elaborate commissions for the *haute bourgeoisie* with every passing year. The banker refuses to discuss his business, which we all take to be a very auspicious sign. I for my part write stories such as the one you hold in your hands, and though I cannot say that I write better stories as time passes, at least I write more of them.

Our traditions at these evenings are simple but inviolable: we meet in the box proper, not in the *foyer*; we do not speak during performance, the merest cough must be assiduously suppressed; and at the midpoint of the opera we take light refreshment in one of the small, sumptuous rooms in the labyrinthine upper chamber of The Gazelle. The *rôle* of host alternates. On the night in question, the jeweler had the honours and gave us cakes of fresh crab with limes, and the flavour was so redolent of the sea, transporting the room of ripe men back to childhood so utterly, that a sudden silence gripped the usual conviviality, for we had all of us begun life in low coastal outports. An intimacy derived from common history cements our friendship, not merely a shared box and a passion for musical theatre that verges on folly.

When conversation resumed, we discussed that evening's performance of Bellini's *Sleepwalker*, an opera we all knew well. The *prima donna* of the House, Ms. Tremonte at that time, had more than adequately acquitted herself in the role of Amina. The somnambulist of the title, Amina leads a peculiarly secret life, unknown even to herself, sleepwalking into strange men's bedrooms, and in a miraculous second-act aria redeems herself before the eyes of the world by unconsciously crossing over a plank at great height, a feat she could never have managed awake. A delightful character delightfully rendered, we all agreed, all except the banker that is.

"You all know that I speak from the position of a faithful lover of opera," he said, "but this sleepwalking woman demonstrates the whole trouble with the thing. Patently incredible situations and characters."

"I dare say many events of daily life are deeply and affectingly strange," said the jeweler. "I don't know if Amina's walk is really so incredible, if seen in the proper light."

"I put it to you that no actual woman has actually walked sleeping into another man's bedroom, no matter how many may claim so, and more, that no woman has dozed through like perils unconsciously."

Our friend the banker, it should be obvious, has endured some training in law. The jeweler was not intimidated, however.

"To those specific cases, naturally I cannot speak, but I do know of one particular female who has passed through a double life and through a darkness which would have made Amina there shake her head in disbelief."

"Now there is a story I must hear," said the civil servant, and the word of a civil servant is after all law, or close enough.

I met her first [the jeweler said] as the wife of Jeroboam Bitterman, the finest, handsomest sailor in my home village, who had tried his luck on the government vessels for two years and had returned, by neighbourly transport, with a new wife. A voice of general rejoicing greeted his return and the goodwill extended to the woman beside him. She was calling herself Dorothy, and soon the village called her Dot.

Well, you know how it is with a wife "from aside." All the village women regard each of the stranger's peculiarites as certified evidence of differences between their own kind and all other women. If a new wife has large earlobes, the fact stands as absolute proof that the village is full to hopping with small, graceful earlobes. If the new one happens to sing well, then the village is unmusical. Dorothy, for them, was a distinct threat, for she was extraordinarily beautiful and elegant, with high cheekbones and a long taille, and all manner of manner. I was a boy leaning towards manhood, but I wasn't alone in drawing in my breath whenever she happened to pass.

The village compensated for her grace by declaring her utterly useless for any important feminine task. To hear the older women speak, she could not so much as sweep out a corner or make a fishbone stew, and while she claimed to have been a teacher when Jeroboam encountered her, everyone considered her inept around children. Our vanity insisted that all other women beyond the pilot rocks of our own covehead were below Crown Standard. Dorothy Bitterman bore the yoke, as the best women do, with a humble smile, cheerful acceptance, and the Christian expectation that even the judgement of women passes.

Indeed, Dot swiftly assumed all of the skills necessary to her situation, and the consequence was that she became one of us within six months. She had a soft gentility in her air when she arrived, I recall, but no man could have distinguished her from the other wives after that half year. And at almost the exact moment of her integration, just after she had managed to sew herself into community with the village wives, Jeroboam died at sea.

The aldermen did offer a party of escort back to her homecove, a perilous journey fully circumnavigating the island, for that was where she told us she was from, but we all breathed a sigh of relief when she adamantly refused it. She was at home with us, she said. She wished to remain with the family of her husband, and asked only to be treated in the same way as any other village widows. The family was amenable and the matter so arranged. All seemed well.

Dorothy Bitterman kept her station for many years. Dot was Dot, a widow among the others, her status as an asider forgotten long ago. If she were remarkable, it was only in her virtue, in that she never listened to those soft, sweet words of romantic callers permissible to widows. She was perhaps a little sickly. Bouts needing bedrest seemed to grip her particularly whenever the geevees hauled into port. Those scenes of joy accompanying the arrival of the mail, the pamphlets, the packages of Port Hope flavours and news, they were never overseen by her gracious presence, not once. But otherwise, as I said, Dot was Dot, and nobody paid her any particular mind.

Several years afterwards, but it could not have been so very long because I was even then planning my own charge into the fray of the city, I did catch the hint of an angle on Dorothy Bitterman. A distant cousin of mine, a fellow with the remarkable name of Frank Virgin, recognized her. He was a worker aboard the geevees and always lodged with us when his ship anchored at our village. We were passing by the Bitterman house when he spotted her at a window, stopped dead in his tracks, and she vanished like a shadow at sudden light. I asked how he knew her, but the sole response I received was a wry smile and the mild reproof that he could never break a secret with a lady.

I recalled the scene vividly when, at the next appearance of a geevee, the commanding officer of the vessel marched up to the Bittermans' door and, without the trace of formality, demanded that Dorothy be given over to his care under Imperial orders. His papers were printed on the blue paper of the Admiralty, enough to terrify the aldermen out of tonguesmanship. She went placidly when called, too; as the Bittermans told it, her bags were already packed, and she left behind gifts for her favourites, complete with attached notes. Parting, she wept profusely, and declared her gratitude for so many happy years, but she offered no explanation. No explanation, in fact, ever came. My memory of Francis Virgin spying Jeroboam's widow merely muddied the puddle, so I never even introduced it into conversation when the gossip inevitably turned, as it did for many months, to the question of the abbreviated village life of Dorothy Bitterman.

They were still discussing the matter when I left. As you know, gentlemen, I ventured my little all in Port Hope, and I have had my little success. The world has danced to me for a quarter hour, it is true. What I learned with pretty shells ensconced in copper wire has stood me well setting rubies into gold. I have prospered, and as I prospered I began to rise to prosperous amusements, dinners for business, balls for pleasure, opera with close friends even.

It was at the opera, at The Gazelle in fact, that I reencountered Dorothy Bitterman, or rather the woman who once called herself Dorothy Bitterman. It wouldn't do to reveal her name of course, nor too much by way of detail, but suffice it to say she is the wife of a powerful man, whom all present would do much to know intimately, and a most admirable hostess. Her father is one of the most august of our nation in the entire colony.

If I may add, to return to our reencounter, the woman appeared not to know me and I have never confronted her about the pretence, if it indeed is so. I have rather engrossed myself since our last meeting but not, I trust, beyond recognition. My distant relative Francis Virgin, who around that time began the lengthy process of drinking himself to death, gave the most extensive explanation I can offer under the circumstances, that the woman had flown from a wealthy life in the city for love of Jeroboam Bitterman and stayed for the simple pleasures of the cove. This woman made our journeys in reverse, gentlemen, and yet her father had to rescue her from the happiness of the condition we fled. Indeed, it was one reason Francis gave out for drinking himself into misery, but there is the bell again, and we really must hurry.

My friend was indeed correct, the bell had been ringing for some minutes, and the boy had passed the door crying, "Seats, seats," on three separate occasions. As we were rising, the banker asked bluntly, "And why did you never confront her?"

The jeweler replied, "Here, among my most durable friends, I may say whatever I please, and there is no shame to my origins, but we are not always among friends . . ."

"This story is as incredible as the opera," declared the civil servant.

"I will oath to every word. Let me tell you that the woman of whom I have spoken, the so-called Dorothy Bitterman herself, is in this audience, and no doubt you all know her real name and would recognize her."

We rushed to our seats with as much dignity as we could muster. In the hush before the singers reentered I whispered half a dozen suggestions to my friend, for I am a preternatural gossip. It is my profession when all is said and done. He brushed the proffered monikers aside with neither yes nor no. "Look for the one with the sad eyes," he said, smiling. That was no help at all of course, since the women in the audience wore melancholy like a fashion. I must admit, though there are few greater admirers of maestro Bellini than myself, I took little from the second act, lost in the thought of how much greater are the dramas performed for us offstage.

UPHEAVALS

AND

INDEPENDENCE

SUFFERANCE ROW

Blessed Shirley

1897 – 1952

Her hands full, Miranda Wisdom managed to open the door and close it behind her with only the nimble movements of her elbows. The narrow closet on her left, hooked open with a heel, received the broom, the pan, the mop and a bucket whose rim was festooned with drying rags. Miranda straightened herself and looked about. A vegetable stew had been left to simmer all day and, finding the warmth too much, Miranda first stowed her burdens and then crossed the room to open a window. The gusts of the ocean breeze were so refreshing that she paused at the sill, leaning out.

The evening sea was calm. The massive transports were not budging in the visible stretch of harbour. Even the shipboarded vessels were barely stirring, seven o'clock postmeridian being the hour for dinner the length of the docks and the men hungry from Wednesday, always a busy day. Three enormous ships, the *Mer-*

cury, the *United States* and another whose name Miranda could not remember, were stationed to load in the sufferance portion of the harbour. They consumed three-quarters of the vista but, between the *Mercury* and the *U.S.*, Miranda could make out a brief span of water glittering purple, red and gold with the setting of the sun. Leaning farther out, she could also see the warehouses of the Row, monolithic flats whose waterfronts lacked any windows.

The ships and buildings deserted by commerce and their usual teemings of men always filled her with a grand sadness. She lived on Sufferance Row, among stocks and stores awaiting a better hour for remittance, resale or redirection. A noise came from below. The stairs to her chamber led directly to the offices, and distinct Britisher voices were audible, the last of the company men leaving the building together.

"I couldn't really tell you why I'm hesitant, although, Lord knows, I'm turning a bit local, a bit native, despite all the efforts of so many kind souls."

"How so?"

"Well, to give you one example, I don't know better than a dog what the cricket's like this year, practically no idea what the summer's been like."

"Practically forgotten the game myself."

"Young Geoffrey Irons was in here the other day telling me that he doesn't feel the least touch of homesickness, what with the steady supply of Englishmen and the climate and all, but I couldn't agree with him less."

"Exactly."

Their conversation no doubt continued but Miranda caught no more of it. With the door's dull thud, the click of brass tongue in oak groove, and the ratchet of the key in the lock, their presence in the office for the day was concluded. That fact, the vastness of the warehouse without a beating heart other than her own, was oppressive. The emptiness of the place rushed in on her like a brisk wind through smoldering tinder so that she had to turn aside from the window and find something to do. "On Wednesday do come visitors," she muttered to herself and began to straighten the room.

Cleaning the floors of an office on Sufferance Row was a full day's toil, but "living above" was some compensation. Miranda took pains to keep the space tidy. The room was single but divided neatly by a long red curtain. Her low bed, oak dresser, and toilet-table could be tucked out of view with a flick of her wrist. In the main area, a plain, solid table with four decent chairs took up one wall, the cast-iron stove and window the other. Crockery, china and linens were all carefully stowed in the large closet beside the door, on a shelf above the tools of her trade. Miranda wanted no clutter in her humble salon. One never knew whom one would be receiving.

After wiping the table, checking the heat of the stove, and tightening the edges of the blanket on the bed, she yet had time to wash her face. Earlier in the day, she had laid out a bar of soap, hair brush, toothpick, cloth and sponge beside the basin of lukewarm water on the toilet-table. Miranda also kept a mirror face down in the shelf of that table. After she had scrubbed her cheeks with the moistened soap and cloth, rinsed her face and sponged off the residue, the mirror came out of its shelf so that she could have a good look at herself. Her age may as well have been inscribed on the tain, the mirror so exactly showed her twenty-nine years. Her deep brown skin was still taut, burnished a little at that moment from the rugged brush of the cloth, but the skin surrounding her eyes was creased, like a riverbed in drought, her lips likewise cracked from salt and labour. Her brow had begun to wear its worries. The first plumpness of her cheeks was being replaced by reserved, wary strength. Miranda's eyes were black inside black, deep recesses in huge limpid white pools, full of solicitous wellmeaning in repose. They fixed the beauty of her face like two tack pins.

Miranda tucked the mirror back into the shelf. She neatened her plain grey dress and pulled the rich red curtain across. The pot of greens and millet sent up a great message of steam when she removed the lid to inspect. A glance at the window revealed the full glory of a reddish sea sunset but enough passages of gold remained to spare a quarter-hour for reading without candlelight. "Well, I thought that I could hope for a visitor as it is a Wednesday and all," she said aloud to nobody. Beside the door was a small bookshelf with a sparse collection of cove pamphlets, a book of family receipts and a Holy Bible. Taking the Bible from the shelf and pulling a chair to the window, Miranda turned to a well-worn passage among the thin, frail, gilt-edged pages. She knew the story by heart but she read anyway.

Before the light had a chance to fail, hoarse shouting from below and an insistent pounding on the thick first-floor door announced a visitor. She lay the book face down on the table and reset the chair in its proper place. The voice was female and so she had no need to hurry. It could only be Gwyn. Miranda was so sure of the fact that she didn't bother with the dooreye at the bottom of the stairs. Gwyn stood back a little as the door opened, surprised. As she lowered her hand, her surprise curled into a smile.

"Upsanddowns, then! I didn't think you were there for half a moment, but then I had to ask myself where you would be otherwise. And another place at this time would not pop into my head, so I thought I might have another knocking."

"I certainly am glad," replied Miranda.

Gwyn followed Miranda closely up the half-dark stairs. Inside the room, she took a kitchen chair before it was offered. The two women were family, however distant, and Gwyn always took advantage of rights which were hers. She was the daughter of the baker whose shop was at the far corner of Sufferance Row, and whose wife related by marriage to one of Miranda's uncles. Few physical resemblances could connect the two women. Gwyn had at least six inches in height over Miranda, and she was nearly a decade younger. Her cheeks were higher, her nose straighter, her skin lighter than Miranda's. From under the Cathedral arches of her brows, brilliantines blazed. Her womanly strength was impressive even when she was dressed in an infantile white smock to do her father's evening deliveries.

She took three flat discs of bread from the basket and placed them on the table beside the outspread Holy Book.

"I'm afraid all I have is the narrow loaves since the Robinsons took another cake just when I came, and the Richstars had a feast for the confirmation of Fortitude and needed ten breads. That was a treat for Father I don't think, and their bill still up in ciphers on the white board."

"I am so lucky," Miranda murmured.

"Also, a portion of glayfish." Smiling, Gwyn handed Miranda the package of fish which had been wrapped in sere saltcloth. "The Jameses offered a double fish as repayment for their tally and we had just come from purchasing a double ourselves, so Father told me to bring you a portion so the waste might be halved."

Miranda took the package to the brief side space beside the stove and began to unwrap it. The fish had been cleaned, its spine removed whole with a proper knife, but still Miranda felt obligated to inspect the firm white ridges for bones. A subtle tremor of its delicate iron-filled flavour rose into the air as Miranda divided the flesh into morsels each the size of a finger, salted them and added them to the stew with pinches of bitter herbs. Gwyn always ended her delivery rounds at these Sufferance offices in the hope of an opportunity to inspect her cousin's room. The romantic heart within her always wondered at the half-widow waiting for her husband Wisdom who had gone to sea eight years before and no word more had been heard of him or the vessel. The man had left so long ago that Gwyn could not recall a single detail of him. The room was extremely clean, and Gwyn sighed within herself, and thrilled a little too, at the thought that Miranda must be keeping it so, so that the vanished man could have an appropriate homecoming at any hour.

"Bread and jam, Gwyn?" Miranda asked when she had done preparing the fish.

"I prefer not to trouble you, but if it is all right, a seat for a quarter of ten minutes perhaps?"

"At your leisure." Miranda stirred up the oven's embers with a pothook. The increased heat meant that she needed to remain by the oven, constantly stirring the mixture, otherwise the glayfish would burn.

"And how is the family?" Miranda asked.

"Father is holding on and the store is keeping. Did I tell you? Mark-Luke is leaving the store now that I'm baking first bread and doing the evening rounds. Guess where he is finding work."

"I couldn't say."

"Right underneath where we're sitting, in these offices. Margison took him under a wing for a handler commission. He's a good fellow, Margison."

"Absolutely," agreed Miranda.

"Soon you will see Margison pointing Mark-Luke where to tote coffee, won't that be a lark? I hope Mark-Luke will take orders, I must say, for the lad has hardly been smooth under a rudder, with Father's mild watch no less."

"Margison is a gentle man," Miranda said.

"I don't worry about Margison but about Mark-Luke. A handler is not child's work, no doubt you know that, and Margison can be a stern man in the greenhouse, so they say along the Row. The boy needs a full meadow when another man says a harsh word to him."

"I am sure Margison understands."

"And what do you think of Margison, then?" Gwyn asked with a sly uplook. Miranda's back flickered and she paused, stirring the fishstew. Flashing her left hand, with the thin silver band on her ring finger, she grinned over her shoulder. Gwyn was again amazed at her elder relative, the amazement tinged with horror, for the patience in the woman was as fierce as newlywed joy.

"Perhaps the chatter would be much better if I asked my young cousin about the attentions of the menfolk of the Row," Miranda said. "I'm sure that is much more the intriguing tale."

A rush of hot blood burned in Gwyn's cheeks and she reached for whatever distraction was close at hand. In this case, it was the Bible on the table.

"You've been reading the Book, I can see," she said. "Or at least a few pages. My, look how these few breezesheets have been rubbed raw. Why have you been reading this one passage so well, Mandy?"

Miranda gave no answer but to stir the pot. As swiftly as the joy had run through her, so swiftly did it run out of her, like water in the sluices of a lock.

"Look, you have near rubbed out these words by finger-reading them."

Gwyn's lips moved as she read. The well-worn passage on

the greyed page was the story of Jonah, the drowned man spat up again, and Gwyn realized the more she read how far was her blunder. With a soft gesture, Miranda rested the spoon on the rim of the pot, and went to the window to widen the crack. Gwyn could see the shudder, the quick hand brushing the eyes, and she replaced the book on the table without a word, shame emblazoning her face. She had dabbled enough in romance for the evening, Gwyn thought. Besides, the light had quite fallen under.

"The light has quite fallen under," she said quickly.

"Can't I offer you dinner?" Miranda asked, returning to her boiling pot without a glance at her cousin.

"No, I'm afraid father will be angry with me for cooling the dinner at home."

"Give my heart to your father and my thanks for the glayfish and loaves."

"Nothing," Gwyn said, standing up and tucking the chair under the table. Miranda put down her spoon again and the two women embraced.

"You're a good woman, Miranda Wisdom."

"Leave the door for me, my dear," said Miranda with a gesture that said no forgiveness would be necessary. "I will latch it afterwards. Must tend the soup."

Gwyn hurried down the stairs for she was indeed quite late for the family, but her delicate skip towards the office stairs ended in her squeal and a man's guffaw. The racket was explained only when Margison's voice boomed out. They must have knocked into each other. Miranda padded to the door and pressed against it to listen.

Margison was saying, "Miss Gwyneth. In a white smock no less."

"Yes, it's just me," Gwyneth giggled after righting herself.

"Did I ever tell you how your father once baked a shilling into a roundloaf he sold me?"

"You tell it me whenever we meet, and I say so every time too." She giggled more.

"And what are you doing here, child?"

"I was just up to see Miranda Wisdom, to give her bread and fish. And you?"

"I am here to settle up the end-of-month accounts. Thursday is the first, you can see it on the wall."

Gwyn began laughing, all her queenly strength lost in the presence of an elder of the other sex, and then she whispered something, something which eavesdropping Miranda could not hear. Margison also laughed.

"No, it is only the accounts, Gwyneth," was his response to whatever it was she had said.

"Well, I must off to Father."

"Give him a blessing with my name," said Margison.

With a parting good wish, Gwyn tore away from the offices, as much from fear as from manners, and sprinted down the length of Sufferance Row towards the bakery kitchen. They were to eat cold pickled tongue that evening and she wanted her full portion. Miranda hastened to her pot and turned over the stew. While she had been eavesdropping, already flecks of burnt brown had appeared on the firm white fish pieces. The latch click confirmed that Margison indeed did intend to rectify the head accounts that evening. He had told Gwyn the truth. The job was beholden to him as chief handler on the first of the month, although customarily the task was managed in the plain light of morning on the day itself. No rule, however, stated that the chief handler was forbidden from working under taper light during time for which he was not paid for working. Miranda could hear Margison taking candles from the low cupboard in the hallway where she had just been mopping. The snip of the wick was following by a struck match tearing open a flame, then the shuffle of blocks and papers at the general writing stand. The accounts rarely took Margison longer than a quarter hour, Miranda knew.

Miranda also lit tapers, and lowered the flame on the stove with three handfuls of dust, topping the pot with a flat lid. When she listened with care, she could hear the scratching of the nib marking the old book, so thin were the office floors.

There was a pause in the cross-checking, then a knock on the wall at the foot of Miranda's stairs.

When she opened the door, Miranda could see Margison there, illuminated by the light of a single candle which diffused his features rather than clarified them.

"Please come up, Mr. Margison," Miranda whispered.

"I hate to disturb you."

"Not the least disturbance."

The naked light of candleflame as he climbed towards her gave his face definition in steady increments. His curly hair was close-cropped, a razor-width from baldness. The creases of his worried brow cracked his face in the flickering shadow. His narrow eyes were kind, however, and the stooping limp of a once labourer on the cusp of his middle years gave him a naturally sympathetic aura. When he smiled, and he was smiling now, Margison could be a handsome fellow.

"Please come in," Miranda said.

"I don't mean to trouble you," Margison repeated.

"Please sit."

"Grace to you."

"Might I offer you a spot of brandy?"

"That would go very well."

One thing had already been decided: she would not offer him dinner. She was not yet willing to share plates with him.

The brandy bottle served as a kind of bookend to support the collection of cove pamphlets on the bookshelf and when she removed it, a few copies teetered over. The crescents, large purple glasses which could each hold a generous dollop of spirit, were in the drawer on the night table. Miranda filled them to near brim, Margison toasted their healths and salvations, and they both flicked a drop onto the table. These preliminaries over, they settled into a conversational silence.

"My goodness me, I forgot to give you this, the reason I came," Margison said, interrupting the pause to take from the pocket of his coat and offer her a bar of cocoa.

"Mr. Margison, that was unnecessary."

"Well, I grimace to give it you really, Mrs. Wisdom, since it was a fluke. It so happened that Tremonte missed a week's payment on bananas for the tenth time in a year, and so the Company overtook a portion of his cocoa shipment."

"How wretched for the trader," said Miranda. "I have heard that he is a decent employer."

"Oh, it's all in the regulations. Beside, it was a bit of good for the handlers. They received a few bars each, over and above pay."

He sipped barely enough to moisten his lips, while Miranda put the bar of cocoa aside, on the bed behind the red curtain. There was another silence when she returned to the table.

"What do you hear from the sailors this week, Mr. Margison?"

"I did hear an interesting story from a Scotchman this week."

"Tell it."

"The fellow was a shipwrack aboard the *Ariadne* and he escaped."

"He escaped?"

"He was the sole survivor, all the rest perished. In the South Seas, this was, and he was taken by pirates without any money to ransom him. One never hears such stories any longer, more like a hundred-year-old tale, not of the twentieth century all in all, and I do have my reservations about its truth. Still, quite the adventure this fellow had, no doubt. He escaped them, he oaths, in Hong Kong and made his way to Portsmouth, as quickly as he could but yet slowly. It took him seven years from the time of the wreck until he arrived on Britisher soil. Yet when arrived there he found wives waiting for husbands he himself had seen perish. He himself had seen them waved to the depths, and yet they wouldn't believe him. That is what this fellow said. They would not believe him. They are still waiting, he said. That was seven years after the wreck."

He sipped his brandy again, his eyes fastened to the soil, and when he peered up again, Miranda's eyes were burning brighter than the tapers, aglint with near tears. "It has been eight years for you," he wanted to say, he should have said, but did not say. Miranda's eyes might have welled up and drowned, the tears spilling over onto her cheeks, but they did not. Instead, she sat staring at the suitor who was too kind to state his suit, shame flitting across her like raindrifts on a road. Her gaze, if it said anything to Margison, said only that she wore a mask underneath her mask. Silence filled the room like the odour of the soup Margison would not be eating that night, until they both had once more sipped their crescents of brandy.

They should have talked about love, but instead they discussed the toings and froings along Sufferance Row. There was the crumbling marriage of the Mastersons off Moses Road to share between them. Their neighbours the Gregors were soon emigrating to New York, Miranda had heard. Margison informed her of supplies soon arriving, Cuban tobacco and rum, an old-fashioned spice ship. They spoke like new neighbours about the petty details of Sufferance Row, where nothing changes or stays, and everything awaits a better opportunity. One must have something to chat about while one takes a sip.

They finished their brandies together and sighed. Both lived alone.

"Mrs. Wisdom, I must go."

"You will come on Wednesday next?" she asked with more than a hint of anxiety in her tenor.

"Most certainly." Margison rose and tucked the chair back under the table. A flattered smile flitted across his mouth, and he stood in the doorframe for a moment, checking his pockets.

"And countless thank-yous for the cocoa bar," Miranda added.

"It was my pleasure."

He half-bowed before closing the door behind him, leaving the company's taper for Miranda's comfort. His limping steps syncopated down the stairs. Miranda listened to his puffing as he clumped down, then she heard the squeak of a hinge, the click of the doorknob tongue, the latch turning, and then silence, the perpetual lap of the sea without disturbance. Miranda was truly alone at last.

The soup was overdone. Most of the glayfish had browned and the rest had dissolved into the broth. Miranda ladled out a bowl, cut a flatloaf into thin strips, and carried the meal to the windowsill. She barely noticed the taste of the dish, so comforting and bland was it with no more spice than a pinch of bitter herb.

The sea had remained calm, the vessels still motionless in the clear night air. The moon had risen, a threequarter milkbowl reflecting onto the water in silver shimmers between the enormous shadows of the ships. The road to the world was laid out on that strip of water, a glittering highway leading everywhere, taking all things away and bringing only some of them back. Miranda mopped up the bowl with pieces of bread. There was still a double portion left in the stove pot, enough for a man, but she was already full. She always made too much. Behind the curtain, on her bed, she found the cocoa bar and broke the smallest fraction from its corner. It would have to last till next Wednesday, after all. With its flavour sharp on her tongue, Miranda returned to the window and her view, quiet vessels, docks, sea, moon.

TWO STORIES ABOUT THE ABANDON TREE

Elizabeth Rushton

1913 – 1965

The Story from the Newspaper

APRIL 28, 1938.—The village of Marginal Cove suffered catastrophe last month when a two-hundred-year-old oak growing on a small island off the covehead was hit by lightning. The landmark, known to local fishermen as "the abandon tree," burned for two days despite the best efforts of the villagers to salvage it.

The tree was a centre of life in Marginal Cove and a physical representation of the village's hardiness and perseverance. Decorating its boughs at the Easter and Christmas seasons were important local traditions. The village sailed to the tree's island to celebrate Good Friday and Christmas Eve feasts.

The bolt of lightning struck the core of the oak, and therefore the teams of rescuers dispatched in the middle of the storm could do little.

Only the black skeleton of the burnt wreck stands today. No plans have been made to dispose of it.

The Story from Me

Green leaves unfurled their living flags, green flags without a country. When past seasons passed, when buds struggled on the bone branches, or withered on the stem, everyone in Marginal Cove brought a substitute ornament. The Abandon Tree at the mouth of the sea uttered a different word each day to the men in vessels piercing the impossible ocean. What the women understood is not for our ears.

That storm night, God's blue finger put down a tongue of red flame speaking up. Red leaves in the night and in the day black clouds as canopy. No green or blue water could that ember quench, island rooted.

Under new light grey ash drifted across, grey-white snow soft on the heads of men and women. Only the children dared look—the bones where the loved one smashed in pieces on the rock of ages, the signal tree become a raised fist to the pilots now.

The seasons have nowhere to turn.

The birds have nowhere to land.

The green sea flows untroubled past the dead thing.

THE MASTER'S DOG

Augustus P. Jenkins

1904 – 1936

More than anything, Mrs. Pamela Worthington found it boring, the twisty drive from the bungalow in the city to the country residence near the village of Jacks. It was too far from the sea, out of view or sound of it. The dense silences of the Tols, that rough scrabble of hills central to the Sanjanian interior, were testing for a discreet British personality like her own. Mrs. Worthington enjoyed stretching out her long, shapely form and, due to the nauseating jerks and chortles of the journey to Jacks, she was forced to curl herself up in one corner of the Victory with her new pet, a German shepherd named Loki, who needed cradling and soothing. When Mrs. Worthington did look out the window of the car, which was not often, the scrub of the Tols, the grey dirt of the hills, struck her principally with its indifference, its attitude of unconcern.

Her servant, Fortitude Jonson, watched his mistress carefully. Sitting bolt upright in the seat across from Mrs. Worthington, he possessed the demeanor and bearing of impassive furniture. Since he rode backwards, his journey was marked by a reversed accumulation of what had immediately passed, and by reflections on Mrs. Worthington's gaze up the road. This doubled judgement at second hand was further hampered by the necessary caution of never meeting Mrs. Worthington's eyes.

The silence of the sea's absence was growing too much for the lady. She began speaking. "So, Fortitude, how do you feel about our return to Jacks, then? How long has it been? Finally we are back now, aren't we? Isn't it good that we are arriving at last?"

"I am very happy, madam," Fortitude said, or more precisely tried to say, as the dog began to bark furiously the moment he opened his lips, its practice whenever Fortitude attempted speech.

When she had quieted poor, nervous Loki, Mrs. Worthington enquired, with an air of polite curiosity, "How long has it been?"

It would be too much to say that Fortitude considered replying that they had been in Port Hope, without a single visit to her husband or his home town, for seventeen months and twelve days, but the truth, after struggling to the surface, fell back and drowned muddily in the style of British hypocrisy he had acquired. "A little over a year, madam," he replied.

"That long? But we are back now, we are back now, aren't we Loki?"

The German shepherd had once been a police dog and did not deal in pleasantries. Mrs. Worthington had rescued the creature from disposal after its tenure at Control. Among the many distinctions which had been beaten into its toughened, muscular body, differences such as black against white, master against servant, strong against weak, there had been no time for pleasant against unpleasant. Fortitude avoided its eyes whenever possible, as he did with Mrs. Worthington.

Mrs. Worthington spoke again, out the window, "We will see what has changed all too soon, won't we? Or what hasn't rather." The last phrase was given lowly, to herself, and with ever so much more violence for that reason. They were definitely approaching Jacks, Fortitude thought. They were near Jacks, near his sweet Lucrece. He too had his questions.

Mrs. Worthington smoothed the dog's coat and tugged the creature gently to the seat beside her. After straightening her summer dress, correcting her posture and reaffixing, just so, a pearl brooch and flower to her front, she folded her hands together on her knees and waited as composed as a schoolgirl. Fortitude saw in Mrs. Worthington's gestures that her previous conversation with him had only been preparation for this moment, that she had pretended such affability to give herself contrast for the theatrical control she would be assuming. When she spoke again, it was no surprise that her voice had altered: they had arrived.

"Have the driver stop, Fortitude."

He knocked immediately on the glass behind his shoulder, and the car rolled to a stop. "Look at it, what a shame." Their eyes peered together at the property: the lawns flopping with Sanjan hay for want of mowing, feckless gardens wild with gold-and-mauve flowers and native mosses, and the tattered grey-shingled roof of the villa at the far end of the drive. To Fortitude, the Britishness displayed on the Sanjanian hillside had inappropriately taken up arms in a mistaken war, its forms protective against the wrong kind of rain and the wrong manner of sunlight, its exoticism foolish and brutal. Mrs. Worthington was noticing the disrepair, the tennis court untended and left without nets, leaving only two grey rotten posts and vague, broken lines in the overgrowth as reminiscences of rules that once had applied. Though it was midsummer, no furniture on the verandah, no table for tea by the rose pleasaunce on warm days, no roses for that matter, no gesture towards civilized, rational enjoyments, and across the common both Mrs. Worthington and Fortitude could see a gap in the once even row of the zareba. A crack had appeared in the fence which divided the house, and the common field and wood, from the village. It must have been opened by workers who had grown tired with the stretch round to the front road. The faintness of the impression on the grass attested to the recentness of the violation, only the beginning of a path there.

"Fortitude, could I trouble you?" Mrs. Worthington asked forlornly.

"I apologize, madam?" For once, he did not understand his mistress.

"I know that this is hardly your demesne, as it were, but could I trust you to repair that zareba? Now that we are back, we must maintain it all again." She sighed. "So will you take care of the fence, Fortitude? The driver will handle the luggage."

"Just as you wish, madam." Too late, Fortitude had recognized that Mrs. Worthington wished to arrive alone at the villa. Hastily, he reached for the door, too hastily perhaps, for in the same instant, the dog snapped, leaping with slobbering jaw and foaming sharp cry at the darkness of Fortitude's hand. The animal was only just restrained by Mrs. Worthington's weak, flexible wrist.

"Quickly now, Fortitude," she said.

"I will see to the zareba, madam," said Fortitude, when safely out of the car.

He watched the vehicle drift up the curved foreroad to the broken mansion, and thought, "I have not escaped, but at least it has chanced that I have a reprieve."

Inside the car, Mrs. Worthington drew a hand through the fur at Loki's nape, and did not smile—she wore a smile. "We must all put on our masks, from time to time," she was thinking. "Nothing can be permanently avoided." The thought was suddenly realized materially, when she saw her husband lounging on the rusted wrought-iron furniture of the verandah, fixing a beard of tobacco into his pipe and squinting into the sun under a matted straw hat.

To Mr. Cecil Worthington, any interruption of his idleness was a travesty, and therefore the arrival of his wife in the black Victory was like evidence of the renewed onset of a forewarned, terminal illness. His thoughts were as strategic as a physician's. "Why has she returned? Why now? How do I prevent her from staying?"

Fortitude Jonson removed his shoes, knotted the laces together, and slung them over his shoulder. From the moment Mrs. Worthington had informed him of their proposed return to Jacks, that is, before the first irritating delay, the second bewildering delay, and the third, resigned delay, he had fastened his prospects onto the sensation of striding unencumbered and barefoot on the grass, which is a pleasure impossible in the city. And here he was doing it finally.

The zareba had been constructed of stakes and wires, left to fill in with brush bushes. To Fortitude's eye, the hole had been worn down rather than destroyed. Nature may have provided a small crack, but the rest had been accomplished by infinitesimal encroachment, the stakes pushed aside little by little, the wires pressed down, the bushes spread apart, a process undoubtedly begun by boys, continued by women, and finished by men. As it was, the stakes by the gap lay in a pick-up-sticks, the wires slunk awkwardly on the ground like embarrassed clothes. Fortitude could sense the feet of women carrying food and water over it, and he smiled to think of the children chasing each other around this cut-through. The transport of goods from Jacks to the villa could be negotiated so much more easily by this little path, but he would repair the fence: Mrs. Worthington had asked him. He did not pick up a stake immediately, only because his reverie had not yet finished with the lushness of the greenery.

Why had no one come to greet him, he wondered. Fortitude was stooping to retrieve one of the fallen stakes, when the question posed itself to him. There was a path here, yet no one was walking on it. This was his home after all. In Port Hope, when strangers asked him for his cove of origin, a unique pleasure had always warmed his heart when he could name Jacks, an interior town. His countrymen, almost absolutely coastal by nature, were amazed that he had never learned to swim, and possessed no strong feelings about the construction or maintenance of vessels. Yet no one had prepared a greeting party. There had been ample warning of his return.

True, he had not once ventured in those seventeen months and twelve days up to Jacks, but the journey by foot was so arduous, and even if Mrs. Worthington had offered him a three-day holiday, which was hardly likely in the best of cases—she would say, "But you are so vital to me, Fortitude"—even then he would only have been able to walk up, have a word, and walk back. For these and other reasons, Fortitude had never attempted the journey, which, despite the strength of his reasons, he so solidly regretted at the moment. For if he had come, if only for a sip of tea, a piece of sugar-soaked tack, a mouthful of solicitous words, his presence would have been sufficient, a glance would have been enough to restore all vows and all friendships.

Then Lucrece entered his memory, and what had been dribs and drabs of regret turned into a wailing tempest. For sweet Lucrece and all his words, yes, he should no doubt have walked up, at least once. She would have greeted him. He recalled the dark cloudiness of the nights when they perambulated, the shape of her body when she relaxed beside the flowers of the reservoir, that too, and her eyes abrim with weeping when he had crept from the villa to tell her, excitedly, that he would soon see the city, that Mrs. Worthington was taking him to Port Hope. No promises were made, no definite promises.

Fortitude donned his shoes again. He had not begun to attend to the gap in the zareba, and would not yet. He left the stakes where they lay, overstepping the broken bushes and tangled wires he would later have to untangle. He would right his affairs in Jacks first.

In the drawing room of the villa, such as it was, Mr. and Mrs. Worthington were partaking of tea. Mr. Cecil Worthington had surreptitiously enlivened his beverage with spirit, and had procured the seat by the window, at the furthest distance possible from his wife, in an attempt to conceal the vapours of the gin. A failed attempt, as it so happened. The room was oppressively silent, and full of beautiful English luxuries which had been left crooked and unmaintained. Loki sat alertly at Mrs. Worthington's feet. Mr. Worthington was staring at the light across the lawn, and Mrs. Worthington posed, much as she had in the car, with her hands interlocked and a mysterious smile playing upon her lips. Both were trying to pretend that they were in England, in the countryside.

"Perhaps we should divorce," said Mrs. Worthington. Mr. Worthington gave no more definite reply than to sip from his teacup.

"Perhaps we should divorce, Cecil, did you hear me?"

"Yes, my dear, I heard you, yes," he replied at some length.

"Would you mind if I enquired how your life is proceeding?"

"Oh, about as well as can be expected at the moment."

"And how, I hope you don't mind me being so forward, but that's why I'm here, how well is that?"

"Right now, as a matter of fact, I particularly need silence and seclusion. And no, it is not," he replied.

"What is not?" she asked in mock confusion.

"It is not why you are here," he clarified.

"Oh."

"You are here, and I mean that cause for which your presence in this room can be accounted, is that you need money."

Mrs. Worthington unclasped her fingers, and sipped her tea precisely. Her husband's face was now turned to her own, the faint hope of advantage flushed faintly upon it, but Mrs. Worthington was clever enough that she took his rebuff as opportunity. His error was engagement, and she saw to exploit it.

"I'm sorry, but in all fairness, I did mean that we are stuck on this Godforsaken darkie island under the imperatives of your career—"

"Which was pursued only by your avaricious . . ." he spluttered while she continued unruffled, "and for that reason have sacrificed mutually enough for the commencement of a career in the Colonial Office, a sacrifice which you have squandered and are squandering even at this moment, and which might have resulted in some further advancement to a higher posting. A higher posting in a different country."

Cecil Worthington looked at his wife with almost bemused defiance. "I don't wish to move elsewhere," he said.

His wife no doubt would have pounced on this ridiculous remark, but Macy, the inside girl—Mr. Worthington employed only one—entered the room to ascertain whether further refreshment was required. After the dog's rage at her had been quieted by Mrs. Worthington's soothing hand, the room was full of silences and English furniture again. Mr. Worthington resumed his inspection of the lawn, his wife returned her hands to their interlocked severity.

"What do you think of Loki, Cecil?" Mrs. Worthington asked.

"He's a German, isn't he?"

"Yes, I took him from the Imperial Police Force."

"One of those brutish black-killers," he said distractedly.

"He doesn't relish darkies, no. Or rather he does," she said with a light laugh.

Mr. Worthington looked with indifference at the dog, as if it were not quite worthy of his consideration, or disgust.

"But to return to what we were discussing, Cecil. We shan't get a divorce, shall we?"

Mr. Worthington spoke calmly after a few moments' consideration. "Why, I wonder, wife of my bosom, more precious than rubies, why are we in the midst of this rather unpleasant discussion? I have considered, up to this point, that we had a perfectly established . . . well, I won't call it a relationship, but at least an established arrangement insofar as you were and are disinterested, nay uninterested, in my existence, though I might grant you to be less so when the question involves my name and my career. You have never loved me. I no longer love you. Tell me how much money you need. Tell me how much. Please. How much do you need?"

Mrs. Worthington had been stroking her dog's head while her husband rambled, and let Loki down off the settee when he had finished. "You are in error, Cecil. It is not money. I demand you to give up this ridiculous do-nothing hermit life of total apathy and move to Port Hope permanently.

"And I hope that you will," she concluded.

Fortitude could hear the schoolhouse before he could see it. A bracken of willow trees muffled the musical sing-song of teacher and students. The very building seemed to admonish him and welcome him. With utter clarity, Fortitude could recall the weather, faint peculiar little cloud pillows on a spread of incredible blue, on that day, years before, when Jacks had built the school. Mr. Worthington had ordered it built, after agreeing to defray the costs of a teacher, and he had supervised the proceedings with noblesse oblige for half an hour before returning to his bottle and library. The elders muttered with amazement to think there would be a whole village of children who read stories each to himself, just as in Hope, just as with the written-down theatrebooks. It had been a day of universal and supreme triumph. His heart fit to burst with the heady mixture of nostalgia, hope and regret, Fortitude crept quietly to the open window and peeked in, unnoticed, to see how the promise of that day had fulfilled itself.

Lucrece stood at the front of a large full classroom, beside an enormous pink and grey map of the world, and such was her concentration that she did not notice Fortitude's peeping gaze at the back window. Seventeen months had plumped her, and her wide eyes, while they retained a general goodwill, registered gained experienced indefinably. Her easy grace still displayed more than traces of the girl who had walked in the dark with him, listening to his unexpressed promises.

"Already, children, we have arrived where we want to be. You are very smart, aren't you?"

All ages of the class were giggling, but in relative unity they said, "Thank you, miss."

"But now hush, on this map behind, who can finger for me where we are?"

The older children's hands shot up, Lucrece chose Georgina,

and Georgina sauntered to the front. She pointed to the spot with a triumphant finger.

"Very good, Georgina, now, can you tell me what country the map says for that spot."

Georgina peered with imperfect eyes at the big map. "Co-Lo-Ny of San-Jan Iss-Land," she asseverated.

Lucrece smiled at the child and released her. "Sanjan Island, yes, Georgina, precisely accurate. You may be seated. Can any other person, a younger person perhaps, inform us of what colour Sanjan Island is on this particular map?"

"Pink!" called out a voice.

"Yes, and can some person inform us, after putting up his or her hand, what other countries here are pink?"

A hurried mélange of competing colonies jostled in the collective child noise: Britain, East Africa, South Africa, America, New Zealand.

"Not America, no," Lucrece corrected, "but could someone, some one, inform the class about what all these pink countries are?" No one answered. "Can some one then tell me why all these countries on the map are pink? Yes, Mellida."

"The British Empire?"

"Yes, and who is King of the Empire?"

"King George," shouted Georgina.

"Yes, but more quietly, Georgina. We do not want to be rude, do we? So, class, who is our King?" The class was silent.

"Who is our King?" No one spoke, and Fortitude thought, "They never see money, so how would they know?" Lucrece looked amazedly at her students. "Sanjan is a part of the Empire. King George is the king of the Empire. Therefore . . ."

When no answer arrived, Lucrece threw her hands above her head in frustration, revealing a fine band of silver on the ring finger of her left hand. Fortitude never heard the answer. Tears rushing with blood pumping from his neck to his forehead, a sob would soon follow the catastrophe of her simple gesture. If it had been another ring or another finger, Fortitude might have heard the answer, but the faint impression of that jewelry wounded Fortitude like the stroke of a battleaxe. It aggrieved him in a way no physical injury could, so he turned, curled away from the painful sight.

As if to smother this conflagration of sorrow, the warm, strong hand of Emmanuel Beaulieu fell on his shoulder. The sudden cruelty of the blow from Lucrece was countered equally by sudden joy at the presence of Emmanuel, Fortitude's oldest, best friend. In Port Hope, Fortitude had seen the novelty of a bathtub in which one faucet ran cold, and the next instant, another faucet ran hot. The alteration of his spirit was just so swift and complete.

After the customary embraces, Emmanuel said, smiling, "I must take you away, so that you don't disturb the schooling."

In the shadowy light of the thicket, Fortitude could see the shining eyes and easeful, almost slothful, relaxation of manner for which Emmanuel was proverbial in the village. Emmanuel's proximity stirred a deep sense of belonging. He was the only greeting party Fortitude wanted or needed. Emmanuel too seemed pleased, but insisted, "Come further. Here. This way."

Fortitude asked, a bit formally, "How fares Jacks, Emmanuel? What news is there?"

"There is good news and bad, as the days flitter," Emmanuel replied equably. "Tell me about Hope, Forty. And why have you not returned these seventeen months and twelve days. We have heard no word but proceeds from the villa, and that is no equivalent for honest letters."

"My friend, there has been no way. It has caused me pain."

"I am sure. Yes. I have no doubts about that."

They kept walking towards the village, but not by the most direct route, Fortitude noticed. "I feel, Emm my boy, like I am beginning to breathe my own air again."

"You are. Indeed you are."

Fortitude could not help himself. "Why do you not take me down direct to the village?"

"Come this way, come this way." Emmanuel fidgeted, leading his friend by the arm down a low embankment, to a grove off the path between the village and the school, a semi-private enclosure. His manner changed from affability to trepidation. Fortitude quivered where he stood like an arrow in a tree.

"Why was no one here to greet me, Emmanuel? Did no word of my arrival pass in?"

Emmanuel lifted his hand in front of his friend's eye. In the light of the clearing, a thin silver band, the same as Lucrece's, glistened on the ring finger of his left hand.

"Why could you not come back even once?" Emmanuel asked despairingly.

Mrs. Worthington restrained Loki until Macy left the room again. The click of the door was like the opening of a broken music box: the mechanical gesture started up a stream of racket from exactly the point where it had been interrupted, but it was Mr. Worthington, not Loki, who was barking.

"How much money do you expect to get from this particular nasty little threat, Pamela? How much exactly? I cannot afford much more, but you know I have always extended myself as generously as possible to oblige you."

"Cecil, it is no longer about money. I reiterate. When we married, yes, I agreed to move to this black-manned life raft in the middle of the North Atlantic, and I agreed to share exile with you, perhaps I even agreed to enthuse about the alteration, but in exchange, if it is really not too much, I demand a husband."

"Mrs. Worthington," said Mr. Worthington, "I will move from this villa under no conditions whatsoever."

"I see. I imagine it would be very hard to leave your Macy."

"What are you implying?" Mr. Worthington shouted, outraged. No doubt the girl was listening at the doorway.

"I am implying, Cecil, that you are utilizing the domestic staff for domestic responsibilities usually left outside the realm of employment in decent society."

Her cold directness deflated the man. The dog, which had been barking more feverishly as the argument increased in volume and intensity, was restrained firmly by Mrs. Worthington's mollifying grip.

"How much money?" Mr. Worthington rejoined.

"Money will no longer satisfy. Cecil. It is time for you to take up your responsibilities as a white man. I cannot be expected to travel the circuits of power alone anymore. It is too, too trying."

"I am sick of this. I tire," Mr. Worthington muttered weakly.

Mrs. Worthington stood up in the fit of her rage. Loki, released, flew into frenzies. "Yes, but you will not be staying. You will come with me to Port Hope, Cecil, and you will be British again. You stupid, stupid man." Loki's hatred, which by ingrained instinct was the only expression of its freedom, closed in on Mr. Worthington. The dog growled and barked at his ankles, thrashing its teeth and moaning in ecstasies of ferocity. Mrs. Worthington said, "I am doing this for your own sanity, as well as my own, you idiotic man."

In a burst of effort, in one complete motion, grip on collar, fist on tail, Mr. Worthington lifted the animal and hurled it through the far window. The world was all shattering glass for a moment, and then, over the splintered shards, Loki's whimpering appeared, and rose swiftly to a yammering, as it searched for the enemy, any enemy, on bloody paws sprinting crazily across the lawn in pain and fury. Following him were the sounds of Mrs. Worthington's squeals, her tears, curses, and her desperate exclamation that the dog had not yet been fed.

Fortitude was contemplating an unhinged stake at the zareba when he heard, in the far distance, the growing sound of the dog barking. He thought nothing of it. Emmanuel had left him to work alone, though they had shared their labours together since they were children. Fortitude had listened with equanimity and patience to the explanation of the courtship, betrothal and wedding of Lucrece and Emmanuel. His friend had explained the matter clearly. Afterwards there was no need to explain why no greeting party had come.

Then Loki streaked by, and catching Fortitude from a corner of its vision, changed course on the fly, careening towards him with a jolt of pure malice. Fortitude had no home any longer. The dog was slobbery with anguished rage, liberated and hence mad with ingrained violence, racing at him in a nameless blind hatred as old as stone. Fortitude too was mindless in his movements, raising the stake with both hands over his head. He did not need to consider. He knew that when the moment came, and the jaws of the master's dog were upon him, pitiless, he would thrust a stake through its cursed, evil heart.

THE CHRISTBIRD

Cornelia Tristanos

1899 – 1986

His thick hair was already matted with sweat. On the water, lacking other company and with no cloud on the horizon, the fisherman covered his head with a sea-drenched towel, and checked his lines—no tension but a trace in the air, faint, certainly not material. "Stay the way I love you," the fisherman said to the waters quickly. The sea listened to him roughly half the time, but now the delicately petalled waves in the distance were winking in agreement. "Calm down, calm." His name was Jerome.

It was nothing so definite as loneliness, less than a smell but more than a vapour. He said out loud, "Something I can eat. Just give me a little fish, a crumb for my love. It's all I'm asking." He was very alone and the sea was very blue. His own words were ringing false to him and he wondered if the sea could be lonely. Again there was . . . but he could not sense it. He said to the sea, "I will draw in my lines for you, if they're scratching." The sea did not disapprove.

He drew up his first four lines easily but the last stuck, and Jerome stared entirely around the undisturbed horizon with suspicion. "What do you mean, darling blue?" he asked the sea with its more mischief than children and old men. The line did not budge even after he had lifted anchor. "What do you mean, winker?"

He tugged the line again—taut as a violin string. Only by throwing his whole strength upwards could Jerome budge it. He tried again, with the greatest force he could muster, moving the line a good fingerlength with the second pull, and it gave more with his next, and yet more with the following. The nearer he brought whatever it was to the surface, the more easily it came, so that his effort changed in a matter of minutes from lugging the line up with the whole of his strong back to drawing it hand over hand.

Jerome did not have time for prayer or thought before the thing jumped from the water onto the floor of the boat. He stared at his shining prize. The sea had given unto him a gold crucifix encrusted with pearls and rubies.

He removed the hook roughly, and shouted at the sea: "I can't eat this!"

In the cool of the evening, in one of the more fashionable houses on Fort Street, last-minute preparations were under way for the Colonial Ball. The Campbells' new girl, Lily, was stitching white crepe flowerbuds onto the floor-length blue silk dress of Miss Jessica Campbell. Most of this stitching had been taken care of months before, but Miss Jessica had spied a few possibilities for improvement as she perused at the dress after dinner. Lily had been the hired servant of Miss Jessica Campbell for an entire season, three full months, and yet she had not developed out of her stupidity in such matters. Ordinarily, such aggravation could be tolerated by Miss Jessica, only daughter of the Vice-Regent of the Sanjan Colonies, Sir Stewart Campbell, but when the Governor's party began in one little hour, Lily's muddleheadedness was beyond trying. Her sewing was slow, and Miss Jessica was dreadfully bored. She could only stare so long at her own painted visage without needing to dance. How she would dance that night!

"Will you hurry up with that stitching?" she demanded.

"Yes, Miss Campbell." Infuriatingly, those seemed to be the only words Lily was capable of uttering: "Yes, Miss Campbell," "I don't know, Miss Campbell," "No, Miss Campbell." After a quarter-minute, mercifully, the girl put down her needle. Her sewing was particularly flustering. Miss Campbell could do the same in a third the time. Master should not be greater than servant in such tasks, especially when the Ball was less than an hour away.

"And bring me the crucifix then, when you're done," said Miss Campbell.

"Yes, Miss Campbell," said Lily.

Jessica Campbell looked in the mirror again, this glance to appreciate the snow-white space between her breasts where that rich ornament would soon hang. How many gentlemen would enquire with her chaperone for the privilege of pressing faintly against her lovely form, as if she were so precious a fabric that a crowd would pay merely to brush it. Without ever having asked the question or having been told the answer, Miss Jessica Campbell knew her role in the drama of life was to tantalize men of adventure and to dance as ephemerally as all worldly glory. Where was that stupid girl? she thought. How she would dance!

Lily was obviously too stupid to find even a large piece of jewelry, and the pearl-and-ruby-encrusted gold crucifix was vital to the ensemble, the very article to gather the eye from the variety of white crepe buds on her sea-coloured dress, and draw it into the blithe perfection of her face.

"Can't you find it, you stupid girl?" Miss Campbell demanded in a burst of irritation.

Lily looked up, hurt and flummoxed. "No, Miss Campbell," she said, and her mistress was more infuriated by her shame. At that instant, Jessica Campbell remembered that the drawer where it properly lay was the one on the left of the escritoire by the window.

"I'll do it myself, if I must," she sighed, standing and swaying to the moonlit alcove.

As she opened the locked drawer that held her crucifix of ruby and pearl, out flew a bird so fast, and in such a flutter out the window, that neither master nor servant could be sure she had seen it. They did not follow the vision. They did not look out the window. When the two women peered into the drawer, there was only a broken, clasped chain.

"Whatever will I wear?" Jessica asked Lily, but Lily had no answer, and said nothing.

The prisoner paced, longing for a sight of any scene but his cell. Endlessly he paced the six and a half steps by six and a half steps by six and a half steps by six and a half steps. Above him there was a window, or rather a small hole that admitted scant moonlight rays. He was less than half a mile distant from the lovely graces of the Governor's Colonial Ball, but he could not have been more removed from its bustles and noises if he himself were on the shining moon.

He sat down on the hard dirt floor. It must be the hour for sleep, he thought, since he was hungry.

As he lay down, he wanted, more than he wanted to live, to be on the open sea in bright daylight, fishing by line. He knew that as long as he could abide this longing and not name it, it would calm and diminish, and then he could sleep.

Sleep was the time for dreams, and in his dreams, the Christbird visited.

The Christbird looks like no other bird. Every colour of the rainbow is on it, and those are the colours of a promise. It never preens when it glories in the light. Rising into the air, the Christbird never stumbles, never runs along the ground. It has no call, but in silence glides upwards easily until everyone can see it. When it flies, no one can say whether it is close up and very small like a hummingbird, or very large like an eagle and just far away. The Christbird never lands. It never leaves. It never remains. It soars away from Sanjan Island over the North Atlantic Ocean and over America and Africa and Europe, but it is always in Sanjan too. The Christbird plunges to the bottom of the sea where no dark shadows are hidden from its eyes, then up to the top of the sky to see everything from above. It flutters everywhere every night, and when the sun rises over Simpson Street Gaol and the Colonial Ballroom and the empty sea, the Christbird vanishes and nobody sees where it was or is or will be.

ULTIMATE TESTAMENT

Ira Rushton

1913 – 1958

1. I, number two thousand, three hundred and twenty-six (2326) of the Inner Island Penitentiary, of decaying body and a firm mind quickened under blows executed by a host of Britisher guards, and having a conscience clear as sky but a soul cracked under many fierce earthquakes of patriotism, despite the above conditions, do hereby state that my current feeble grandeur and resolution amount to an approximate soundness. Therefore I, two thousand, three hundred and twenty-six (2326), do set forth my last will and ultimate testament.

2. Pursuivant to the intent of said will and testament, here follows an enumeration of the undersigned's possessions:

[i] suit of prison clothes, badly frayed
[ii] prison body, worsely frayed
[iii] love of country, good as mint

Beyond the above three (3) possessions, the undersigned is unaware of any further ownership, unless the Britisher masters would care to allot him, in his lifetime, a homecountry.

3. As to item one (1) of the list outlined in paragraph two (2), the item referenced being a suit of prison clothes, badly frayed, I wish to divide the tunic equally, along the concave beltline, between my brothers, that they may, in their wisdom, and under their own discretion, further diversify the rags among the tenderest of my home village. I hope that they will accept my apologies for the stains which are only prison dirt and human fluid, both of which dissolve after a washing.

4. As to item two (2) identified on the list in paragraph two (2), the item referred to as "prison body," let it be divided and subdivided several ways. As for the skin, I would prefer it flayed off by a registered taxidermist, and donated to the Queen of England, or to her trusted servants in Sanjania, who loved so much to beat it during its period of use to me. It is my hope that they will beat my flayed hide instead of another's whenever the urge to strike black skin falls upon them, which it so frequently has done in my experience. As for my blood, I hope that my brothers will display it in vials to the commonest people of Sanjan, so that they can witness themselves that it is no different in quality or kind from the blood of the mansioneers and profiteers who abuse them, but after the blood has been so displayed, I allow it to be given again to the Britisher Queen's servants, so they may spill a quart of mine, instead of another's, when the urge for spilling blood is on them. There will remain my skeleton, which will pass, in lesser circles, for ivory, and so I would ask

my brothers, again, to carry every bone to the Pomegranate Inn on Fitz Street, Port Hope City, and to divide it there among the men and women of that brandyshop as repayment for my sundry debts. You may give my largest bones to the women I owe. As for the offal, donate it widely to the truly wretched. Perhaps a bonnet can be fashioned from my lungs, skipping rope from my intestine, two bouncing balls from my kidneys. I leave the matter in their hands. My heart, however, I offer fully, without reserve, to my sister. Let her keep it and let her decide whether it is the heart of a patriot or a criminal.

5. As to the last item on the forementioned and enumerated list, item three (3), being my love of country, I will never give it to anyone. It belongs to me, prisoner two thousand, three hundred and twenty-six (2326), over and above and beyond death. This last will and testament is witnessed by the signs of smudged fingerprints of my other cellmates, there being no other nor no better ink, and if these words escape the prisonkeepers (there are five [5] paragraphs to this, my ultimate testament, inclusive of this), permit me to assure my heirs that all futures are invalid. Here contains all that I have.

TO BE READ AT THE HOUR OF INDEPENDENCE

Leonard King

1932 –

> *This version of Leonard King's classic is taken from* The Sanjanian's Own, *an anthology used in grammar schools from 1966 to 1985. When originally published, in June of 1959, as a one-page broad, the introductory passage in italics was not included. Caesar Little's government-in-waiting printed over ten thousand copies in the run—it was sold a dozen for a penny on street corners—and at the Independence ceremony, on July seventh of that year,* The Trumpet *reported, "it seemed everyone in the crowd brought a copy of the King story with him."* —S.M.

I write in the dark. At dusk my pen begins to move along the page, and in recent days, I can write only in the dark—quite a gift, quite a skill, let me not grow vain about it. I only mention it so that you will forgive the blots and the errors you find, I am sure, reading my works under the full light of the hour of Independence, the new day . . .

At this moment, the dead and the unborn are meeting on Sanjan Island. The unborn is the first to speak. "What do you bring me?" the unborn asks.

The dead replies, "On the contrary, you should carry gifts to my absence instead, since I was the one who suffered for this hour of Independence."

"I don't know what I could bring you. What will you bring me, though?" the unborn asks.

"You always want more," the dead remarks.

"I do, yes."

The dead examines the all-consuming North Atlantic before speaking again: "I bring you mud, and bones on the bottom of the sea, and out-of-date fashions and dry riverbeds and the flightless Sanjan swallow. Lost cargo manifests that demonstrate a trade in human flesh across the sea. I bring you the slaves' whipped beaten backs, and the laughter of the masters as they trade off the last dozen souls for a jangle. Small packs of survivors, and the privateers who dumped the booty of prey on this desolate shore, and others, many others . . . who did not catch even a glimmer of what the unborn might be. Consigned to shine on the bottom of the sea, they learned to flourish on an island gripped in hand and rattled. Otherwise, I have only the rush of blood to the cheek, marriage and trade and conversation, the wealth of empire transferred through its accidental colony like wine through a sieve, and the rest."

The dead expectantly looks at the other for an acknowledgement or a refusal. "You want me to speak?" asks the other, the unborn.

"Yes," says the dead.

The unborn replies, "I can only give you a murky outline, an impossibility, an unknown fish circling at the bottom of a cloudy pool. I owe you nothing. You acknowledge my lack of debt. If I offer you a gift, it is mud, marriage, conversation and trade, the rush of blood . . . There is desire and love around it like a stem with petals . . . More ships arrive, more plague, and more bones litter the sea bottom, and more shipwreck survivors tie their lives to the stable flotsam of this island . . ."

"Is that all you have?" asks the dead.

"Also, I will join you with everything later," the unborn replies.

"Yes. In the meantime, let me cherish this hour for which I laboured in unconscionable labyrinths and deserts," says the dead.

The dead and the unborn fall silent.

In their eyes, the glorious hour of Independence turns out to be as mundane as any other hour, and the rivers do not cease babbling, rushing through time to their appointment at the sea's mouth. All Januaries flow into the moment and past it, and the sea remains the same, even when the dead and the unborn are meeting, and the place of their meeting is only another island, here, which is perfectly ordinary ground. Now the Britishers have rolled down their flags, and the crowds are milling for speeches, bread and desire. The meeting of the dead with the unborn in our life matters, even if it is only for a moment, but after this hour, the hour of Independence, Sanjania will be a nation among others in the world, and a nation among others in the history of nations, another river babbling to the sea, another half-child of lies and the essence. The dead and the unborn will never again meet here, in this place.

All nations will be one at their next encounter, that final hour, when the world's on fire. Let us pray, if prayer matters, now for when there are no countries. Let this and every hour be the anniversary of that other certain and unnamed hour.

AN OLD MAN MOURNS FOR HIS BLIND DAUGHTER

Morley Straights
1890 – 1964

The old man's daughter had earned her fame singing faithsongs in the inns, and over four hundred fantasticks attended the funeral. The old man was a cooper and never went to inns. He did have a memory for weather, though: the evening sky was the same July turquoise it had been five years earlier when his wife had been buried at St. Matthew's. Circussers, bandits, innkeepers, gypsies and other faithsingers cried and they moaned for his daughter. Casks of brandy spilled open for her sake. Floods of tears downpoured. Great flights of eloquence soared. The Jews tore their hems. There were to be celebrations all over the portlands for the Inndweller, the Faithful Evocation, the Blind One, the Girl with the Gold Guitar. The old man stood in the fluxes of others' grief with his barrel-making hands crossed in front of him. He did not quaver at the motley crowd. He did not flinch as the sextons shoveled in the soil.

His eyes had been dry at his wife's funeral too. Fellows had thought that he did not mourn for his wife at all. She had been a cruel woman and betrayed him moreover. His grief nonetheless had been real then as it was for his daughter.

After the funeral, the old man wound his way from St. Matthew's past the mall into the neighbourhood of Lammas Hill.

These were respectable streets. The houses wore respectability on the lintels. No step went a morning unswept. No gutter clogged with leaves a quarter-season.

Neither man nor woman stood out on the clean corner to meet the old man at his return from the funeral. They never grieved for other than kin. By keeping the children indoors, they had shown their respect. The grocer was the street's ambassador. He was leaning in the doorway of his store, a stocky man who ate his portion. With a nod and the offer of a cigar, the grocer stopped the mourner. The old man accepted the tobac but not the lit match.

"No smoke?" The grocer wondered if it were grief. He lit his own.

"I will take it later."

The grocer nodded his head.

"A great blessing to have such a daughter as you had."

"Yes."

"I don't mind to tell it how we pitied you and the wife when the word came round how a blind one had come in your house. My lady, she bowed her head in prayer, and said what Jesus Christ gives is given to mercy, and that what right hand takes the left hand distributes."

The old man turned his cigar round in his fingers. Finding neither resistance nor acquiescence, the grocer continued.

"Marcia allays wanted what to know how a blind girl could play guitar."

The old man replied, "The same as another."

"No, I mean, she meant, how could the daughter learn the thing."

"A guitar has frets. To feel." The old man concentrated on his cigar.

"I see. Yes, and I suppose it's no question. A blind one can be beautiful in a way. A voice doesn't need eyes too. And what voice! O companion, tell me in privacy now, did you ever off down the portlands for a brief cluck, to hear faithsongs?"

"No."

"No? Well, what a sign, and many a broken heart will shatter its pieces tonight for the Blind One with the Gold Guitar."

The old man seemed to feel responsible for speech. "There were many at the burying."

"I expect. I expect there were. What a voice! And what beauty. The good die young for pity, and we're not all of that constitution that says fantasticks salt their body ground. No! Not but at all."

"I see you."

"I hope you do see me . . . "

The grocer continued smoking. He smoked and watched the old man stride down Mott Street. Nothing in the old man's manner or gait betrayed him. The grocer wondered if the old man kept in mind how the young boys used to throw stones at his daughter. They had thrown stones when she first became fruitful on Lammas Hill. He might have forgotten. The grocer doubted it. He watched the old man turn onto Crescent Street.

Crescent was more deserted than Mott. These were not people to seek out sorrows, their own or others'. They paid respect in absence. The old man understood them. He would have done the same. He plodded towards the flat he had shared with his daughter.

The block was working people. There were mine-widows, bargemen and cargomen. They would never acknowledge the shame of a blind child, or the redoubled shame of a faithsinger blind child. The averted gaze was charity by their lights. Only when his daughter flourished into the rites of womanhood had their eyes briefly overcome reserve. For a fixed moment, for an hour, they had stared.

On the stoop outside his flat, the landlady was waiting for him. She was shucking greenbins into a bucket. Her ugly face was entangled in age. She squinted into the light. Her gauntness was poorly hid by a shapeless flowerprint. She wore builder boots. The old man tried to move past her to the stairs. She spoke as if they had been chatting for hours.

"It won't be so much as I minded the tunage, but the neighbours, man, think of the neighbours! And what how I always took in only the 'spectful, only the geesies of the decent working families. What would they say? And me with only this place to keep stranger animals from the door. So I don't take it badly, none of Jesus' creature but lives a purpose, not so we view it, but there. I'm saying, nothing dies without cause either."

The soft beans made a tapping noise when they hit the inside of the bucket. The old man said nothing. The landlady resumed her conversation.

"I mean, what music is is a nasty affair. It means men and ladies no good, so there may be a glimmer of comfort far afield from the storm of this horror what that the sound of that gold guitar won't be strumming down. And how the girl rebelled, now. For a blind one, she greyed her mother's hair. And there was a woman, the mother. Not too hesitant with the stick I grant, but what reason not to keep a family in embraces. Yes, she were solid as granite rock. True as goodness itself. To be burdened with a blind faithsinger! It makes me ask what name comes over respectability. And yet I wonder if it weren't a flaw in her womanflesh made it."

"We will never know." The old man interrupted. The landlady was surprised that he spoke.

"She was a good woman, your wife. Always a grin for a lady of substance."

"We will never know." The old man repeated.

The landlady nodded and said no more. She did not turn to see the old man unlatch the door. He padded up the two stairflights to the flat. But he was no different in grief. That is, not that she could see. Greatest among his features, she thought, was his piety. You shall and you shall not: he followed them truly. Being his landlady was a richprize, and she knew it. Your servant, she scribbled on her bills to him before signing.

The lock clicked behind him. The room was bare. The Gold Guitar in the corner would never again give any sound. Without changing his mourner's clothes, the old man sat down in the chair by the corner. He was facing the window but could not see down to the ground from his angle. The only sound was the soft piff-paff of greenbins on tin.

The old man lit his cigar. There were no clocks in the room. As he exhaled the rich smoke, like a sigh, the street outside began to fill with the sounds of people gathering.

FLOTSAM AND JETSAM

Caesar Hill

1945 –

Taking the Bible from the shelf and pulling a chair to the window, Miranda turned to a well-worn passage among the thin, frail, gilt-edged pages. She knew the story by heart but she read anyway.

—BLESSED SHIRLEY

They were utterly loathsome, the oleaginous used books, and so were secondhand bookshops loathsome, particularly as they contained secondhand bookmen, who are all the worst dregged scrapings of the life of the mind, the rankest filth from the worst-timbered barrel bottoms. So Antony Percival Percy thought to himself as he stared blankly at the smoky front of the Hope Mall Library and Emporium, a store as nondescript as the suburban London street it inhabited, its windows stuffed, seemingly at random, with the spines of rejected old tomes whose only use now was to block the sun. How fetid, he thought, and grim, but in the torn pocket of his raincoat, he unconsciously fingered his motivation for entering and, with a sigh, descended the few steps of walkdown to the door. A question about the book in his pocket was pressing desperately in on Antony, and the answer could only be found inside.

The interior of the store was no more prepossessing than the exterior, the shelves disordered, volumes stacked two deep without visible contiguity or any obvious use of the alphabet. The books themselves were grubby, as the owner bought principally much-touched, much-annotated copies, paying almost nothing for them, and these accruals of grime and commentary were disgusting to Antony, reminding him of nothing so much as dirty fingernails. He only patronized the establishment because it was the cheapest secondhand bookshop in London, and the owner, a man he knew only as Remus, was a fellow Sanjanian, and would accept ten per cent. less than the marked price. Antony's soul surfeited with bitterness that he was now being forced to ask his countryman for more than the ten per cent., and he alleviated the resentment with a further sigh.

As if in reply, from the alcove of a back room, Remus boomed out, "Well met, compatriot, how are we? Fine? Good? Or I hope, excellent? Outstanding? How are you taking to your time in exile? I am flourishing in mine, thank you. You will no doubt be happy to know it, although my family in Port Hope, and also in Brunville, claim they are anxious for my return. I myself wonder if they are not anxious that the money I wire to them is drying up. Cash is low, cash is terribly low, but still there is some hard money in the City. Yes it is better to be a live dog in London than a dead lion in Sanjania, haha, haha, ancient wisdom, modernized, my boy. If it were only that we didn't hate these Britishers, but look round, look round. Take your time."

During this monologue, Remus had processed, teacup in hand, from the dank squalor of the back room to the fetid throne of the slightly raised cash register beside the door, smiling vaguely in Antony's direction, and waving him towards the store contents. When he had set himself down into sufficient comfort, he accompanied his smile and greeting with a parody of a Sanjanian gesture of greeting, dipping the little finger of his left hand in the tea and spilling a few drops on a handkerchief. Their shared nationality embarrassed Antony: it implied intimacy, and intimacy with Remus hurt him like rending. Remus was fat and disheveled and sweaty, gross in the archaic sense of the word, and thus at one with his bookshop, his face spotty in splotches of black and tan, his eyes brownly gelatinous. An audience to Remus was merely an occasion to speak more loudly to himself. There was the faint odour of urine in his presence too, a fact which Antony found degrading even to recognize.

Nothing would have been more to his taste than to rummage among the books, unpalatable as they were, and so escape the all too human bookseller, but instead, he gingerly pushed the slim volume from his pocket onto the counter, and mumbled a question that was not quite intelligible. Remus peered briefly over his teacup, registering instantaneous delight in his puffy eyes, and took the book up with his whole concentration, for here was a genuine opportunity to let oratory resound.

"Ah yes, you have brought me something. A book. How delightful. *The Tempest* by William Shakespeare. Yes. A particularly interesting drama, even by the lofty standards of the Bard. Many claim it to be the last play that master craftsman ever skillfully whittled from the vast timbers of general human motivation. The great play about the joy of renunciation, much as *Lear* is the play of its agony. But I am afraid that I cannot buy books now, compatriot. Wrong season."

"It's not for selling," Antony mush-mouthed. Remus sipped his tea imperturbably and examined the book in his hand, which was small, fadingly blue and crapulent. He himself had sold it to Antony not a week before, and so could not denigrate the physicality of the specimen as much as he might desire.

"Though Shakespeare's ultimate, or perhaps penultimate, work of the imagination, it is given pride of place in the First Folio, foremost in that exemplary collection. Clearly a demonstration on the part of Heminge and Condell, those most elaborate editors, so full of their own ideas, that hidden within the drama, within *The Tempest*, was some key to the identity of The Author. Yes. Shakespeare's identity. The all-important question. But, as I said, I cannot buy it. Besides, this price is in my own handwriting. You purchased the book here."

Antony mumbled an affirmative.

"Yes, but surely *you* must be cognizant, you with such a brilliant brain between and above your shoulderblades, that I can hardly buy back books that I have sold once already. Bad business, compatriot."

The door opened, ringing a small bell over the counter, and a small, pretty English girl had entered, in neat bohemian clothing, red beret, sleeveless grey blouse, black pleated skirt, any of which pieces instantly identified her as a university student. She nodded at Remus, who beamed pacifically in response, and excused herself past Antony through the narrow passageway by the register that led into the cramped labyrinths of the shelves. Even though he had never seen another customer at the Hope Mall bookshop in his many months of custom, Antony paid no mind to the blonde, so possessed was he by his concern for the frail, blue book.

"I do not wish to sell it," Antony said distinctly.

Remus looked at him for the first time with mild interest, the veil of his narcissism lightly blown aside by the refreshing breeze of Antony's lack of mercenary motive. His thick jaw opened sideways, and a thought entered surreptitiously.

"You have heard of my theory, then." Mistakenly, Remus

assumed his young countryman was visiting the Hope Mall Library and Emporium for intellectual discussion. "That *The Tempest* is clearly the product of a Sanjanian."

The milkwhite blonde stepped with mannered tread up the rickety slatted staircase which led to the bookshop's second floor, distracting Remus' attention momentarily.

"No," Antony said quickly.

Remus had put his tea aside, and was beginning to price books, penciling numbers on the inside covers as he developed his argument.

"Of course critics," he uttered the word with scorn and with more scorn he added, "scholars, drydust philosophers, will tell you that reclaimed panegyrics to the newfounded colony of Virginia provided the model to Old Bill. Not so, I say, for could anything be plainer than the fact that *The Tempest*'s actions precipitate upon an island?"

"I see yes but . . ." the junior scholar interpolated.

"Not Virginia, and there are others who wonder where Shakespeare's youth passed. Where are the products of genius in youth, they demand. The cry goes up, 'Whither young Shakespeare?' But we know, you and I know, that exactly coincident with that period of Shakespeare's absence from the record, Martins was first breasting that uninhabited profitless shore not yet known as Sanjan Island, and Martins, of course, like the deposed Duke of Shakespeare's play—first in the First Folio, bear in mind—was Neapolitan."

"Martins was Portuguese," Antony said shrilly, drawn into the argument despite his better judgement. "It is known to every schoolboy on Sanjan Island that Martins was a Portuguese adventurer."

"By adoption, and by that ridiculously improper term we currently hold to, naturalization, he was indeed Portuguese. True.

True, good fellow, but on a casual glance at the *Almanach de Gotha* and a few of the lesser-known sources of supporting documentation, one discovers that Martins' father had been, was in fact, a scion of a family longstanding among the nobility of Naples. There is unassailable evidence on the point. There are also, however, irregularities in the line which have led to confusion among amateurs and neophytes."

Remus suddenly put a chubby finger to his fat lips. They both could hear the young woman pacing overhead. The floor deprecatingly creaked, and Remus continued noting prices in the inside front covers, barely scanning the volumes as he did so, and holding court contentedly.

"Besides, the answer is in the text. As always. The descriptions are of a piece with our lost home. 'On the curled clouds.' 'In a cloven pine.' Where do those exist but on the North shore of Sanjan Island by the hills? What else are curled clouds and cloven pines but our island species? I grant you, my evidence is circumstantial, but men have hung for less conclusive aggregations of facts. Facts, furthermore, as I said, in the text."

Antony raggedly contained his disdain, since he could not afford to offend the bookseller, but in the slight pause in Remus' concentration while he examined a slightly curious volume, Antony inserted his question. "I wonder if you could tell me . . . I wonder . . . you might know, or remember I am sure, who sold you this book in particular?"

Remus jotted a figure in the margins. "There is also the rather intriguing problem of Shakespeare's premonition. For instance, the issue of the release is one and the same with our history. Prospero, on this island, far from the experience of Europa on Virginian or Bermudan or Jamaican shores, is an emancipator, not an enslaver. 'Into a cloven pine, within which rift, imprisoned thou didst painfully remain.' That is for Ariel and also for Caliban. 'Therefore wast thou deservedly confined into this rock, who hadst deserved more than prison.' And then there is Sycorax, literally a blue-eyed Algerian devil, identical to the Spaniard. The whole journey of *The Tempest* is from the reign of the slavedriver Sycorax to the dominion of Ariel. The same might be said, though the gesture is not yet entirely concluded, for Sanjania."

"That is all good. At least, I am sure you are correct," Antony said more firmly, summoning all his reserves of manly courage. It was possible that his countryman had not heard his earlier demand, he had spoken it so shyly. "But I want to know who sold you this copy of the play."

"Interesting." Remus put his finger to his lips again and stared out into the middle distance over Antony's head, and they listened to the woman's steps twisting the wood floor overhead again. Remus whispered, "She is moving from drama to poetry and back again, much like our beloved friend. But," here he resumed his dissertation in full voice, "the beginning of that gesture is in Shakespeare's early contact, in young adulthood, with Sanjan Island. *The Tempest* is the first drama in the First Folio. It is an identification. 'Hell is empty and all the devils are here,' how true that is, not only in the contemporary political debacles of our time, yes, for which you and I have so much suffered, but also for the devils of creation, those demons which pursue the artist, for Sanjan was the wellspring of the Bard, just as of our own uniquely rich heritage. As they say in other countries, 'there must be something in the water.' Eloquence runs through Sanjan like diamonds in Southern African states."

"A Sanjanian must have owned this book," said Antony.

"How do you know that, friend? If I may ask," Remus whispered. Antony leaned over, spread the book at Ariel's song, and feverishly pushed it towards his compatriot, who betrayed only the mildest curiosity. The passage was thickly underlined.

> Full fathom five thy father lies
> Of his bones are coral made;
> Those are pearls that were his eyes,
> Nothing of him that doth fade
> But doth suffer a sea-change
> Into something rich and strange.

Beside these lines, in a looped feminine hand were inscribed the words, "Revolution. July 7, 1959. Sinking of the Diver-For-Pearls."

The gross bookman rested the book with seemingly magical skill on his paunch to consider the poetry and its commentary, and such was his fascination that minutes passed, in each of which Antony's loathing for bookmen increased exponentially. When, at last, Remus lightly snapped the book shut, it was to address the female student, who had descended from on high. "Will you be buying anything today, miss?" he enquired with an obsequious smile.

"No, thank you," she said politely, and shyly smiling at Antony, who stepped out of the way for her to pass. "Farewell, Miranda," Remus said as she left, throwing a querying glance over her shoulder, and as the chimes above the portal clanged at her departure.

"And you wish to meet the woman or man who made this particular annotation," Remus said to his only remaining customer. "'You taught me language and my profit on't is I know how to curse. The red plague rid you for learning me your language.' Learning me. Double meaning, you see, compatriot. And here is an intriguing literary anecdote, for I know you collect such curios, that in Melville's copy of *The Tempest*—though he was an American I am quite sure his travels aboard North Atlantic whalers touched into our lovely Port Hope—Melville annotated the following brief speech of Miranda's, 'O wonder! How many good creatures are there here! How beauteous mankind is! O brave new world that has such people in't,' with the cutting phrase, 'O terrible innocence.' Almost as cutting as Ferdinand's tart response: ''Tis new to thee.' Incidentally, I have held Melville's copy in my own hand."

Antony's squirming abjection, which to then had been frothing behind his teeth, suddenly found expression in anger. "You will not tell me then," he said sharply.

Remus ticked off a price on the counter. "Of course what is never uttered is the obvious truth that Miranda's description of braveness and newness is of Europe, not of Sanjan Island, or Sanjania as we must now call it. I am telling you, compatriot, I am telling you, we are the Mirandas, we are called back to praise this Europe, we exiles are."

Remus paused, and Antony's anger caught a snag, his eyes shifting suspiciously. Remus glanced hintingly out the door through which the woman had vanished. "Europe is a strange, new world, isn't it? The books of Prospero are a terrible cipher for it, and you and I must be the Mirandas then, I suppose."

Ding-dong-bell went the chimes of the door, and Antony, having run up the half-flight of stairs, was again on the nondescript street in London. His flummoxed vision could find no milkwhite, ricepudding English annotator Miranda, the European woman who somehow knew the details of the history of his home island. The fog had rolled in, thick and factory-made, so thick that he could not see his feet, so thick that his family in Sanjania, who lived by the sea, never believed his descriptions of it in his letters home. Antony Percy could see nothing on the street where her possibility loomed, but he could hear himself panting. He could hear himself wanting. His Miranda had vanished.

EXILE

AND

RETURN

MEN

Charity Gurton

1954 –

Three different versions of this story exist, each authorized. The original was published in a student literary-society journal and differs from the text printed here in lacking any punctuation. I have selected, chronologically speaking, the second story—the text found in Gurton's collection Men and Other Stories. *A rewritten "Men" appeared five years ago in* International Eye, *with the rich city dialect simplified and the speaker's narrative broken into paragraphs. For an introduction into the debates surrounding "Men," see the selection from Octavia Dickens's book* Tongues of Fire *in the criticism section below.*—S.M.

The old woman said:

His name wa' Marvelous and his women call 'im Marvelous o' Marvely but when th' man come back fram th' war fellows keep 'is name Marvy. Marvy on the docks. Account to some Britisher what monickered tha' man so. Took up and married full wi' a woman named Meg, foreshortened Magdalene, follow me. Marvy loved Mags deep true, fo' in the prewar, wha death we' coming and Adolf wa' prawlin' the sea, the stars brightened, catch me, the night darkened. One way or tother, seasound no doubt we' singin' sweeter 'cause we all know tha' Adolf's boaties could run unner waves, yes, and they did too. Right into the city too. So many the baby forged in the forge of danger, and 'smany thousand time the loves. Meg and Marvy we' hammered so. Marvy come back fra war, survivin', young and live. Every fella we' handed the gift free of 'varsity education, know, but Marvy don' want. He want life fore th' war loving sweet Mags o' workin' the docks 'mong the vessels of God knows wha'. Strong back! Maggy agog wi' him, marryin', lil twiste' settlement 'n more than naught for a living. Mags' belly open up like an old topmast, you know. Surely, in four month, trouble come. Maggy say, "Marvy, I don' feel so well then," and Marvy say "wha' you want, sweetest angel, name it and it shall be thine," and Maggy say, "I'm afeared I do need a woman wi' th' touch." A woman wi' touch is a mi'wife, follow. Best mi'wife a' tha' tune we' Goody Swallow. She ha' the touch, sell it fo' price. Fair's fair. Maggy grew sick' 'deed too. Cannot walk, belly full, jus' lying in bed so that Marvy we' scared to he' death of it. Marvy does hire Goody, wha' knows plenty to do with medicinery, and Marvy stay out late workin', workin', where the work be wherever. To get money fo' the mi'wife like a good lovin' dockman. Well, now a sketch o' the life of Goody Swallow for ya. Ask a one for miles round, Goody we' good toucher, a good one wha' women clamourin' far. "Come and stay til it off, Goody," the knocked women say, and th' men follow sure. "Come stay ya." So after th' wa' she live family 'a family, just til baby born. The fellas give 'er room and bread, leaf an' suga', touch it off with a bouncer and she dons a 'tuity. She save too, Goody does, smar' girl, but she too ugly and her womb seize up when she we' youn', so no babies, and fo' such twin reasons, na husband and na need. That's Goody. We turn back now, follow. Knocked Maggs sick, so Goody 'n the house, follow. Goody 'n the nex' room. Night-soun'. Nothin'. Goody hear a real soun'. Soun' of a man. Soun' of Marvelous. He come in her room. Goody's room. He saying, "You moniker is Magdalene, honey sweetness, me honey Maggy, give'm a dose." That's what the fella saying in Goody's room. Goody lookin' straight in the eye and seeing, no, he's na blin', na chance he's blin'. And na ev'ry day does ugly barren Goody Swallow ha' a strong dockma' tendin' bedside. Goody thinkin' "No threat of a nuisance, he's clean or keepin' it a lil. No gossip will bekeep me fra' th' houses of tothers." "Welcome to a lovin' bed," she say o' good as. Why na. Goody we' a brilliant kiddie, and the' run no risk of gossip, sure, fa' Marvy in love with Maggy, no neighbour doubts. Else why woul' he ge' mi'wife and work twice the hours? And the woman Goody has an ugliness, so why woul' the fella ran with he', and it's all perfect, follow. Follows. With the probs that it do not follow 'tall. Cracks in walls are big 'nough for small ears. Next day, Maggy t'rew he'self into th' seaness, divin' straight down into the water, pocketsful of stonies and tears astrewin' 'er. When Marvy fish 'er out, she say, "I will ne'er forgive ya," and he say, "I beg ya forgive me," and she say "never." Wha' she home, Goody heard an' gone with her touchin', and Mags bled out the life in 'er, it's as ne'er was. Goody go' and lef' town, left fa' inland Sanjan. "Can't stan' to hear the sea namore," she tol' neighbours. An' Maggy won' look at Marvy, and he can' hard stan' to look at hi'self. A dark time in the daylight. An ill wind won' be ke't indoors. Marvy won' be 'llowed in th' house, he paid fram dockwork, but an ill wind dies dow' too. "Lemme in house," was beggin' Marvy and Maggy was forever silent as stars. Men are runners round, but they does love too, and Marvy was deep true with Maggy. "Lemme in, I beg ya," he say 'very night, and never a word ta him. Ev'ry night, he lyin' on the floor outsi' tha front wantin', cryin'. This's the same ma' wha ran with the mi'wife while 'is wife in bed sick wi' his son. Not unhear' of since you hear it now. Still 's the veteran 'n th' doorsill sayin', "Forgive me, I beg," dunn'd up in ashes and sa'cloth, wailin' for the lost kiddie too. In the morn he's up a' th' docks, a man far work for sure na'. He put money unner he' door, and she say nothin'. She ta'es. She ta'es and then she gives and surely so the door opens, and Marvy's walkin' through. Lemme sketch y'out that too, 'cause young beautiful love must be a 'flection of some corne' fo' heaven. That was married life 'tween 'em, and he brought he' th' money, an' never took, and she give a little fo' his lunchin' dow' docksways, and they two spen's the 'vening together, talkin' and luvin' and card-playin'. Never an' natime was Marvy out drinkin', whorin', or otherwise like a Sanjanian dockman. No children, but he brought all his money. A good man. Strange t'follow how Marvy never brought hi'self to mourning when Mags died. Na grieving, and tha's what I mean to say 'bout men, th' tother creatures. Yes, she died. Time she died of, and you woulne'er ha known fra th' look in Marvelly's eyes, na, he didn't frown. Na tear coursed down the stone of his cheek. Stone of 'is heart I thought. But I heard, I did hear, 'ow he foun' Goody, went into the island centre Tols. He said to Goody, Goody now, "Honey, sweety, sweetness Maggy, Magdalene by moniker, give'm a dose," and Goody thought to he'self, "Tha man's got strength, and's wife's passed." That's his sorrow, follow, his grievin'. He recalls his dead wife by the feelin' of cheating, follow. Brought Goody back to Hope wi' 'im and she's toucher here now. He brings 'er 'is money. She don' ask if she a ghost in his arms, so's he find it in he' arms, what I 'magine. Yes, the innocence of men is like nothin' else. Crooked wood crooked ashes. For all Maggs' dead and Goody's in the dockman's arms. That's men fo ya. Men. Ha. Men.

UNDER THE SKIN

Trinity Hopps

1967 –

Monica couldn't help but tear away from her mother's hand she was so curious about the tattoos. For just a glance she tore away. Suns, snakes, pierced hearts, eagles, bottles, labeled monikers, painted ladies. At the dusty corner of Main Mall Street, the café-fronts spilled out sailors and other less predictable drunks: canvasses. Mother said no, out of the question, but Monica begged, begged, begged. She had held her mother's hand so obediently along the esplanade, right until the sailors' part. Thoughtlessly Mother wrung her hands, but said yes, right, what harm could be done, be quick about it, Monica.

The sailors offered their skin pictures in coarse terms to the young daughter of the statuesque lady in the lovely white Colonial dress. They permitted Monica to touch, ease to her, sure. The tough ones were so tender. Faint ridges, so gentle, so real along their arms, their necks, their backs. Stare at this piece, this is the true finery, kiddie. Big round laughter.

It was the day before Monica first heard the word divorce. Sometime in the late seventies, in a more or less new country called Sanjania.

That night she slept well in the nostalgic arms of her old big bed.

And awoke to the complex and always novel smell of chaunticleer. In the odour of that dish, the creamy morning lemon soup, in that odour, or rather exactly the abstract sensation of that odour rousing her from slumber, she was loved. She was that instant home.

And at the thought that Salamona might remember how she liked a drop of coconut milk in her morning soup, Monica tore away from her bed, stripped it, tossed it off, left its nostalgia crumpled and abandoned. She tumbled out, down two flights of wide wooden steps, enthusiastically creaking cheers for speed, yes, yes, and through the poor quarter's portal with its spectral welcome, into the expectant basement kitchen. There was Salamona! There was a summer morning!

The house servant's arms were magically comforting, lovely pillows laid out on the boughs of a strong, high tree so that Monica could hang improbably in the air. The embrace between them was longer than a greeting. Better and longer.

Salamona remarked how tall Monica had grown, not a kiddie at all these days, wasn't it? Well, she was twelve now, and Monica said that Salamona was the same exactly as she had remembered her. Salamona smiled, saying mildly that she was not past vanity. Monica set herself at the small deal stool, for a bowl of fresh chaunticleer made before dawn for the returning girl. Was there by any chance a spot of coco milk, Salamona? Just a drop. For the prodigal. Such good manners these days.

What with the soup and the colossal map of the nation behind the counter to stare at and all the local gossip about fellows who Monica didn't know or care for, Salamona's speech was like a warmth in the air she felt not heard. The soup was busy with flavour, demanding attention, and the map too, on the wall, was so curious. The Defence Ministry, where Pappa worked, made that map and it showed every place where everyone lived. Different size dots for different places. Port Hope, a bullseye. For what dart or arrow? It had such elegant borders of the land around the sea. Three white lines, for waves. No sea in Switzerland where Monica had been going to school. Sad. A spinster country. Sanjania was lost in the sea. Monica lifted her bowl and drank, and thought about how the country was like a tattoo on the ocean waters.

Monica couldn't read the names on the map. She tried, squinting.

Run along, Salamona was saying. You cannot listen anymore, and your soup finished, they did not teach you to listen, I witness. Monica insisted that she had been listening, intently. You more alive with that map, I try to give you the news, but go and look at another. Just come back for lunch. Monica said, Oh yes, I will, I will Salamona and thank you for the chaunticleer, it was delicious. Divine. Salamona laughed and said, I did see that you are not so polite now you cannot toss it up and lick a bowl clean. Go then.

So much day, that day, there was so much of it. There was so much home!

On the first floor, there was the large dining room, the small dining room, the yellow sitting room, the blue sitting room, and the library, which was better than the other rooms. The public rooms were cold maiden aunts who shook your hand and disapproved. The library was the warm rich uncle who let you jump in his lap. Monica thought, if there is one room in the house in which I will be married, it is the library. Everyone knew she went to the library. The whole world knew she went to the library every day. "Booking," Salamona called Monica, disapprovingly. Her mother looked away nervously at the subject, uncertain whether to disapprove, but not Father. No. He smiled. His study was off the library, therefore the library was his, and therefore she should naturally love it.

No one would notice her curled up into the far corner of the large room. Like one of the moths the teacher had displayed under glass in the botany lesson the previous autumn, she instantly camouflaged into the varied landscape of book spines. Two bright eyes only. At school, she had longed for such mothish invisibility. Then, from the next room into the warm solemnity of bookish silence tapdanced the tin sound of her father beginning to type. He was in his study. The strange arhythmic running of his words. A telegraph warning. Tap-tapTAP-tap. Tap. Stay away, stay away. She did not run to him. He would be happy to see her later.

Instead she took down an atlas the size of her torso and began to flip through the pages of Europe to find the town in Switzerland where the school was. She found it. There it was. She looked up other countries and other cities. She spent maybe twenty minutes, maybe two hours. The atlas was like a new girl with pretty clothes who had come to visit with one of her parents' friends, a new girl with nice stories who liked to go on talking.

Then Mother swept into the library like a sudden cloud.

Pausing briefly for composure outside the study, she removed her round spectacles made of thin silver wire, breathed deeply and rubbed her eyes, then lay the spectacles on the shelf next to the study. Preparing herself. All the while, Monica stayed still, since every second of not speaking made her more guilty and so less likely to speak and so more still. At last composed, determined, Mother made her entrance into the study. The typing stopped. The spectacles remained on the counter.

Monica waited for shouting. Fighting, she was used to.

Monica could take the spectacles and bring them in to her mother. That would be a reason. I saw your spectacles and I thought I might bring them to you. Better yet, I thought they were Father's spectacles, they look so much like a man's. I did not know you were here.

I just thought you should know, Monica heard as she picked up the spectacles. Her mother speaking. And her father, yes, yes, I suppose I should know. But why did you let her run off like that? She is curious, Mother replied, they were only tattoos. Father remarked that the men behind those tattoos should have frightened them both, and Mother asked why, and Father said you know damned well why. And Mother said, that is your fault, not hers nor mine, and the sailors know that well enough. The sailors don't know who she is regardless. You are so naïve, he said.

There was pain in Monica's hand. She was gripping the spectacles too tightly, she realized.

When shall we tell her, Mother asked. That, I don't know, I don't know, Father replied, it is a hard thing, it is a confusing thing. It doesn't make sense to me, and to a child . . . he faded. Divorce, her mother said finally. We shall tell her tomorrow, her father said, it is better to be straight and out with it. Mother demurred with a moan, she is away for Switzerland in two months, perhaps a letter . . . Her father was adamant, not a letter, no, your own daughter, woman, it's disgusting, we shall tell her. Her mother said, I am not disgusting.

Monica almost thought she might hear the typewriter start up into that silence. She moved away, still gripping the spectacles.

This business with the tattoos, Father said, it's just like you, you know. Mother asked, Whatever can you mean? Always out with the people, you know, always slumming. Under the guise of curiosity. He chuckled. It's just funny. Mother said, I find it funny how she is reading all the time, very ladylike. You have encouraged . . .

Monica crept back to her blind of a library shelf. Perfectly still. She was either hunting or hunted. Divorce. The new word. That was the word of the decade for Monica.

A minute later, her mother passed through the library without remembering her lost spectacles or seeing her hidden daughter, and Monica heard again the tapTAP, tappitytappitytap TAP-tap of the typewriter. She had never seen the typewriter. Heard it only. She replaced the spectacles where her mother had left them and went back to the basement kitchen.

No Salamona. Empty. There was the map. More vague than before, the points on the surface were bleeding into each other, the lines were blurring, the names grown indistinct. She walked up close to inspect the metamorphosis, to see how and why the map had so strangely altered.

Then she realized that her eyes were full of tears.

That was the nineteen-seventies in Port Hope for Monica. Now it is the eighties, in London. A party in a flat in Soho. "I think of writing as staining the world, bit by bit, page by page," Monica is saying.

"Like a tattoo?" the stranger asks.

"Show him, my lovely," Monica's girlfriend says.

She turns around and pulls her shirt up halfway. On the small of her back, there are three small, modest designs. She explains each, looking back over her shoulder. "The map is the outline of Sanjania, so I will always remember where I'm from. The spectacles are to remind me that my vision is never perfect."

"And the typewriter? That is a typewriter?"

"I am a writer. I stain with words."

"Monica, you are so full of surprises." "That's too funny." "They are so well drawn." "Beautiful." "What do the spectacles mean again?"

This is London. These are explanations. But there are tattoos, Monica knows, that can't be seen or explained. Written too deep under the skin to be read.

HISTORIES OF AENEA BY VARIOUS THINGS

Leonard King

1932 –

Things. Aenea was a thing among other things. Like her, there are mirrors, coffee cups, pens in marmalade jars, white candles, a telephone, a map of Vienna. (This list of objects I have rather lazily received from the near corner of my writing desk.) Aenea was a thing like them. Forgetting all categories for a moment, if I were to reach out to touch anything, or simply to hold my pen more snugly in the pocket of finger and thumb, I would be and am touching Aenea's fellow thing. In paradise, every thing is held in everything, and I forget Aenea in such paradises. I remember her in things.

Cats. Cats always took to Aenea. From a very early age, she naturally sympathized with all felines. Tomcats would abandon a chase to curl their tails around her ankles. Voluntarily the most haughty and regal of Persians would forgo privilege for a few moments of her fingers' skill in the secret places of his chin hairs. Despite the attraction, Aenea never once owned a cat. In fact, never once did she so much as offer a saucer of milk to a stray tabby. Her relationship to cats was strictly tangential, if I can put it that way.

Those young men in her home cove, who felt for adolescent Aenea much as the cats did, attributed the feline attraction to a kind of sympathetic magic. Aenea's lean litheness and unconscious grace were catlike in a way, and her peripatetic nature a byword. Aenea confessed to me privately, in the connubial bed, that the reason cats loved her was her reserve towards them. "Cats respect you when you assert the dignity of your species," she said. Cats have always despised me.

Wine. She loved red wine, but only drank it in Europe. Every night, when we lived in Rome, she would not sleep without her glass from the café Noli Me Tangere directly under our flat. In Sanjan, she never bought it. I brought back a bottle of claret from a lecture in Paris, and she never opened it, was uninterested in drinking it. The bottle sat in our cupboard, slowly covering with dust until it disappeared, just as if the dust had swallowed it. Domestic objects had an easy way of dissolving from space under Aenea's care. They just wouldn't show up one day. I foolishly did not ask my wife why she refused to drink wine on our home island.

Still life. We owned only one still life painting, by the North Coast artist Good John Dome. Bananas. Tomatoes. An avocado. In a silver bowl reflecting a plain wooden table. We bought the piece in the Lintako gallery on Shuter street in 1971. Aenea liked it more than I did.

There is something ridiculous to me in the fact that I can still look at this image made by paint on canvas when she cannot. I don't know why.

Ants. When she was a half-year old, rolling in the beach sand of her home cove (Little Harbour, on the West Coast), Aenea accidentally crushed her first ant. The ant world was diminished by a count of one. In the span of her life, thousands upon thousands of the insects would be assured of their mortality through her.

As a child, a dirty boy named Ramon taught her to kill ants with the focused beam of a magnifying glass. Such specific and controlled brutality was not like her, but finding a sizeable anthill, she readily enjoyed the chaos her scattering foot caused. Out of a similarly random curiosity, she once ate a living, squirming red ant. Finding the bitterness to her taste, she consumed a whole line of the things, the next after the last, as they marched in an orderly fashion to their doom.

When she came to woman's estate, ants were worthy of attention only when they sallied through cracks in her various homes. When a solitary explorer discovered the expanse of her flesh, she would casually fleck it away. She did not spare ant life. She did not seek its destruction. If there is God among the ants (and the ants are certainly intelligent enough for divinity) she could have been a source for Its Image: engaged but unthinking, cruel only in passing. "Inconsiderate" is the right word.

Now that I call it to mind, when she was dying and I was too troubled to maintain the house in full repair, I once oversaw her carefully watching her steps to avoid crushing the ants.

Cigarettes. How elegant I thought she looked with one. Curls of grey. Curls of blue. Vanishing.

Ages. January 6, 1928, to December 26, 1982. Aenea died eleven days from her fifty-fifth birthday. The time between these dates is the age of Aenea. It is not the age of the Depression or the Second War or the Cold War. Not being the postmodern age, it is neither the age of Auschwitz nor the nuclear age nor the age of anxiety. To her lover, it is the age of Aenea (1928–1982).

Our ivy plant. It keeps growing up the side of our south wall, despite the fact that she does not observe it. Again, I find this bizarre.

Clouds. We were vacationing on the West Coast in a removed village the locals identified as "Portuguese Cove," though I doubt you'll find that name on the national maps or in the office of the registry of names. The happiness of our love at that time was so great that strangers smiled at us and widows spontaneously prepared us meals because of the joy in our eyes. We were not even young, but Mrs. Spooner, I remember, gave us a roof for free and I would sail out with the fishermen for their stories, and the women would look after the children from Aenea's first marriage. We would make love behind a small fence beside the sea.

At one of these events, after we had exercised ourselves thoroughly, lying on my back, I spotted a cloud in the shape of an open book. She could not or would not see it, and it was really, obviously there. We spent the rest of that day (a considerable portion of that summer, actually) examining passing clouds for shapes she might recognize. She never did. "I just see clouds," she would say.

Twelve years later, Aenea and I were flying to Rome. At thirty thousand feet, she looked down on the clouds and said, "It looks like a whole city in that embankment of fluff there," and when I looked down I couldn't see it at all.

Cancer. Flower of death. "A growth," the doctor said. My utter panic at the diagnosis. Her utter calm. A quiet slowed explosion in her left breast. After the doctors had removed the deity, there was a frantic white scar where before there had been the calm dark sun of her breast that I loved.

Herring broth. In some homes on the West Coast, herring broth will be cooked three or four times a week. Aenea loathed it. The soup was never to her taste, not even when she was a child. It must have had something to do with the physiology of her mouth. She was always very lean, verging on too skinny, and perhaps this distaste for herring broth along with its ubiquity as a dish was the cause of it. When I looked at her thin body, the old women of my mind were silently imploring her to eat her broth.

England. She adored England, or London, to be more exact. We lived there for three months in the late seventies.

Anna Karenina. She was reading it when she died. Aenea sat in the red armchair, dying, reading *Anna Karenina*. The strata of thin white seams on the fat black spine, from bending it, stop suddenly at three-quarters width.

Money. Since we live in a world of things, we must deal with this thing from which all things can be derived. To the child Aenea, money kept its primitive innocence. In the world of Aenea's childhood, money had the cultish place it should still hold in our faded, stilted, tangled minds. Danger and possibility: like a shape-shifter, cash could take on any form because it had none itself.

In those days, the pound was printed in bright magenta. I am speaking of Sanjanian currency, naturally, and only of the one-pound note, since Aenea's small village would not have seen any other denomination. Even the local tavern accepted labour and produce in exchange for doses of its substandard brandies. Most other exchanges worked on the same principle, although many maintained mental accounts of credit and debit, the tenders and payments of which were always and endlessly deferred. Perhaps she might have caught an occasional glimmer of magenta stuff passing from the hand of one fisherman to another. She may have discovered a small pile of paper strips hidden in her mother's kitchen. Perhaps even a few flashes of blue, but such extravagances as orange could only be afforded by the likes of smugglers or tourists.

But I am forgetting that Aenea left Little Harbour for Port Hope, and that to make the journey, she must have needed money. I imagine her, teary-eyed, exhilarated and clutching the shreds of colour. Money too can be experienced as freedom. There it is, practical freedom in the palm of her young hand. In the city, after her marriage to a brutish first husband had ended, money became a series of fresh problems, and fresh solutions to old problems. Debt, which was so easy a habit and so readily disposable in Little Harbour, took on the vague menace of institutions and the immediacy of property and sustenance. No adult can be sane about money with the sanity of a child.

She found a job sewing linings onto clothes bound for England. Later, she found illegal work and was able to survive with her children and without her husband.

After we married, she told me clearly that she wanted me to handle all the money. It was soon after the wedding, and we were staying in Little Harbour. I told her that the issue was much too important to her interests and her future to be left solely to me. She told me then that if disaster were coming, she wanted it straight out and simple. We were in the bar, drinking rumtotos. I never spoke to her about money again.

Clothing. Aenea's amber skin was so smooth and luxurious that it made every outfit seem superfluous. Even dying, her loveliness outstripped her decorations. The barest hint of Aenea's surface made the faint turning of silk or the rough honesty of denim or the crusted politesse of flannel seem like unnecessary refraction of a glory they obscured.

Death. She watched her mother die—agonizing months of daily and nightly expectation. She learned of her father's death by letter—the butter knife tucked under the exposed flap, the hearty tear to open it. Her own death somewhere between the endless and the sudden.

Elephants. In Paris, at the circus with the children, she lectured easily and fluidly, for roughly thirty minutes, on the biology, history and global cultural significance of the elephant. Facts at her fingertips included the daily consumption by weight of fully developed bulls, both African and Indian, how many piano keyboards could be made out of one tusk, and the latest research on the legends of the elephant graveyard. I was more enraptured than the children.

When I enquired when and where she had acquired these elephantine details, a coy smile was her sole response. I remember not one fragment of her statistical knowledge of the creatures, but I recall her subtle smile exactly.

Running shoes. She always owned running shoes and never went jogging. Her last pair is still in our closet, and I never asked why she bought them.

Jacques Derrida. He was a graduate student at the time, and we met him at a dinner with Rivero. He was honoured to meet me, so he said. After one conference or another. Man and the Self? Something on Marx? I cannot precisely recall. He was, by then, married to Marguerite.

At any rate, Jacques, like everyone at first meeting Aenea, was both deeply attracted and unsettled. He sat beside her, trying and failing to make conversation. Eventually, he looked up from his mumbling and verbal shuffling to make the following declaration: "Your name, it is a palindrome." His comment, and the situation in which he made it, coloured my entire reading of *Grammatology*.

Leonard King. Her second and final husband, Leonard King was the negative of her first husband, in suffering and joy. His quietness was gentle and his isolation was stupendous and ungracious. The first husband was the generator of her children, but they called Leonard King their father and he called them his children. Her blood was his blood.

Of all the countless men into whom Aenea had cast the image of her person, she penetrated into Leonard King the deepest. Her light was strongest inside him.

At a ceremony, in front of two hundred people, he was asked if he would forsake all others for her, to which he said, "I will."

There was his body, on which she feasted and glutted and starved.

There was his library, which required massive effort to transport when they changed houses, when they changed countries and continents, driven by what sense of exile in him? There was another burden of letters for her to carry just above the shoulder. One might also add that through Leonard King she was introduced to the literary scene in Port Hope, the post-Independence

Sanjanian intelligentsia. Without Leonard King as go-between, Frederick Christopher might never have written his "Ode to Aenea." She would almost certainly never have seen Paris or Rome. And to see Aenea in Paris was to know that dust wants to be two things: cities and Aenea. Cities and women are the only quintessences.

He was her most durable lover.

He dedicated two books to her: *Love and Football* and *Melody*. Critics assumed that the title character of the latter novel was based on her.

He watched over her death.

He watches over her children.

Bicycles. In Little Harbour, there was only one bicycle, and it belonged to the telegraph man, who guarded it so closely that it slept under his bed at night. No one but he ever had a chance to ride, so when the boys of the town tried to steal it for joyrides, their adventures always ended abruptly. They didn't know how to balance. Aenea therefore had no direct experience of bicycles when she had to teach Christophle how to ride one. She had to learn to teach what she had never learned to do herself. It was a double victory then when Christophle's velocity escaped the need for her guidance. Joy! It can be done! We progress! We progress!

Tea. Strong black tea. From Ceylon. No sugar. No cream. No lemon. Four pots a day for as long as I knew her. Her greatest everyday luxury.

A photograph at the Trevi Fountain. I recall it was the early autumn of 1967. "What are you thinking, my darling?" Her smile was almost melancholy as I set up the camera for the shot. "I was thinking that the birds don't know they're at the Trevi Fountain, and I was wondering if we're as blind as they are, but about other things we don't know." Click.

Mice. Aenea's hatred for mice was fanatical. She always respected rats, but despised mice. Related to her feline sympathies?

Numbers. Her autodidacticism started and stopped with novels. She did sums with a thumb on her fingertips.

Loves. I would like to say that our love was the centre, or the origin, or the end, but Aenea's loves were disparate, and uncontained too. She loved her children to folly, and her parents beyond duty. She loved her first husband to the point of idiocy. She loved me. She loved boys in Little Harbour, I am sure. And I must ask a widower's regrettable question: Was the ending of our love by death a blessed prevention of love's passing?

Love in Aenea. She is fifteen, in the shadows of the pines outside of her village commons, embracing a now-forgotten face. That face and hers, as with all others, vanish into oblivion. It is one version of mercy.

Sun. Sun will never admit limit to its dominions. The light of the sun flooded down on Aenea, and it made her and the grass she lay on. It made the ants on her skirt and the hem of her skirt too. It was shining in the sky a million years before her birth. It is shining now.

Red armchair. We bought a red armchair from the furniture maker whose boutique was (and possibly still is) on Pitt Street. It cost fifty-seven pounds, I recall. Aenea adored it. It found its place in the strangest angle of the house, what appeared to most people at first glance to be an architectural flaw. Off the kitchen, the wall jutted out oddly to capture a weirdly placed window. In the winter, in midmorning, the seat caught direct sunlight, and at night, when the sky was clear, one could read in the intensity of the moonbeams.

I wrote practically all of *Melody* in that armchair. Also, when *The Trumpet* arrived on Sunday morning, I would carry it to the armchair and wait for the children to descend and read it with them. During Aenea's sickness, I would find her there, always after searching everywhere else in the house. She would curl up into the red armchair with a book and fall asleep in the darkness.

We did make love in it, once.

Moon. The moon sucks up reflections, and leaves whatever blankness it can. The moon takes, as a single impression, Aenea curled into the red armchair with *Anna Karenina* on her lap. It will reflect a thousand years after her death.

Bells. What I hear is one long peal, an effervescent pleonasm of sound, but in Aenea's life it was the warning bell in Little Harbour, ringing out danger, and the bell of Saint Jerome's in Port Hope, ringing out celebration, and the bells in London and Paris, ringing out for others, not us, others.

Chess. Though she never learned how to play, she liked to keep a board set up as decoration wherever she lived. Another question I did not ask her.

Nothings. There was the nothing before her, and the nothing after her. There was the nothing from which she emerged without parallel, unlike anything or anyone else, and there was the nothing into which she dissolved, the same as everything and everyone. While I remember her, that is something, until I am nothing. While the story is, that is something, until it is nothing. One can see they are things by the nothing and the nothing.

A WEDDING IN RESTITUTION

Cato Dekkerman

1966 –

The sound of joy in Restitution rang all the way up to the hills and all the way down to the sea, the whole town shaking like a tambourine when it heard the news, and it seemed that everyone heard at once. Children's squeals and women's laughter mixed with the pleased shouts and snorts of the men, all of it reverberating over the town in an uproar of . . . Well, what *was* the uproar about exactly?

"What *is* that uproar about exactly?" asked Alderman Charity Barker, who sat in the village hall with Alderman Virgin, also forenamed Charity, trying to enjoy a game of chess in peace. "Why the racket?" Barker was already irritable because his opponent had blockaded his white-squared bishop and posted a knight to the sixth rank.

Alderman Virgin left the hall to ask a hardscrabble boy who spent his idle hours trying to knock over a row of green-tinted bottles with blue stones beside the Alderhall wall. When he came back, he had to whisper the news, he was so shocked: "Caesar and Endurance have announced their engagement!"

If Alderman Barker wasn't so stunned by the news himself, he might have thanked providence for its timing: the two men couldn't possibly finish their game now.

The children in Ms. Moonthorple's long school giggled a lot about the uproar over the engagement. Which does not mean they understood what was going on. So they sent an emissary to the teacher's desk, "a polite but not interstellar girl" as Ms. Moonthorple had described her in the term report, a "teacher's pride" to the students, Sylvia Romani by name. During quiet hour, when the class was all bent over their copies of the *Sanjanian Reader*, Sylvia crept up and asked her question. "Ms.?" she asked.

"Yes."

"Ms.?"

"Yes, Sylvia, out with it."

"Why are Caesar and Endurance getting married? Why is there an uproar about the engagement of Caesar and Endurance? Why wasn't there a fuss when Aeneas and Romana were married last month?"

The whole class held its breath. They could tell Ms. Moonthorple, who was stroking her cheek like an old private king holding judgement, wavered between telling and not telling. Her long stare deepened the expectation, but Ms. Moonthorple at last decided that she most certainly could *not* tell the tale to her kiddies. "I think you had better learn to read while you are at school and leave idle gossip to idle gossipers, little girl. Back to your desk."

Later Ms. Moonthorple reconsidered that she could at least have told them that Caesar worked at the Scala, the town tavern, and was the only tavern keeper of the masculine persuasion in town, and that Endurance was the only female sailor in the whole world so far as anyone knew. Those little morsels might have alleviated some of the poor dears' curiosity and saved Sylvia Romani some schoolyard shame. Ms. Moonthorple was tenderhearted, you see. She could afford to be very tenderhearted once she had left her classroom.

Oh, the pinches, the cloth-tears, the crooked names Sylvia Romani suffered after last bell, for these children had *no* use for failure when it came to piercing the veil of adult mysteries. It turned out that they just had to wait until dinner. Husband told wife or wife told husband (depending on the marriage) and little ears rustled at the table-edge.

The thing was, the uproar, the great sound ringing up the hills and down to the sea, it was because the whole town had always wanted Caesar and Endurance to be married. It made you want to giggle and laugh and shout, they were so perfect for each other. They fit together like a turbot and a turbot-pan.

Consider the facts: Caesar and Endurance were Restitution's two orphans. They were born on the *same exact day*. Both their mothers had died in childbirth. Both children had been named after the mother's suffering. Ms. Carpenter and Ms. Saltdate, Restitution's midwives, would never talk about those births to anyone but each other, used to wince at the mention of their names, and once were overheard, slightly tipsy at the Scala, to say that Caesar and Endurance were born on the foam of a sea of blood. Those were their exact words: "the foam of a sea of blood." They refused to spell out exactly what they meant and so the town's imagination took over.

Then there were the other stories. About the christenings, to take one instance, there was the story . . . well, it was the story that determined their whole *lives*.

Their christening was a double ceremony since they were born on the same day, so Caesar's father was lifting the boy all in white and overhead down to the shore while Endurance's father was just bringing her down to the font. The town was still clad in mourning for the mothers, but everybody cheered and a bottle of brandy was unstoppered and handed to Caesar's father for a toast. All more or less the usual scenario, until the child—Caesar, that is—grabbed the bottle in his baby fingers and toasted his own life by pouring it out on the sand. That was where the town's astonishment began but not where it ended because the bottle spilled and spilled and spilled out and spilled out some more and in a minute the father was standing in a *puddle* of brandy. In three minutes the whole congregation was standing in a drunken *pool*. The whole *world* might have drowned in brandy from that one bottle. Then a sudden cry from the church pierced the air, and poor baby Caesar dropped the bottle and started bawling. Inside, at the christening table, Endurance's father was displaying her back to a room full of sailors.

At first glance, it looked like some scoundrel had scattered a handful of white scars over her smooth, light skin. The dots were evenly spread over her front too. "The stars! the stars!" her father was shouting, and he was a navigator, so it meant something. Yes, with a closer look every sailor there could see that the pattern over Endurance was the same as in the heavens. Her skin somehow was a map of the asterisms.

So those were the miraculous stories of their christening. It was easy to see why the whole town thought from the beginning that their marriage was inevitable.

A few days after the christening, the fathers both sold their children, one to the Scala, the other to the good ship *Monroe*, left town in a single boat to seek their fortunes in Port Hope and were never heard from again. Caesar poured unlimited brandy to the tavern owner for free (the rate to the customers at the Stairs was only just reduced), and Endurance was forced to live up to her name on the sea, where her flesh was spread out on a mariner's table like a shifting map, even when the sky was clear and there was no need for her. A miracle is an extraordinary piece of furniture, Restitution discovered, and it was not a misfortune to either of the children, when their miraculous abilities evaporated with adulthood and, after adolescence, they were just a perfect masculine tavernkeep (who didn't have a single tattoo at that), and a well-battened, strong-timbered sailorine.

Then they decided to get married.

Whether or not there are miracles marrying, or mothers dying, or children listening to elders telling stories about orphans, when the sun tilts over in Restitution, the men are at the boats with fixed tender lines, their eyes on the horizon. The morning after the announcement was not a Sunday, and so down by the piers the men prepared themselves for the sea just the same as usual.

Endurance was reining in her tackle. She burlapped her forearms. She tightened the laces on her boots. None of the sailors could see any change in the woman. She was still dressed in her dirty fishing weeds, smoking her owlshead pipe to cover the reek of scale and pulled guts. Her eyes were still fierce as a deepwater fish, and she hadn't traded the rough hub of her sailor's mouth for a girly portico of soft lips as far as anyone could tell.

"How are the waves blowing?" hazarded one of the men.

"See them for yourself," replied Endurance, head-pointing to the shore. Orange light licked the darkness steadily like a panting dog at a trough. She didn't want to talk about the future. She wanted to talk about fish.

"Maybe we'll catch a tuna for your *wedding*," he said.

"Or your *funeral*," Endurance shot back. The men laughed, then they threw themselves into the ships, singing "Keys and Plenty."

At the same moment, the women of Restitution were streaming down from their houses towards the market. That path, which is taken "more for the chat than the chits" as they say, neatly passes the Scala, where Caesar, as he had done every morning, was sweeping the covered terrace with a switch. Today was no different from others, and it was Caesar's trade always to greet the wives and misses with their proper names and to remember whom he had seen and whom he had not. This was the heart of his profession.

"Caesar," called out Estella, who happened to be the eldest woman in the village.

"Yes, Estella."

"How is our fine *groom* this morning?"

"Fresh as a sea rose. Do you have time for tea, Estella?"

And as they came along, Caesar invited all the wives into the Scala for a sit down and sip. The gossips gossiped that day about where the ceremony would be (at the pier church, naturally), about what Caesar might wear to it (his best church suit, of course), about what would be served at the breakfast (the ordinary wedding dishes of lamb and mountain spring grasses), and then about other marriages (successes, failures, battles, truces). But it's a fact of life that even gossip ends. The women filed away in dribs and drabs, ones and twos and threes, for shopping and stewing and gardens.

As for the children, at lessons that morning they were stunned to learn, from Ms. Moonthorple's mouth (who just *couldn't* resist this once) that Caesar and Endurance had been "deprived an education," as she called it. "Only the tavern for him and belowdeck for her, children. Consider how *lucky* you are." The children might have done so, had they not been so deeply overwhelmed with jealousy at the couple's deprivation.

At dinner that evening, the wives said to the husbands that the wedding of Caesar and Endurance was the responsibility of the *whole* town and the husbands granted that yes, they supposed it was, and the wives said that they hoped they *would* say it to the Aldermen and not lose courage at the meeting that evening, and the husbands mumbled that they would not lose courage at the meeting that evening, and the children listened in wonder to it all.

The church bells rang up and down the hills and out across the sea, and all the men from the town left their dinners and went to the meeting with the Aldermen Charities, who were once again forced to put aside a game of chess to discuss the wedding of Caesar and Endurance. The meeting was rather brief for a Committee meeting and rather unanimous. Alderman Charity Barker suggested that the wedding of Caesar and Endurance was the responsibility of the whole town, and Alderman Charity Virgin seconded his point. All the men, in fact (certainly all the men who were married), agreed with the statement. These poor children had been born from the foam of a sea of blood, said someone from the back. They *deserved* a town wedding, shouted another robust voice. A quieter speaker mentioned quietly that Father Nuncet was due at the end of the week.

Father Nuncet! They had all forgotten about Father Nuncet! Disaster! Disaster!

The men flooded out of the church down to the waiting shores of their homes. "The priest is due at the end of the week!" they shouted. The wives gasped: "At the end of the week?" The men nodded. "He's not due for another three months after that," they added, needlessly. Everyone already knew that, even the children.

They had four days. Well, it would *just* be possible. They would have to clean the town, dress the bride, prepare the feast, but it *could* be done. With great faith and every hand pulling, there would be time enough. *Just* time enough. First, a good night's sleep.

The next morning, there was much thinking to be done, much weighing in both hands, many decisions to be sliced *thin-thin*. It required tea and sugar, and there was no better place for those (and to keep Caesar out of it) than the school before the school hour. Ms. Moonthorple brewed a fine sip.

A white dress for the bride was essential, of course, and only Charity Virgin's wife Trin had the cloth. After a few cups and nudges, she offered it relatively gracefully, to more or less free applause. Secondly, it was agreed that Romana Lambden, the youngest bride in the village, would oversee the roasting of the lambs, just for the charm of it. Laurentia Tapamount, for her part, would lead a battalion of wives into the bakery for her tricolour hat pastries, and send another battalion into the hills for spring grasses. Ms. Moonthorple sighed and volunteered to cook them on the day itself, just like she had done for dozens of weddings which were not her own.

As for the cleaning, there being nobody else and no other time, the *men* would have to clean the streets. There was nothing else for it.

Business concluded, tasks assigned, rigourous matters dispensed with, a less practical question came up: How had Caesar and Endurance found time and place for a rendezvous? The boy lived in the Scala, slept in the back of the tavern, and the waves of a boat were the only cradling lullaby the girl had ever known, so when could they have managed a session?

Answers were swirling thick and sweet as fume over the teacups until Trin Virgin solved it: they had made love in their *dreams*. All the wives were convinced utterly and instantly, those two thin little beings rubbing into one another like silver spoons in a drawer, and all over the town too (that's where dreams happen). They must have made so much friction in the street corners, their enormous dream backs lying down like fakirs' on the points of the rooftops, their sweet moans caught in all the dishes slow-cooked overnight in the whole town's kitchens. Yes, that must have been why all the food had tasted so savoury these last few months.

There was *men's* business to be taken care of as well. That evening they tightened their buttons to their coats and tucked their liquor money under their belts with deeper conviction than usual. There are words that must be passed from fathers down to sons, and since the whole town was Caesar's father, and since they were the town . . . The love between men and women needed *explanation*, and poor Caesar was an orphan.

On any other day, from the first drip of liquor, the Scala was a spontaneous festival, but that night it was lined with gloomy, silent men. Only Caesar was rattling on in his continual tavern chatter, but eventually even he stopped.

"Caesar . . . " began Goodman Jones.

"There is something that we . . . " Joshua Asmith continued.

"That we should discuss," concluded Praisegod Gallant.

The men were mute after their little choric impersonation. Caesar waited to be illuminated, and then put down the glass he was hand-buffing. "What is this *something* that we must discuss?" he asked.

No answer came, but at that moment Charity Virgin was standing up from the chess table, where he had forked a rook, leaving his co-Charity to contemplate the series of poor choices he had left in his wake.

"What must these scholars of life discuss with you, Caesar?" he asked.

"I haven't the shadow of a notion."

Virgin looked at the bashful men. He looked at young Caesar.

"I think they want to give you the news about the love between men and women, Caesar, but what they haven't noted in the tiny logs inside their brain vessels is that the tavern was a cradle to you, and there isn't a dirty book printed or not that you haven't at least skimmed."

"I see," said Caesar.

"Best give them a sample," said the Alderman.

Caesar took a breath before he began speaking. " 'A young wife to bed is like a goat to the meadow.' 'A mother looks to the belly, a wife to the back.' 'A disorderly wife is better than to remain a bachelor.' 'A wife's clothes are the price of a husband's peace.' Shall I go on?"

"No. That will do," said the wise Alderman.

The first Charity returned to the board to see what bad choice the other Charity had taken. Caesar went back to polishing his glass. Later the fishermen upped their jaws.

At dawn the following morning, the women of Restitution (or rather seven representative women of Restitution) rushed down to the shoreline and gathered Endurance up in their skirts before she could run away. She shouted to her fellow sailors, "Help me,

I'm feeling lucky for bluefish today!" But they could do nothing for her. Though each of those steadfast men who sailed with her would have dived past the sea teeth for her sake, they couldn't *possibly* save the future bride from their own wives, and left her to the struggle.

It lasted the whole day. By the late afternoon, Endurance was leaving the tailorshop in gloves, under a parasol for practice. (It was one of Restitution's particular traditions that a woman in bridal costume shouldn't be touched by direct sunlight on The Day.) Endurance smiled, and each of the seven women stared at her modest pleasure in the white muslin with a long look, but there was *no* time for looking.

There was no time at all. *Absolutely* no time. There was barely time enough to let the zap of the thought that there was no time zip through your mind. If every second was a minute, and every tick was a tock . . . there wasn't enough time to complete the metaphor even. The wives told the husbands, and the husbands told the Aldermen who reported it to the fishermen and their wives: "There's no time."

"So?"

"So, tomorrow all the women will go together up the hills for spring grasses and spices and to talk to whatever shepherds they can find, Nobby or Christian or Luke."

"And the men?"

"The men will clean the town."

The women's laughter was sudden and bright, a fish leaping from a reed boat, and so it was decided that the women would leave for the hills before dawn, since once the men had started they would *never* be able to tear their eyes away.

Give them their due: the men didn't flinch. They set their

staunch backs to cleaning the town, all of them. All except Terence Olive, that is.

Terence Olive refused not to fish. He said, "If I don't fish, I will fall apart from my ankle," and nobody knew what he meant, so they let him go. The rest of the good-hearted, strong-backed men went to work with shovels, pails, mops, brooms and rags, until the dusty streets had been raked, the whitewalls reflected like shells, the wood walls gleamed like new, and fresh green garlands hung in tight-fisted bunches over the porticos. The women, coming back from the hills with the slaughter when the sun was slipping, said nothing.

The men said, "How do you find it?"

The women said, "Oh, wonderful, but . . ."

"What is it?"

"Well, it's nothing, it's just that . . ." But the thought will never be finished because Terence Olive interrupted it, calling for witnesses, chasing down the raked streets *howling* (still in his fishing gear too), and all Restitution ran after him down to his vessel. There a monster fish was still slapping almost the *length* and *breadth* of his little-man boat. "I had to sit on it to row home," he said between pants. The fins were a sleek yellow, and its fatty, silvery sides hadn't even been torn by netting. But the cast of its eye was the strangest part, like the dying fish could smile. The bottom of the sea had sacrificed itself for the wedding of Caesar and Endurance. That was so obvious to everyone it didn't need telling.

"How did you land it?" was the first question.

Fisherman Olive couldn't say. He just didn't know. He didn't know why he didn't know, either.

Ten men carried the beast to the public square, where the women stuffed it with slushleaves and bitters and packed it in buckets of salt. Its heart was still beating when they laid it down in the pit behind the yard of the Scala, at least that's what Cecilia Barker and Ms. Moonthorple said.

The men cleaning, the women's trip to the mountains, the fish, that all happened on a Friday, so the Miracle of the Smiling Fish That Leapt into Terence Olive's Boat was doubly, maybe triply, significant. The date was *certainly* remarked upon.

Saturday afternoon was the appointed hour for the circumnavigating priest to arrive, and Father Nuncet was always punctilious. He was a tight man, Father Nuncet, young and shipshape, tall and thin, cleanly shaven and neatly cropped. A bit *severe*, he was thought on the coasts, but generous, proper and serviceable. Always on time too, and there's not more a cove can ask from a priest.

Charity Barker went alone to fetch him from the next cove over in the local Ford, and he drove back slowly to let the gleaming town hit the priest full in the eye. The whole covetown looked like a bride's house before The Night.

"What's this, Charity?" the priest asked when he first glimpsed it.

"What's what, Father?"

"This." He gestured to the town, and its beauty.

"A wedding tomorrow."

"Ah, good," said Father Nuncet, and swallowed the fact that none of the covers ever told him about ceremonies that called for special sermons until the last possible *hour*. Then again, there was no way for them to notify him yet, despite the built roads from cove to cove. He would just have to use the ceremony and sermon from last month, which had worked at the wedding in Openroar, though it was maybe a tad long.

"And who is to be married tomorrow?" he asked.

"Caesar."

"The tavern man?"

"The tavern man."

"And to whom?"

"Endurance."

"Not the little sailorine?"

"The one."

"Ah, good. So the two orphans are to be wed together?"

Charity Barker nodded and Father Nuncet turned his view back to the shining village. "My, my," said the priest. "My, my, my, my, my."

Father Nuncet arrived Saturday night, the wedding to take place next morning, but still the priest barely had time to put his carrying case in one corner of his churchside chamber when a *storm-patter* of knocks on his door started falling. He opened the door and it seemed like the whole town tramped into his little suite.

There were so many stories, and so many people to tell them, that the priest had to bring in *all* the chairs from the kitchen, and as more people with more stories came, he had to lift in the *bed* so a few elder Aldermen could recline on it, and later there were children lying in the *corners*, and men squatting on *footstools*, and a standing crowd too. All to tell Father Nuncet about the massy fish that jumped itself into the Olive boat, or the men cleaning the village, or the lovedreamcovescape where Caesar and Endurance had made love or the miracles after their joint communion (*those* stories the father already knew), or that they had both been born from the foam of a sea of blood.

It is a well-known, long-established fact that stories put people to sleep.

Sitting, standing, leaning, kneeling, their voices calling out, or asking somebody else to explain, or to clarify or just to repeat, they fell asleep talking, the priest too. He told his stories and dozed off like the rest.

The next morning, where there would usually be the muffled sound of the women ensundaying themselves, now only a snore was drifting over Restitution. Nonetheless, Caesar dressed himself in his steam-pressed wedding suit and stood in the doorway of the Scala, waiting for his coterie, but there were only a few young children playing in the streets with wheels and winks, and they were as confused as he was. The sun was already high.

Endurance was already wearing the white muslin dress, minus gloves and parasol. She waited, slung in a low hammock among the tackle and netting. Having once herself been a miracle, Endurance was rarely surprised, but even she was a little mystified by the town's silence.

They were all dreamlessly asleep . . .

Only when the sun ran up the mountain, and *ten*, and then *eleven,* showed on the tick-tock clock in the priest's cabin (the only timepiece in town other than the one in Charity Virgin's pocket), did Caesar and Endurance begin to tremble a bit. The problem was that tradition in Restitution held that all weddings *must* finish in the morning, which, if their fellow covers remained opiated by stories too much longer, would shortly be impossible. Then it would have to be another Sunday. Then the priest would be gone. One feature of time is that there's always less and less of it.

Restitution's sleep was broken by the laughter of children. Ms. Moonthorple rose to scold them and her startled scream, seeing the tick-tock, was like a bell. Everyone woke up. Everyone looked where she pointed. The clock read a *quarter to noon!*

In the confusion that followed (nobody admits it but it's still true), several of the less necessary, more time-consuming traditions were not exactly maintained. For example, without time for a sip to clear their heads, the wives ran to the tavern to get

Caesar while the husbands fetched Endurance from the ships. There was also no time, in the fury when the whole town ran to opposite ends (market and pier) and then ran back, to sing the traditional songs. No "First Ray of May." No "Kings and Queens." The bride and groom, who remained serene throughout, were *pushed* through the church doors, not introduced with gay stateliness. There was also no one but children in the church aisles, where Sylvia Romani said, "It's a lovely wedding, isn't it?" to her neighbour Marsha Walpole, and Marsha Walpole said, "Yes, isn't it?"

Naturally, the necessary sacred words were uttered, if a bit hurriedly. It wouldn't count as a wedding otherwise. Father Nuncet's wedding sermon, however, was abbreviated sharply: "We all know what is going on here. God is Love." Which was not the sermon he had given a month before at Openroar, but was enough. "Kiss-kiss," Restitution shouted. Caesar and Endurance kiss-kissed. "I now declare you husband and wife," said Father Nuncet. One interesting fact is that at the word "wife" the last toll of the clock sounded in the next room.

It was *exactly* noon. Without knowing how, without being able to remember what they had done to push it through, the villagers of Restitution had married Caesar and Endurance. The grown spectators were standing in the church aisle, still in the clothes they had slept in. The children politely applauded.

A feast followed, a feast of the flesh of the fantastic fish. Ten men carried it out of its grave. Ten women washed the salty dirt from its back. They roasted it over a bed of burning spindles and thorns, and the smell of the smoke pouring over those monstrous sides sent up a gentle, hastily smothered moan in the crowd around it as the aphrodisiac fume flooded the streets. In the mouth and on the tongue, its flesh was soft and giving, rich and delicious and unlike any other seameat any of the sailors or their wives had ever known.

"As if compassion had a flavour," said Ms. Moonthorple, who had read a lot and had been fidgeting ever since the first waves of its scent.

Another woman at a completely different table said it tasted to her more like mercy.

The meal began at dusk, and as if to make up for the hurried ceremony, it went long and slow, with *every* song sung and *every* ritual performed. Like the streets themselves were the bride's sitting room, Caesar and Endurance were kept at opposite ends of the market, following the rite of keeping bride and groom at opposite ends of the wedding chamber. There was also a speech by Alderman Virgin (from the groom's party) about the beauties of the bride, and there was a speech by Alderman Barker (from the bride's party) about the strengths of the groom, but both thinned out in the tide of gossip, and general toasts, and the rest of it. Even the most traditional let the feast take its course from that point.

The children watched the scenario brimming with delight because it reminded them so much of a dream, the town using the public square to eat in, and Ms. Moonthorple bibbling too much, and the massy fish skeleton with its stuffing stretched over the bones, and the two orphans as king and queen, and the whole town giddy.

That fish *should* have fed the town for a week, but it was already gone by the time the whale tapers were being lit on the tables and set on the branches of stonetrees. They devoured, off the bones, the stuffing of slushleaves and bitters, ate it right from their hands. Everyone had to rush home for a session, or rather every wife just remembered some chore that was pressing, and needed the help of her husband at home. The only people left were fidgety Ms. Moonthorple, who was looking up at Father Nuncet, who was looking down on the ground, and the children (sick with hilarity) gathered around Caesar and Endurance. "Will you make love tonight?" "Can you see by the stars on your back?" "What names will you give the babies you're making tonight?"

The orphans offered no answers but Caesar did pick up an empty bottle and poured continually, poured a whole *pool* of brandy around their feet. Endurance tore off a strip of white muslin to show them by torchlight that her back matched the constellations. The children giggled, the priest and the teacher gasped, but they never spoke to anyone about The Last Miracles of Caesar and Endurance. There would be no others but nature.

Slowly the growns came limping back from their homes, a bit weary, frailer, tinged with sadness. Father Nuncet remarked on it to one of the Charities (he could never tell them apart). "Why do we all seem so suddenly melancholic?"

"Besides the errands we have all so hastily had to run?"

"I cannot see why that should sadden the group, but yes, what besides those?"

"The boat," said Alderman Charity.

"Ah, good. What boat is that?" asked the priest.

"I suppose you could not know about the wedding boat. It is a tradition only in Restitution."

"Please explain."

Charity opened his mouth to answer . . .

The cove spoke for him by performing it: they lifted Caesar (the men), and led blindfolded Endurance (the women) down to the shore. Father Nuncet and his companion followed behind the crowd, who tenderly placed Caesar and Endurance in a vessel, threw in oars, a blanket, pillows, and pushed it off.

"What does it mean?" asked the priest.

"The tradition," answered Charity.

"But what is the tradition? What happens now?"

"Now we wait all night to see if they return."

The town was silent as Caesar and Endurance drifted into calm waters and slipped beyond the haloes of the tapers. The quality of that darkness was unique. It wasn't an absence or a presence but a possibility, and possibility isn't black. It's sort of brown and sort of blue. The people sat on the border of the sea. The children played "Tangerine and Trouble" in the courtyard. Will they come back? Will they be destroyed? Will they bring us a gift from the sea?

Father Nuncet tried to stay awake with them for their vigil. (They told no stories that night.) He tried to stay awake because he could sense that the covedwellers were contemplating memories of their sins and virtues, and that is when a priest is really *needed*. The food weighed him down like a sinkstone though, and he nodded and nodded and could not quite manage to keep himself on the right side of the border.

At the hour of snails and nighthawks, he was asleep and *nobody* could wake him. They would not wake him.

In his dream, Father Nuncet felt a hand on his shoulder, and a swift wind at his back, and then he felt as if he had been bundled in a sack and was being carted by a heavy workman up a series of ladders. The priest did not struggle. His release blew him upwards into the infinite heavens of Jehovah, into the empyreal realms of Paradise, to the seat of God Himself. At His Right Hand, Jesus Christ sat in judgement, and His judgement was perfect. Light was turning in heavenly orbs infinitely outwards in waves of perfect love and utter mercy. (This is how the priest described it when people asked him later.) At Christ's feet were Caesar and

Endurance, and then they were carried up to His Right Hand by engines of angels. The priest went unnoticed, a spy of the Last Day, wondering what the judgement would be and angels stared past him into the abyss. Then Jesus, who was about to speak, opened His mouth: the roar of a crowd came out and Father Nuncet awoke into a bright dawn. "My, my," he said.

The uproar in Restitution rang up to the hills and down to the sea, as Caesar and Endurance, embracing, let the waves carry their vessel to shore. Charity Virgin and Charity Barker stopped. They had been playing chess to wile away the hours of the night. "We will have to build them a house now," muttered the one Alderman to the other. They sighed, put their game aside, and joined in the uproar.

THE MAN FRIDAY'S REVIEW OF ROBINSON CRUSOE

Marcel Henri

1978 –

> *In the history books the discoverer sets a shod foot on virgin sand, kneels, and the savage also kneels from his bushes in awe. Such images are stamped on the colonial memory, such heresy as the world's becoming holy from Crusoe's footprint or the imprint of Columbus' knee. These blasphemous images fade, because these hieroglyphs of progress are basically comic. And if the idea of the New and the Old becomes increasingly absurd, what must happen to our sense of time, what else can happen to history itself, but that it too is becoming absurd?*
>
> —DEREK WALCOTT

To the casual reader, the full title of Crusoe's memoir, *The Life and Strange Surprising Adventures of Robinson Crusoe*, may be a little misleading. All that is strange and surprising here takes place during Crusoe's isolation on an unnamed island at the mouth of the Oronoko River, when nothing at all "adventurous" occurs. The surrounding plots, in effect, are just persiflage and should be skimmed, if read at all.

Unfortunately, there is quite a bit of persiflage to skim over here. The latter two-thirds of the book are of little interest to anyone other than the most devoted student of biography. The return journey to the island is full of boring self-aggrandizement, and the concluding reflections on morality highlight a tendency to empty platitude on Crusoe's part.

The first of the three parts, however, is wonderful, and not just the sections in which I appear. (Full disclosure: I am the same Friday mentioned in the book.) The figure of Crusoe alone is genuinely fascinating, not least because of one paradoxical aspect to his writing: despite being rife with factual errors, the choicest materials of the work are all descriptive. Others have pointed out many of these mistakes before. Crusoe stuffed his pockets full of biscuits after he had undressed for swimming. He saw the eyes of a goat in the pitch dark, a flat-out impossibility. The Spaniards gave my father an agreement in writing when we did not have pen and ink. There are many more such inconsistencies, not that the number of them matters.

In the past, I have made no secret of the fact that Crusoe has misrepresented myself and others, but those who scoff at him on account of these technical trifles are missing the point, I think. Crusoe, when I knew him, was near-blind and half-deaf. His physical weaknesses were unfortunately combined with absolute self-certainty, and I believe the combination of these traits perverted his memory unconsciously, without his being capable of recognizing the problem. Like history, *The Adventures of Robinson Crusoe* has to be understood despite its author.

One particular scene comes to mind, the moment when Crusoe has built his boat nowhere near the water, and cannot push it to the shore nor build a canal. He writes, "This griev'd me heartily, and now I saw, tho' too late, the Folly of beginning a Work before we count the Cost, and before we judge rightly of our own Strength to go through with it." To those who know Crusoe, the absence here is the key: he does not mention that he has been an idiot, that any child could have figured out to build a boat near the water. At no point would he ever inculpate himself.

Take another example, the scene of our first encounter, which I will have to quote at some length: "I halloed again to him, and made Signs to come forward, which he easily understood, and came a little way, then stopp'd again, and then a little further, and stopp'd again, and I cou'd then perceive that he stood trembling, as if he had been taken Prisoner, and had just been to be kill'd as his two Enemies were. I beckon'd him again to come to me, and gave him all the Signs of Encouragement that I could think of, and he came nearer and nearer, kneeling down every Ten or Twelve steps in token of acknowledgment for my saving his Life: I smil'd at him, and look'd pleasantly, and beckon'd to him to come still nearer; at length he came close to me, and then he kneel'd down again, kiss'd the Ground, and laid his Head upon the Ground, and taking me by the Foot, set my Foot upon his Head, this it seems was in token of swearing to be my Slave for ever."

Just so—Robinson Crusoe was the kind of man who could see, at the drop of a hat, a gesture of eternal servitude. He could imagine one as well: I know that I never kissed his feet. As for my kneeling down, he had proven that he was willing to use a gun, and was waving it liberally in my direction. At my first view of him, I could tell he was blind. In short, I was ducking.

The misrepresentation of myself is far from exceptional. When Crusoe says anything, it is always best to turn it sideways, reverse it, cut it in half and believe a third.

The second and third parts of this work expand Crusoe's misbegotten certainty into the domains of religious sentiment and the colonial impulse. His complete self-assurance is distasteful when accompanied by power, but in the first part the vulnerability of his condition mollifies the arrogance. This man, we think, could after all die at any moment. Not that he notices the fact. The enormous, terrible silence of "eight and twenty Years, two Months and nineteen days" (ludicrously precise and entirely incorrect arithmetic, by the way) seems to have bothered him about as much as a mild, recurrent rash.

Nothing seems to have bothered him much, and nothing excited him much either. The adventures on Crusoe's island are really about avoiding adventure: rather than explore the novelty of a new world, Crusoe sets about re-creating the life of England's small gentry, an insane desire undertaken with complete rationality. At the gateway to a new continent, all he wants is tea and biscuits.

In one of the autobiography's most noted scenes, Crusoe is astonished by the discovery of a naked footprint in the sand. He asks neither where the walker came from nor where he might have been going. We are left to ask those questions ourselves; we are left to wonder at the opaqueness of a man who didn't need to ask—an obliviousness more remarkable perhaps than the footprint itself.

THE END OF THE BEACH

Octavia Kitteredge-Mann

1946 –

My mother's face. Also, I remember the end of the beach.

We are lying in bed. His hand brushes along my side like a blush. Staring together at the foggy Paris spring. It is a garret apartment, time is no enemy, and we are happy.

"What do you remember about your home, about the place that you come from?" he asks. My mother's face. No. I have already forgotten everything and I remember every detail, but I say to him, I say, "I remember the end of the beach."

From Sanjania, from the East Coast. Lawson. Like perhaps another hundred towns, it is nestled safely at the back of a shallow cove. Leaf-thatched huts press close together.

As in all such covetowns, the women's lives are spent talking, cooking, cleaning, healing, raising, ordering, gardening and tidying, and the men's lives are spent fishing. Between the women in little homes and the men on the vast ocean, the pebbly, sandy sleeve of the beach leads to a rocky outcrop, a craggy, solitary place, next neighbour of the sea, full of slime, crabs, pools among flat rocks. The women watch beyond it to see who is returning. Who is not.

My mother and other women are always cursing it silently and out of sight, fearing and hating the end of the beach.

It is Paris, as far away from Lawson as I can go, and in Paris, I find myself being asked by my French lover, "What exactly do you remember about the end of the beach?"

An odour. In the hour following the hottest part of the day, when the children have been delivered from school and the men are about to be delivered from the sea, Lawson is overwhelmed by the odour of fish soup. Women cooking. The boy children gather at the beach to prepare lines and tend to the boats, and the girl children separate to their own houses to help their mothers.

My sister Julia is sixteen. Four years older than I am. Old enough to hate walking home with me past the boys with their busy glances, but we are the same to my mother. So when my mother speaks to Julia, she is speaking to me as well.

"Don' go dow' end of beach, Ju," she says. She has been saying this every day at this hour since Julia's sixteenth anniversary.

"Yes, Mamma," Julia says.

"You hear me?"

"I do hear you, Mamma."

"All girls in town, this one wanna go always dow' to the end of the beach. I see it."

My mother thinks our family is better than every other in

Lawson because she was born in the city, and vaunts over them, although she would never dream of living anywhere else, her life circumscribed by the town gossips and the quarterly deposit of pamphlets from the geevees. I see the limit etched on her face most clearly at this hour.

Making fishbone soup is a demanding chore. My task is always to strip the vegetables. Slimy. Seedy. Juices crust in the crevices of my quick and nails. Julia undoes the fish morsels from their skeletons. Mother strains the broth for bones and seasons it. Even in a bowl of fish stew, there are dance steps and hierarchies. I am a quick learner, my teachers say.

At the kitchen hour, mother's eyes are always going back to the sea. It is like a flower turned away from the light. A moment later, it faces the window again. Mother looks to the sea to reckon who will return and will not. Ju looks up with her, I look up too. Three women awaiting twists of fate at the border of the sea. Three women making soup, staring past the end of the beach.

"Julia?"

"Quiet. Sleep. It's night."

"Julia? Why does Mamma forbid us from going to the end of the beach?"

With my Parisian lover, I never have to answer. I never have to speak. The silences between us glow, luscious and fecund. I may ask him what we are eating for dinner at night, or what the word for penknife is, or if we should drive up to Normandy on the weekend. He will answer me, while I never have to answer him. The definition of gentleness.

Arm in arm, our togetherness is something like new love, an overwhelming wave of comfort and tenderness, *la tendresse*. He doesn't say much. When we go out walking, in Normandy, at the sea's edge, there seems to be no end of the beach.

With Jerome too, my "firstboy" in Lawson, I was always asking questions. Forever in my soul, wherever it travels, it carries the image of Jerome as a thirteen-year-old boy: thin lips and an overly mature, brooding forehead. Between them a wee nose and kind, solicitous eyes.

"Jerome, tell me what happens at the end of the beach?" I ask.

"We hunt crabs. We splash little pools. Hide and seek. You know it." His soft answers are asking for an explanation of the question.

"But others. Tell me, Jerome, what does Julia do down there?"

He says, "I don't know." Quickly. A lie. He would fabricate if he didn't know. A suspicious flicker at the playful parts of his mouth. His eyes have turned wary. He does know. He will not say. He knows.

These thoughts, and the first hint of my anger flaring, dispel his reticence. I don't even have to repeat my question. He whispers close to me, "They go there to love it. Your sister does too."

Disbelieving, I suppress my denial for the sake of more knowledge.

"You know it. One hears the grunting in the rocks at evening, echoing like."

My anger suddenly fades, without the time to make a flush. Because now I know. I have heard. I know what happens at the end of the beach.

In Paris, in the graduate seminar, I am not listening to the professor. My lover is wearing an elegant grey pinstriped suit, cavalierly without a tie. We are in the same class at the university, he is across the room, staring at me out of the edges of his eyes. What might be called thought in me is not even the sense of my lover's gaze, but a memory of the weight of Jerome's vision on my nakedness a decade before. The professor is asking, pressing the point, "But to what end? To what end?" The answer, given silently to myself, is "To the end of the beach."

In time, Jerome and I "loved it" among the jagged rocks and tide-coughed seaweed. To look out at the waves and dread where they will carry me. I learn home and body and self in uncomfortable twisted limbs on stone, stolen ecstasies, the smell of the ocean, risk and another. I learned these things with Jerome at the end of the beach.

I remember. My memory is so strong the other children call me "elephant." I am the best student for mathematics, grammar, geography, physics, but history is my best subject. My skill will serve me well later in my study of philosophy. I have consumed every page of every book in the small library. There is some talk of sending me off to Port Hope, to the new university. Perhaps Europe. The word rings like a bell over my life. Europe. Julia will soon be finished school. There is no talk about her.

What I remember. My sister leads me, without a word, away from school, along the sand. I follow. We are halfway down the blond pebbly strand. Julia stops me, and turns my whole body with both her hands to face the town. There are tears in her eyes and I am afraid. "Look over town, Elephant," she says. "Look over it because here is where I am going to die."

I stared into her face, mute, uncomprehending.

"See it, Elephant. A bunch of houses away from the tide. You see it?"

"Why?" I ask her. "What is killing you?"

New life and young death are confused in her laugh. She is pregnant, she tells me, patting her belly, which has not yet visibly changed. Julia has taken me walking to tell me, "Remember this. That you must leave. That this town will never be enough for you. Tell me that you swear to leave."

Jerome, who will be carried off by the sea in a week, has already been holding me in his smooth and taut adolescent arms. I swear nothing. I smile shyly and move along the sand towards the end.

"Promise me that you will leave," Julia insists. "Promise to leave."

I say nothing. I promise nothing. We arrive at the place. The rocks seem distorted, menacing, otherworldly, the pools filled with exoskeletal scuttling and slime. We turn our backs from the ocean, from the wide world, and to the little smokes from the fires of our village. Julia and I stare and keep staring at the shade-partitioned houses where women are toiling. We watch Lawson from the end of the beach.

"Why did you choose France?" he asks. He is proud of his country in a gentle way. I did not choose France. I chose not to go to England.

"Why did you not choose England?" England was too close to my home, too close to Sanjania.

It is not true. I do not know what is true.

"Why did you leave Sanjania, though? May I ask you that?" He may ask. He may always ask. I sit up on the bed. I look at Paris. The fog. I surprise myself by weeping. His hands move calmly, imploringly, across my back, white on black. My French lover's body is rich and strong, but I miss the splendour of my young dead Jerome. I have learned to love snails in garlic butter, but only fishbone soup could satisfy me now. When I stop and wipe my eyes, I tell him my stories about Jerome and Julia, and how I learned the meaning of the end of the beach.

I will never forgive the wide world. I will never forgive. Because Jerome was swept out past where the mothers look to, swept out past the end of the beach.

My mother, my sister and I prepare fishbone soup for me on the night before the geevee is to carry me off to adventures in the wide world. Port Hope. A city in which I do not have so much as an aunt. I can barely stomach even the idea of dinner.

The silence, like the soup, is pungent, heady with unstated flavours, defiant, crisscrossed and patterned with the meaning of its sources. My mother is ladling soup and silence out for us all. I think, God has granted me a visitation at my own funeral. Julia keeps one arm in mine except for when she must tend to Hope, my now three-year-old niece. I may be Hope's introduction to absence, I think, the absent metaphor of loss.

As mother ladles out my portion, I watch her carefully, to remember. For the first time, I can see that it is a face full of disappointment, weeping, fury. I see in my mother's face Julia's need for me to leave Lawson. I will leave. I will keep leaving. I will be leaving my entire duration on earth. The exact architecture of Julia's sorrow is displayed on my mother, Julia betraying hints of how mother once was. I see it. When mother says softly to herself, "It is the end," I cannot imagine that she means "the end of the family," or "the end of you," "the end of the soup," or "the end of the world." I assume she can only mean "the end of the beach."

The beaches of Normandy are white. There are fields of graves without end, Sanjanians among them. White crosses. "I want to know where you are from," he says.

I am from nowhere. Pretend I am from nowhere.

"Then tell me about Jerome."

Jerome is in the country of the dead. Not elsewhere.

We could walk forever, but we stop at flat stones and look together at the unifying North Atlantic, the monstrous one. "Tell me about France," I say.

"You are in France." Yes. That is true. I am alive, in the wide world which is not Lawson, the world beyond the end of the beach.

I will never open the book of my exile, not for my Parisian lover. He might recognize that it is a book, but he will never be able to read it. He says, "Please explain to me what our differences are." All right. For you there is the beach, but for me there is only the end of the beach.

The plane lifts off. As if I willed it off. Up from the ground of my home. I watch out the window. Upwards there is the blue of heaven, and I am going to Paris in Europe, to learn a new tongue. I say that I will choose the wide world, and I say that Lawson will always be there. I should look at the blue, over the blue also. I should be looking forward, but I find I'm looking back, at the land of my country, my home. Until it is only a strip. Until there is only a line. Until the end of the beach.

CRITICISM

LETTER FROM ERNEST HEMINGWAY TO JOHN DOS PASSOS, WRITTEN AT BONIPOINT, SANJAN COLONY, AUGUST 12, 1929

Dear Dos:

Where am I? I'm cold and drunk in the Sanjan Colony that's where. I was going to say I wish you were here fishing but that would be fibbing. There's no fishing here. Still I wish you were drinking with me, dam you, you're a fine son of a bitch Dos.

Jesus it's been raining. I thought God put the rainbow in the sky as a promise there wouldn't be more of this sort of thing. Don't you believe it. Every morning I go to the door, open it, stare out at the dam sheet of water outside, curse Waldo Pierce who suggested this dam trip, slam the door and return to drinking. I'm steadily improving at drinking at least.

Marooned. That's the word I've been waiting to use. I've been marooned.

Oh well. Anyway let me tell you about this neat trick here. They rub brandy into their chests to keep away the frost. I know you will be happy to learn a new way to bring alcohol on board so I'm passing along the bit of business. Dos, don't think me a shite for only writing because of the weather and drink. You have got to understand. I wake up in the rain and the fishermen tell me the bass love it after the rain and go back to drinking brandy. You can picture it. They sit around reading and stinking of brandy and I can't write and I can't fish. It's hell. I would kill for a lonely trout stream with no Sanjans around. I would hunt down and murder Waldo Pierce for free.

Back to Madrid in two days. No tarpon. What a waste. We'll be in Paris in the Fall. Please write to me Dos. It's not as good as drinking with you but it's something.

Yours,

Hem

[ATTACHED NOTE:] I'm sending you some amusing Sanjan pamphlets. Pirate stories and ladies of leisure and handy conclusions with neat morals. I bet Alice B. and husband would love them. I must bring back a few. Why are whores and sailors so florid in their expressions can you tell me Dos? Still better than the shite in *The New Republic* I suppose.

[Used courtesy of the Dos Passos Collection, Manuscripts Department, University of Virginia Library.]

* * *

SELECTIONS FROM "ON THE MOTIF OF THE SHIPWRECK AS HISTORY," BY SHERLOCK COLE, A LECTURE PRESENTED AT THE INAUGURAL CONFERENCE OF THE LITERATURE DEPARTMENT OF PORT HOPE UNIVERSITY ON JULY 9, 1961

The whole of Japan is a pure invention. There is no such country, there are no such people. One of our most charming painters went recently to the Land of the Chrysanthemum in the foolish hope of seeing the Japanese. All he saw, all he had the chance of painting, were a few lanterns and some fans. He was quite unable to discover the inhabitants, as his delightful exhibition at Messrs. Dowdeswell's Gallery showed only too well. He did not know that the Japanese people are, as I have said, simply a mode of style, an exquisite fancy of art. And so, if you desire to see a Japanese effect, you will not behave like a tourist and go to Tokio. On the contrary, you will stay at home and steep yourself in the work of certain Japanese artists, and then, when you have absorbed the spirit of their style, and caught their imaginative manner of vision, you will go some afternoon and sit in the Park or stroll down Piccadilly, and if you cannot see an absolutely Japanese effect there, you will not see it anywhere.

—OSCAR WILDE

When our Prime Minister, just over two years ago today, remarked in his Independence Day speech that we could now begin imagining our country, I remember thinking that the comment was, to say the least, imprecise. We had been imagining our country for decades, if not centuries. Independence was more a rite of passage than a birth. But if not with Independence, I wondered, when was our story born? And how? And why? To these grand questions, and on such a grand occasion, I want to attempt a somewhat quiet answer tonight, through some very old stories and a very new play: we were born through shipwrecks.

Ira Hardley's play *The Shipwreck*, which was performed for the first time during the Anniversary of Independence last summer, is a newborn masterpiece. It cracks open the truth of our history through four neatly symmetrical acts representing Sanjania's four most significant shipwrecks: the *Diver for Pearls* slaver whose survivors, in legend, formed the first communities on the East side of the island; the *Hercules*, with thirty-two fishermen, the worst accident in Sanjania's maritime history up to that point; the *Walker*, sabotaged by patriots during the 1936 Rumourstown riots; and the *Tremendous*, lost with all hands including the departing Sanjan Colony's last Governor a year and a half ago.

A critic in *The Times Literary Supplement*, writing at the time of the play's first performance in London this past spring, described the play as an example of the "exotic apocalyptic," a view which can charitably be described as limited. Because for one thing, *The Shipwreck* is not exotic, at least not to us, and for another, the term "apocalyptic" implies a vision of history in which a complete meaning to all action awaits us at the end of time in a great revelation, and nothing could be farther from Hardley's vision of history. The reviewer was closer I think when he described the work as "an exquisite portrait of victimhood without knowing of whom or what one is the victim." In short, Hardley is a catastrophist. Sanjanians are catastrophists.

In the opening act, the slavetrader Smythe's deranged Christian piety expresses itself in explicitly progressivist terms, with outbursts of "onward and upward, onward and upward" as the storm gathers around him. When the commander strides onto the deck of the *Walker* at the beginning of the third act, and declares, "more tonnage, mon frère, more power, more knottage, more slice along that fine keel," we sense instantly his connection with the slaver, not least because the actor playing the Commander plays Master Smythe in the first act. For Hardley, the idea of progress begins as an excuse for evil and develops into a kind of fetishism of machines.

When I saw the performance at the New Theatre last summer, the most devastating moment of the production was Captain Smythe's final question of the first act: "Why am I made to suffer so, sweet Christ Almighty?" After the slavetrader has casually murdered and raped his way through the previous scene, his self-pity reveals evil in all its massive obliviousness. But of course Captain Smythe's question is also the question of the slaves underdeck: "Why am I made to suffer so?" In the fourth act, with the sinking of the *Tremendous*, both the innocent servants and the Colonial Governor suffer the horrors of watery torment. The world without justice in *The Shipwreck* inspires a kind of massive sympathy, a sympathy which I believe Hardley would extend even to the slavedriver. The only truth is that we are all destined for destruction. Which is what I mean when I say that Hardley's vision is the opposite of apocalyptic: none survives therefore judge none . . .

Our blindness towards the future is as absolute for Hardley as it was for Sophocles. Because you and I know our schoolboy's Sanjanian history, we are aware that the catastrophe of the *Diver for Pearls* will mean new life, new liberty to the Eastside survivors, and that, for the slaves, what looks like a catastrophe is its opposite. The third act with its carnivalesque exultation in the act of sabotage—following the by now standard comparison of the *Walker* sinking with the Boston tea party in the United States—is transformed by the knowledge that the sinking of the *Walker* led to the Crackdown, and the subsequent two decades of vicious Imperialist oppression. The only thing we know for sure about the future is that our current ideas are wrong. As an aside, Hardley sketched this irony a decade ago in a wonderful poem from his first collection, "Myism." I am thinking in particular about the final lines:

> Not downwiththemism, not upwithusism,
> Not endisnearism, not newbeginningism,
> Whowouldhavethoughtism. Whowouldhavethoughtism.
> That's myism.

But what does any of this have to do with what we might describe as a Sanjanian voice?

Unprogressive, ungodly, openended: these adjectives perfectly describe his play, and may fairly be said to represent the exact opposite of the rest of Sanjanian literature. For nearly three decades, Sanjanian writing has been intimately bound to progressive proletarian politics, published in large part for and by dockworkers with trade unionist sympathies; we might add that Sanjanians have always been attracted to modernist literary development as well. Sanjanian writing is religious to its core, its piety consistently sleeveworn from the earliest pamphleteers to the latest modernists. And finally, Sanjanian fiction has never been able to resist the platitudinous, pat ending, the easy and complete closure.

So, is *The Shipwreck* a rejection of Sanjanian writing? Are we seeing Hardley, as newly decolonized Sanjanian, breaking with the old literature of the Sanjan Colony? I must admit that even Hardley most likely believes the answer to be yes.

And yet.

Identity can be, sometimes it must be, discovered against our intentions, against the grain of whatever we might imagine to be our real desires. Which is why we employ psychoanalysts and critics, to shine their rays of light into the dark, quiet corners we don't like to look at. And so I would like to turn now to the Marlyebone stories, dark and quiet corners indeed. I am aware, two years after Independence, that we are all trying to forget them, but it is exactly the dreams one tries to forget the hardest that are the most revealing . . .

We read, for example, in two different Marlyebone stories by Hector Lanickston, the line "I am the shipwreck Marlyebone," and "I am the shipwreck." In an anonymous work written, I believe, only a few years after Lanickston's "Infamous Life and Notorious Death of Marlyebone, the Private King," we find the usual tale with the unusual opening line "Born was I on the Shipwreck Sanjan Colony." Again, in the short piece on the "Destruction of the Private King" by F. R. Fisher, one finds: "Avoid the Finger of Oblivion, that's half the bigness, two-thirds of the surface of the earth Oceanshrouded, the horror of it."

Humanity is flotsam and jetsam in these stories. History is a shipwreck.

Plato said that learning was not the introduction of novelties onto the mind but the more and more profound remembrance of ideas already present within us. What I have to say today, as we begin the struggle to understand ourselves through our literature, is that nothing can be invented, least of all a nation's identity; it can only be remembered. Ira Hardley uncovers those old tale spinners, and brings with them the whole of the Sanjanian vision of the catastrophe. For there has always been in Sanjanian writing, behind the progress, behind God, behind the fulfillment of history, something or someone other, something or someone undeclared. You can find it in the stories of redeemed prostitutes which revel more in the sin than in the redemption; or in the war poetry, supposedly about glory, which concentrates on stupidity and defeat; or in any of the characters that fall apart like crumb-cake as you're reading them. At its worst, the national trait I'm trying to identify can be nothing more than disingenuousness or murkiness or outright lies, but at its best it shows a hardy reserve toward the accepted and the unchallenged, and an awareness of the possibilities which dwell just past imagination. For whatever it is lurks silently beyond us, a word on the tip of our national tongue, a smell nearly recognized, perhaps the breath of a breeze behind a curtain slightly open. The time has come for us to put forward our hand and pull back the curtain. Thank you.

* * *

"WHY IT IS IMPERATIVE TO PAY CLOSE ATTENTION TO DETAIL," BY BLESSED SHIRLEY. *THE REAL STORY*, ISSUE 6, EASTER 1932

Lieutenant William S. Sanders writes us—his letter takes pride of place in the "Correspondence" section at the rear—to call out the lack of patriotism in our pages. By his lights, we are "abandoning the proud traditions of pamphlet storytelling"; we are promoting "fusspot fiction" in place of "decent, manly tales"; our ideas are "pseudo-European nonsense" which "[we} couldn't begin to understand"; and the like. Our hope here at the magazine had always been to spark debate, and now it seems we have done it, in spades. Lieutenant Sanders at least cannot accuse us of false advertising. The magazine in which his letter has been reproduced is, after all, entitled "The Real Story." The authors we carry, while divergent on questions of style and content, are united in their careful attention to what is really happening. We cannot and do not and will not apologize for candour.

Let us be forthright about the true source of this tempest in a teapot. Lieutenant Sanders is peeved that we do not print pirate and ghost stories, and comedy tidbits and prostitute parables with shiny endings. All of these things have their place, in *The Sanjan Trumpet*, to which Lieutenant Sanders subscribes we have no doubt. Here at *The Real Story* we do not print such material because, simply, we want the world, Dickens and Scott notwithstanding. We will no longer dream the feverish dreams of imprisonment; we will walk out among the fields; we will glut ourselves on the sheeny arc of the crocus; we will look at the beauties of a workman's hands or a chaunticleer stew or a bit of old rope; we will have the world's ugliness too, its starving children and flogged backs and opium dens and punchy husbands and unfaithful wives; we will not look away. How can we? The creative artist, once he has set himself to look into reality, cannot return to the old tomfoolery. The hieroglyphs of ancient Egypt no doubt meant a great deal to their carvers, but who would continue to carve them once he has seen a rendering of the human face in all its glory? Who will reference Ptolemy after peering through one of Galileo's miraculous contraptions? Science everywhere is expanding human happiness and piercing the dark clouds of superstitious adherence to timeworn convention with the light of close observation, and we are seeing the enormous benefits in Russia and elsewhere. Who would choose to return to the old oppression and misery?

At *The Real Story*, we have taken our stand. A work of art

should be useful just as a life should be useful. It should not serve to titillate or to stir up passions but to communicate an observation of truth. A rational perspective on the world often looks into uncomfortable realities, and stories for Lieutenant Sanders and his ilk must be above all as comfortable as the Spaniard's afternoon siesta. We respectfully submit to our readers that between *The Real Story* and Lieutenant Sanders, the choice is wakefulness over sleep, consciousness over oblivion, in short, the choice of life over death.

I might add, as a further, obvious defence, that we do not forbid our readers from subscribing to other publications.

* * *

"COMPARATIVE BIOGRAPHIES OF ELIZABETH AND IRA RUSHTON," BY RICHARD WILLIAMS, FROM *THE POLITICAL TURN: SANJANIAN FICTION IN THE ERA OF UPHEAVALS*, OXFORD UNIVERSITY PRESS, 2000

The Rushton twins were born, Elizabeth first and then Ira, on January 31, 1913, in their parents' home in Whitesmoke on the Western shore. Their father, Samuel Rushton, was an itinerant tax officer, responsible for prosecuting smugglers in the West Side coves and raising funds from subsistence-level fishermen. These nearly impossible duties kept him away from home for weeks at a time. The twins' mother, Mrs. Glory Rushton, taught at the local Whitesmoke school, providing the family with a second income. The Rushtons were one of the more well-to-do families along the West shore.

Both parents had attended the King's College Secondary School in Port Hope, where they had met and become romantically involved, and both threw themselves wholeheartedly into the education of their children. Neither were they disappointed. After a great deal of expensive tutoring and a long journey to the city for the examination, both Ira and Elizabeth successfully attained full scholarships. That two out of the ten students admitted to King's College School from the West shore were from the same family even excited comment in the pages of *The Sanjan Trumpet*.

We possess almost no record of the Rushtons' careers at King's College School because of the 1946 fire which destroyed its library and archives. The few surviving letters between the twins and their parents contain nothing more than the standard "letter from school," and are of no interest to us. The parents pray for their children's safety and hope that they dedicate themselves to their education. The children insist on packages filled with local delicacies, which for Ira and Elizabeth meant "chicken bone" candy. The twins' stellar academic success must have continued because, at the conclusion of their baccalaureates, Elizabeth received her Status Certificate and a full scholarship to St. Magdalene's, the teacher's college, and Ira was offered a substantial sum to attend Cambridge. Six such positions were made available to the Sanjan Colony annually. Ira Rushton was the first to refuse one.

He never received a response from his confused, heartsick parents, whose fondest fantasies he had dashed with this single swift kick. He wrote to them:

> I hope you will believe me when I say no arrogance broached my decision—I more than know what has been sacrificed for my little bag of bones—It is only that the university in Britishland can only be more of the same to me, a search after effect and not truth, which I do not need—Moreover

> the effect, father, for which they are searching is mere Britishness—To me, and I know to you, Britishness leaves a great deal to be desired as a *summum bonum*—You have always wanted me to be a nation builder but how can I build by leaving?—Think, at least, I shall visit[1]

Ira never returned to Whitesmoke, throwing himself instead into the theatrical life of Port Hope.

Meanwhile Elizabeth's career continued at St. Magdalene's, where she successfully pursued coursework towards a three-year teacher's degree. In her diaries, she referred to this period of her life as "the great unclouded April of my soul." With the help of her brother, she published her first story, "Two Stories About the Abandon Tree," in the 1932 Christmas issue of *The Real Story*, which was sadly to be its last. She insisted, as she would for the rest of her career, on a pseudonym: Glory Samuelson. Her diaries note the sarcastic commentary of her brother: "Ira made a great deal of an unreal me in the real story. More fun at my expense because of the parental allusion."

After receiving her teaching degree, Elizabeth was hired as an assistant at St. Magdalene's, where she performed minor administrative duties and taught a course on French grammar. She and her brother ate Sunday dinners together at the College, when she would share her fiction with him and he would recount the vagaries of the Bohemian life for her amusement. Despite a rocky start, Ira was already making a name for himself on the stage, with his performances as Morrison in Sloane's *The Rebel Daughter*, Bocaculo in Gomes's *Masterful Madness*, and finally Othello, which made him the toast of the Port Hope Scene. From 1934

1. All correspondence in this article is used courtesy of the Manuscripts Archive, Ledman Library, Port Hope University.

to 1936, Elizabeth produced eight of her twelve surviving stories, and Ira wrote his two dramatic interludes and his historical melodrama *The Clocktower*.

This period of creative ferment for the Rushtons ended with the Rumourstown riots. Ira himself wrote what is generally agreed to be the best account of the event, and even managed to publish it in a handbill before the Crackdown proper began and the presses were closed.

> They come upon us in squalls of horses, wailing wind batons, bullet hail, threat and curse hail. Human fury mimics nature's forces. A man. A child's face. A woman's straining limb. On a city street, amazed, hurled through the air, the names cried out inchoate. Such a struggle to remain human.[2]

Rushton mirrored the general incomprehension at the English response to the riot. Ben Stephens in *The Upheavals* describes the transformative nature of 1936 on the life of the country:

> While the structures of the Colony remained identical to their pre-riot forms, the reality of its underlying violence, which had been revealed by the Crackdown, deranged all political life. Governor Bellingham who had been regarded more or less as a birdwatching eccentric was now a tyrant, with rumours spreading that he indulged in nightly orgies of prostitutes and plum. Middle-class functionaries, who before had been exemplars of the nation, were now the traitorous servants of a cruel enslaver. "Fishermen fished. Children went to school. Churchbells rung. But all in a mist."[3]

---

2. *Documents of the Upheavals*, ed. Richard Williams (Port Hope: Port Hope University Press, 1997), 22.

3. Benjamin Stephens, *The Upheavals* (Port Hope: The Sand House Press, 1992), 3. He is quoting the Rushton handbill, op. cit.

The twins had opposed reactions, reactions which reveal the courses open to Sanjanian writers after the Crackdown and during the early years of the First Interstruggle Period. Ira emerged from prison six months after the riot and threw himself once again into the theatrical life of the city. Elizabeth, shocked by what she had witnessed and terrified by the imprisonment of her brother, gave up her position at St. Magdalene's and returned to Whitesmoke. In their correspondence, which dates from this moment, Ira castigated his sister for leaving "just as interest is sparking," as he put it, and for accepting the government's half-salary at the village school with their mother:

> You remember Praisegod Streets from the school—Last eve I knocked out my bit and left the LS [Leopard's Spots, the theatre] solo—I came across him staring up at a jewelers [sic] shop—The fellow couldn't keep his eyes off a gilded gigglegaggle in the window—I say to Praisy, What are you doing here?—I'm enriching myself, says he—I say, How's that ump?—He says, That diamantry must be worth a thousand pound—So?, say I—So, says Praisy, I come every postmeridian for two hours, two out of twentyfour is twelve, one out of twelve of a thousand pound's nearly eighty quid, eighty quid's rich—Poor Praisy hasn't figured out you own something by shutting it up in a dark hole—Our parents have figured that out

For the better part of a year, Elizabeth replied with nothing but bromides about the simple pleasures of home:

> Mother and I tend the students as best we can, and yet I think a teacher's lot may be fruitfully compared to a new homeowner who watches spring roll into a winter-purchased garden. He waters and mulches but cannot say what bulbs

> the previous owner may have planted. The appearance of the children's abilities is exciting in just this way.

Nonetheless, in the spring of 1938, Elizabeth sent her brother two new stories, "The Night" and "Open Umbrella," which he managed to have published in the English literary journals *The Leader* and *The New Imagist*. "Open Umbrella" was published under the pseudonym that Elizabeth had used for "Two Stories About the Abandon Tree," but Ira, with his typical disregard for privacy and other people's feelings, instructed the publisher to attach Elizabeth's real name to "The Night." His explanation:

> I am sorry but I am not v. sorry—The pseudonym wasn't even very good, Zabs—It was such a bloody wonderful story I couldn't stand to leave it on the orphanage doorstep in a basket with a note round its neck—I couldn't leave the story to blunder out its life in obscurity—Besides Mama will never hear of a rarefied Britisher journal anyway—Unpossible as Maxy would say—Come to the city pet—I have a garret—I have excellent friends who read your work regularly and pass it hand to hand—We'll be a country unto ourselves

Elizabeth responded with what for her amounted to fury.

> I will only say that I have enough trouble keeping my writing a secret from Mother, as you know that I must. I suppose you cannot imagine the weight of that responsibility. I write in the supply closet at the school because it would be impossible to justify having ink and paper in the house. More than once I have destroyed the sole copy of a manuscript simply to avoid being caught. Let me attempt an explanation you might understand. My life is like one of those aristocratic mansions built with false walls, trapdoors under carpets, sliding panels, blind alleys, and hidden closets, and you have blasted a trumpet

> into what I believed to be my place of greatest secrecy. It was my folly to assume that a Bohemian like yourself would know that diseases spread by tongues, even rare foreign diseases.

Over and over during the next two and half decades of political repression, Sanjanian writers would use one or the other of the Rushtons' strategies. The more political writers, with Ira, found subterranean communities that were inherently nationalistic and Independence-minded. While they might remain focused on aesthetic concerns rather than political projects for periods of time, they prepared the way for the revolutionary Independence movements which exploded in the late fifties. Other writers, particularly the fictioneers who, unlike dramatists, did not need communities in order to create their art, more often followed Elizabeth's way of hiding, finding security in utter privacy, limiting their art to only the most necessary expressions, and its dissemination to only the most select circles. The fog and nightmares of the upheavals could not extinguish every guiding light.

* * *

A NOTE ON A CODE IN MORLEY STRAIGHTS' "AN OLD MAN MOURNS FOR HIS BLIND DAUGHTER," BY ARCADIO SKELTON, *SANJANIAN QUARTERLY*, SPRING 2003

During the period of the "repamphletization" of Sanjanian fiction, following Bell's definition of the term,[1] political writing hid

1. F. Seeker Bell, "Repamphletization: Themes and Modes," in *Essays on Sanjanian Fiction During the Upheavals*, ed. Richard Williams (Port Hope: Port Hope University Press, 1998), 78–103.

in plain sight. Writers like Lewis, Starkey and Malleson resorted to ciphers cached inside seemingly benign romances, whose solutions would then be passed around by word of mouth,[2] while Wolfhead and the Straights of 1961 and 1962 set their stories of tyrants and cruelties in ancient Rome or in ancient African kingdoms. This latter strategy, as Wolfhead explained in an interview in 1982, "forced the censors—either leave us alone, or explain to us, please, in the best detail, how much like Nero Prime Minister Little really is. Sheer genius."

Morley Straights' last story, "An Old Man Mourns for His Blind Daughter," does not utilize either of these elusive strategies. Arcadio Barley, in his definitive article on Straights' late fiction, describes the piece as a "kaleidoscopy of allegories which fit for a second and then fall apart."[3] A reading of the story's opening paragraph bears this opposition out, filled as it is with small significances whose connections are never clear. The sky is described as turquoise, which is a reference to Biddy Little's distinctive jewelry. The funeral of the blind daughter is held in the month of July, which Caesar Little had declared Independence Month, the time for forced national jubilation. The old man is a cooper, and "Cooper" was the surname of the minister for the portfolio of culture appointed in 1962.

There is general agreement (Barley, Carverson, Mallick) about the story's larger meanings. The "geesies," the landlady's term for the bourgeoisie, have betrayed art in the figure of the girl with the golden guitar. The middle class has become indifferent to the

---

2. Goodfriday Bennington, "Oral Literature and Literary Orature: The Case of the Coded Fictions," in *Essays on Sanjanian Fiction During the Upheavals*, ed. Richard Williams (Port Hope: Port Hope University Press, 1998), 56–77.

3. Arcadio Barley, "Only the Cigar Is Just a Cigar: Codes in Morley Straights' 'An Old Man Mourns for His Blind Daughter,'" *Sanjanian Quarterly*, Winter 1995: 234.

"great silence" after the closing of the press houses. Given these overt political meanings, and the story's "kaleidoscopy" of allegory, as well as the fact that other encoding authors were using out-and-out ciphers in their fiction, I would like to propose a new reading of the third to last paragraph in "An Old Man Mourns for His Blind Daughter." It reads:

> The landlady nodded and said no more. She did not turn to see the old man unlatch the door. He padded up the two stairflights to the flat. But he was no different in grief. That is, not that she could see. Greatest among his features, she thought, was his piety. You shall and you shall not: he followed them truly. Being his landlady was a richprize, and she knew it. Your servant, she scribbled on her bills to him before signing.

The awkwardness of these sentences inside the otherwise easy flow of Straights' writing begs for decipherment, and after a few passes it may soon be found by the attentive reader.

> The landlady nodded and said no more. She did not turn to see the old man unlatch the door. He padded up the two stairflights to the flat. *But he* was no different in grief. *That is*, not that she could see. *Greatest among* his features, she thought, was his piety. *You shall* and you shall not: he followed them truly. *Be*ing his landlady was a richprize, and she knew it. *Your servant*, she scribbled on her bills to him before signing.

The full cipher then reads: "But he that is greatest among you shall be your servant." It is from the gospel of Matthew 23:11. The most obvious interpretation is that Straights is referring to the events of the month before the story's publication, when Caesar Little published a new tax charter under his freshly enlarged official title: "Prime Minister of Sanjania, Head of the Sanjanian People's Independence Party, Mayor of the City of Port Hope, Master of the North Atlantic Seaport." The last title, which had never existed before Little invented it, was the most recent sign of his megalomania. The political motivation becomes clearer when one looks at the verse preceding the reference, Matthew 23:10: "Neither be ye called masters: for one is your Master, even Christ."

That Straights would quote gospel may be surprising to his critics, who know him as an engaged freethinker and an anticlerical essayist. The reader of his letters, however, realizes that his perspective on Christianity was always much more complicated than his newspaper articles on the subject would suggest. He wrote of his admiration for the fundamentals of the gospel as early as 1958:

> Jesus's politics is so, so radical, if one really takes up and reads. It's well to left of the likes of me. I'm no anarchist! But what I'm talking about redletters the hypocrisy, mother. Read the sermon on the mount and tell me that it isn't Christianity itself, Christianity itself, that hasn't been the cruelest obstacle to the fulfillment of Christ's teaching, which calls for nothing less than the complete abolition of all private property.

Matthew 23:12, the verse following the allusion in "An Old Man Mourns for His Blind Daughter," might even be said to contain a perfect expression of Straights' political hopes: "And whoever shall exalt himself shall be abased; and he that shall humble himself shall be exalted." Tragically, such hopes were soon dashed for Straights. Two months after the publication of his last story, Straights was taken from his home by the carpenter troops and never seen again.

* * *

SELECTIONS FROM "LANGUAGE IN CHARITY GURTON'S *MEN AND OTHER STORIES*," BY OCTAVIA DICKENS, FROM *TONGUES OF FIRE: LANGUAGE AND DISPLACEMENT IN SANJANIAN WRITING*, ROUTLEDGE, 1995

4.2

> *No democracy without literature; no literature without democracy.*
>
> —JACQUES DERRIDA

Historicizing the writings of Charity Gurton (as we will now proceed to do) demands the recognition that resistance in Sanjanian discourse has always been couched in expressly universalist, enlightenment terminology, and with the end in mind of literary English as *lingua franca*. Pre-Independence writers believed the capture (or liberation) of the covetongues in dialect to be an aesthetic alibi which they longed to displace with a linguistically purer, politically purer "clean style." The "great silence" which sclerotized Sanjania as a nation reinscribed its literature as of and in exile, and Gurton rejected "plain speech" writing as language "pub(l)icly shaved of its embarrassing Sanjanity."[1] Ira Feingold and Martha Simpson add:

> [Charity Gurton] stands opposed not merely to the monstrosities of the Little government's form of populist totalitarianism, but against the entire program of Western generalization and the mode of Western coherence inherent

---

1. Charity Gurton, "Exile, Language, Dialect: Correspondences with Charity Gurton," in *Postmark London: Letters from Women Writers in Exile*, ed. Abraham Sloane (London: The Love Supreme Press, 1986), 167.

> in the "clean style." Women's voices and the narratives of the underclass are outright celebrated.[2]

Others found in Gurton's rebellion against the "clean style," which she conceived as the exile's nation-constru(ct)ing responsibility, yet another example of the imposition of foreign modes on a native aesthetic.

> The idea that the Sanjanian writers of the thirties and forties indulged a mania for generalization or for excessive plainness is wretched nonsense. It's wretched because it ignores a tradition we have possessed in good standing for over a hundred and fifty years. It's nonsense because we never really achieved anything more than rough comprehensibility to one another.[3]

King goes on to posit a "Westindianification" of Sanjanian writing through Gurton's writing and the critical community surrounding her, which he further implicates in a false confluence with Jamaican and Trinidadian literary traditions, and therefore an homogenization. . . .

4.7

It will prove to be useful, always bearing in mind King's warning against homogenization, to tease out the problem of cove dialect and Sanjanian nationhood with the aid of the dialect studies of West Indian communities. R. B. Le Page describes a node of discourse much like the one Gurton inhabits:

---

2. Ira Feingold and Martha Simpson, "An Introduction to Charity Gurton: Sixteen Theses," *National Con(text)* 4 (1987): 29.

3. Leonard King, "Letter to the Editor," *National Con(text)* 5 (1988): 3.

> The first technical problem, therefore, which the writer has to face is, what variety of West Indian speech he is going to try to use in his writing. If he uses the parochial dialect with which he is most familiar and perhaps most easily at home in a relaxed manner for telling stories or other intimate purposes he may find that he has only a parochial audience. Once he tries to aim at a slightly larger audience (that, say, of his part of the island, or of his island, or of the Eastern Caribbean, or of the Caribbean as a whole) he enters upon a process of normalization, of finding the ingredients which are common to two or more parochial dialects of West Indian English.[4]

In other words, the imaginary of any writer of fiction cannot be claimed under the aegis of a narcissism which the reader, through an accident of privilege, "overhears" in a Romantic sense. Rather, the speech acts of a writer like Gurton can only be comprehended within a communicative model of language grounded in adequate conceptualizations of creole as migrant experience. One brilliant study which supports my point, approaching the origins of Sanjanian writing, is Nathan Villon's *Vagabond Tongues*:

> The pamphleteers had themselves passed from isolated coves, whose economies rarely encompassed more than subsistence fishing, into Port Hope City, a metropole with literally the world at its door. The English language is a burr on such journeys and Sanjanian writers were, if anything, overly aware of the discrepancy between speech in the city and in the cove they had left behind. . . . One finds, in the earliest pamphlets, country writers living in the city writing in language they half-remembered from their country days.

---

4. R. B. Le Page, "Dialects in West Indian Literature," *Critics on Caribbean Literature*, ed. Edward Baugh (London: George Allen & Unwin, 1978), 126–27.

> Never has Locke's dictum been truer: "Imagination and memory are but one thing, which for diverse considerations hath diverse names."[5]

Following Villon, Le Page's communicative understanding of dialect in which ever expanding categories of speech acts integrate ever larger communities explicates the "clean style" as the end process of universalization in the Hegelian sense of cancellation. However, the "bargain" which the writer must strike with her communities ensures that any "clean style" maintains its self-consciousness as a solution to dialect. Hence, rather than an opposition, we are left with the Janus-headed reality of language itself. Both Gurton and the clean-style writers connect, through a communicative model of language, the real and the private with the social and the national, but given the total irresolution of the relations between the particular and the general, and between the individual and the nation, communication between them (dis)achieves itself from the beginning. In other words, universalization is a ladder that can be descended as well as ascended, and the writers are left in the permanent limbo of play. Gurton inhabits a double ground, in which the dialect(ic) of general speech and contingent speech is not merely Janus-headed, but endlessly self-replicating. The act of writing becomes play within pre-set labyrinthine structures of endlessly multiplying significance. . . .

4.8.2

It also will serve to recall the opening words of Gurton's story "Men": "The old woman said." The gesture of distancing is simultaneously a veil over the speech act itself, a revelation of its cos-

5. Nathan Villon, *Vagabond Tongues: The Origins of Sanjanian Speech* (Port Hope: Port Hope University Press, 1997), 249.

mopolitan reality (and therefore its half-false consciousness) and recognition of the "doubleness" of its own speech. One hears the echo of Homi Bhabha:

> If, in our travelling theory, we are alive to the *metaphoricity* of the peoples of imagined communities—migrant or metropolitan—then we shall find that the space of the modern nation-people is never simply horizontal. Their metaphoric movement requires a kind of 'doubleness' in writing; a temporality of representation that moves between cultural formations and social processes without a 'centred' causal logic. And such cultural movements disperse the homogeneous, visual time of the horizontal society because 'the present is no longer a mother-form [read mother-tongue or mother-land] around which are gathered and differentiated the future (present) and the past (present) . . . [as] a present of which the past and the future would be but modifications'.[6]

In this metaphor, language becomes, in effect, the alibi of time, or as Samuel says in Gurton's story "Havers": "Tongue is rive', tongue is sky, tongue is downfallin' rain 'tween."

* * *

TWO REVIEWS OF *A WEDDING IN RESTITUTION*, FROM *THE TRUMPET*, JANUARY 28, 1992, AND *THE NEW YORK TIMES*, FEBRUARY 3, 1994

> A Wedding in Restitution *was released in January 1992, to widespread acclaim. It swept the Port Hope Film Awards, taking a*

6. Homi K. Bhabha, "DissemiNation: Time, Narrative, and the Margins of the Modern Nation," *Nation and Narration*, ed. Homi K. Bhabha (New York: Routledge, 1990), 293.

record seven Good Angels, and went on to show at over eighty film festivals, where it received eighteen nominations and six awards.

"Wedding" Cake Crumby, L.K., *The Trumpet*

Not so much a film as a shot of saccharine committed to celluloid, Cato Dekkerman's latest, *A Wedding in Restitution*, paints a tourist-trap portrait of cove life which would be more appropriate on a souvenir plate than on screen. The fishermen never lack for work, the children are all in clean, efficient schools, and two kindly Aldermen watch over the town government. There aren't even any widows. People did laugh at the screening I attended, but not at the comedy.

Somehow, the plot manages to be even more simplistic than the setting. Two magical children, Caesar and Endurance, get married with all the expected surrealistic silliness. A fish jumps into a boat. The food at the wedding feast makes everybody run home to bed. The priest has a vision. And so on and so on. And so on.

The actors blunder about in this nonsense as best they can. An endless array of "cheery covefolks" and "strongbacked fishermen" required a massive cast of placeholders and ciphers. Ira Portstanley and Jennifer Tear, who play Caesar and Endurance with nuanced understatement, are exceptions but their performances get hopelessly lost in the film's overall blather. Imagine two preserved cherries under a bundle of pork crackling.

Sherlock Cole famously said that "because we have no tourists, we have to become our own." I can't tell whether it's a blessing or not that he didn't live to see the latest proof of our sickening cultural myopia. Safe to say, if there's a cinema in heaven, it won't be playing *A Wedding in Restitution*.

In its final scene, the whole town gathers around for a ritual supposedly peculiar to that town. (Anyone who has visited the North knows different.) The town sets the couple adrift at night and waits for them to return by morning. For once, I was thinking, Dekkerman got a scene right. Just like the couple, the film is adrift and asleep. I just couldn't bring myself to care whether it ever made it to shore.

A Wedding Worth Celebrating, S.M.N., *The New York Times*

Most of the time, a wedding is a surefire way to ruin a weekend. There are the awkward speeches over the bland food, the chicken dance over the lousy band, the morning regret over the night before. The drunk mom, the bitter bridesmaids, the unfortunate relatives, it's all a little too much, and much too little. So when a really great wedding comes along, it's not just delightful, it's surprisingly delightful.

A Wedding in Restitution is just such a film. It comes out of nowhere—ever heard of the Sanjanian film scene?—but manages to be both a profound affirmation of life and a heck of a lot of fun.

Caesar and his fiancée Endurance are the couple at the center of this celebratory comedy, which opens today in New York and Los Angeles. Born on the same day and orphaned almost immediately, their childhoods are both, literally, miraculous. At his christening Caesar, played with great understatement by the young Sanjanian star Ira Portstanley, grabs a bottle of liquor and starts pouring. In his hands the liquor never stops flowing from the bottle. The birthmarks on baby Endurance's back are equally wonderful. They change with the constellations overhead (or "asterisms," as they are called in the film's richly suggestive Sanjanian argot, which sometimes has to be subtitled).

The story's sublime magic runs into hard-headed realism early on. Both children are more or less sold into indentured servitude because of the profitability of their gifts. (One of the film's more fascinating sidelights is what the nature of a "gifted child" might be.) Caesar goes to the local bar, where his abilities reduce the liquor bills to zero. Endurance's father sells her to the owner of a fishing boat who finds her back useful for navigating on cloudy nights. "A miracle is an extraordinary piece of furniture," as the film's narrator says. Caesar and Endurance are relieved when their gifts disappear with adolescence, and so are we.

Years later the townspeople, as if to make up for their crimes against the children, rush to prepare the entire wedding by week's end, when the "circumnavigating" priest will arrive, not to return for three months. As it turns out, the ceremony is more or less forgotten about due to an all-night story session which leaves everybody asleep at dawn, but weddings aren't about the ceremony, are they? The party is all that really matters.

And Restitution gives one heck of a party. An enormous fish throws itself into a fisherman's boat in one of the film's most enchanting sequences, and it makes an appropriate main course. The taste of the fish, even more appropriately, makes everyone in town so frisky that they all excuse themselves from the meal for a bit of stolen love. Only the new couple, the priest, the spinster schoolmarm, and the town's schoolchildren stay to celebrate the nuptials.

I won't give away the ending, but it is hugely moving, even with its explicit Christianity and an overt didacticism which was a bit much for this First World viewer. But then, besides being a film about the miracles of love, life, death, birth, pain and joy, *A Wedding in Restitution* also manages to be one of the year's great films about the miracle of storytelling. It arrives in America trailing awards from a dozen of the world's premier film festivals. What could be more miraculous than a strange little story from an island no one has heard of moving the hearts of people all over the world?

Like all good magic realism, *A Wedding in Restitution* recounts the extraordinary in the most matter-of-fact way and the matter-of-fact in the most extraordinary way. Toward the end of the wedding party, Caesar and Endurance briefly recover their magical abilities and show them off to the town's gathered children. By that point, the gestures are redundant. The narrator promises, "There would be no other miracles than nature afterward." Such is the power of this film's exquisite wonder that we're convinced that nature is all the miracle we'll need.

* * *

AN INTERVIEW WITH OCTAVIA KITTEREDGE-MANN, *JAPAN FOLDERS*, WINTER 2003

Octavia Kitteredge-Mann, author of the internationally bestselling short story collection The End of the Beach *and the Ivey-winning* Apples and Oranges, *answered questions at the kitchen table of her apartment in Charlottetown, Prince Edward Island, Canada, where she is the Distinguished Visiting Professor at the Institute of Island Studies, the University of Prince Edward Island.*

JF: *Apples and Oranges* is a remarkably precise novel. How clear were its central ideas when you sat down to write it?

OKM: Precision, right. I believe that's what people say when they mean it's a short novel. *Apples and Oranges* was short, precise. It's the same thing with the word "details." "It's a very detailed book." To me that just means the writer was paying attention, if you know what I mean.

JF: There are some very unusual details in *Apples and Oranges*.

OKM: I think that's what happens when you're writing about decay, simply because so few people have written about it or even notice it as they go about their daily lives. Rot is very expressive and varied, like the powder you get on fruit or cheese, black mold under wallpaper, gangrene, tasty mushrooms, and so on. That's speaking just physically. I wanted to talk about national decay too, urban decay, which people do notice, but the decay of ideas also. These were my subjects anyway.

JF: And families.

OKM: And families. Families, I discovered, do not fall apart the way other things do. A man who beats his wife, as James does in the book, that can keep the family together. Whereas real love, without a trace of violence, like the relationship between Tammy and Watson, it can collapse under its own strength, if you know what I mean. How love rots was fascinating to me.

JF: Would you say the town rots in *Apples and Oranges*?

OKM: Nothing could rot that town. No such luck. [Laughs] Or maybe it's already completely rotted away, rotten to the core.

JF: Is the town in the book the same as the town where you grew up?

OKM: I call it Tattoo in the novel, Lawson in some stories, Redmethod in others. I called it Mothshead in one story. That's a bit close, but I'm not sure I ever published that story. Its real name is Moorshead. I grew up in a small village on the east shore of Sanjania: that is the basic fact of my life.

JF: Is it the basic fact of your fiction?

OKM: I hope not. I mean, *Apples and Oranges*, as I said, is about rot, about how things fall apart, which happens everywhere, and remember half the book is set in Port Hope, which is very far, the opposite of cove life. And "The End of the Beach" was about what it means to come from an island. About living on an island, and all that entails. And leaving the island too of course.

JF: Since we're here at the Institute of Island Studies you had better talk a bit more about that.

OKM: To justify the grant. [Laughs]

JF: Both grants, yours and mine.

OKM: All right, then. This is good actually because I've been thinking about islands for a term, and I'll be able to get it out.

JF: Go ahead.

OKM: Islands share a kind of common interiority, a personal sense of space that is just not possible to mainlanders. When you live on an island, all of it belongs to you, whereas on a continent, you have to share, you have to establish borders. That is not for islanders. Along with that goes a sense of the emptiness of the world, because on an island you could just disappear and who would notice? No one is watching. You could just fall into the sea. That's more and more true the smaller the island. For islands like Sanjania or this one, Prince Edward Island, where you're never far from the waves, the bloody pounding waves, where you're just looking all the time at . . .

JF: The harsh North Atlantic?

OKM: The universe does not care, that's the point, about one island more or less, one planet more or less. No one is watching. Perhaps that is truer on islands in the North Atlantic, like Iceland or Newfoundland or Sanjania, or more remarkably true. One of the first things I noticed in reading children's stories about islands in the Caribbean is that the moment people arrive they try to figure out how to leave. The pirates or whatever show up, dig some treasure out of the ground and get back to Bristol. You strand people on North Atlantic islands. Whereas in the South Pacific, the sailors show up and never leave, never even dream of wanting to leave. The whole idea of a trunk of treasure seems to resolve itself into a dew once you set foot on a South Pacific island.

JF: And Japan?

OKM: The islands of the North Pacific are the ones you have to kill people to get on, hence very mysterious.

JF: Indian Ocean?

OKM: Spice Islands. Uninhabited and unreal. Inhuman. Magical. Fairy-tale islands.

JF: Australia? England?

OKM: Australia is a continent, so it doesn't count, and the English . . .

JF: Yes?

OKM: Martin Amis, I think, said that the British lead the world in decay, which is something I thought about a lot when I was writing *Apples and Oranges*. I don't know what to make of the English. I don't think anybody does. The way they believe, they really believe, in class for example, but even the most pious don't believe, don't really believe, in God. A nation of shopkeepers, OK, but they have clearly proven that shopkeepers are much more dangerous and, I guess the word is "vivid," shopkeepers can be much more vivid and bloodthirsty than the rest of the world. And yet the word "ardent," what could be less English? They are the least human people on the planet, I have come to the conclusion. They seem to me to be an enormous, absurd play. Everyone pretending. Everyone in a big Dickens play.

JF: Dickens didn't write plays.

OKM: Exactly. [Laughs]

JF: Does Australia not count as an island, by your terms, because it has the bush? Because it has frontiers? Where does a frontier start?

OKM: I find it interesting that you should choose that word.

"Frontier." Because there are no frontiers anymore. Nobody believes in outer space. There is no frontier in America anymore, either, which is interesting. Sanjania was once on the frontier. I will say one thing, there is one feature of the island, everyone stays on the borders, on the sea. Very few people live in the mountains in the centre. And so the mountains are the frontier.

JF: So the frontier is interior?

OKM: Exactly.

JF: And this is a feature of Sanjanian literature?

OKM: I think perhaps it is not only Sanjania that has the limit inside. I think it is also perhaps Japan. I think it is also any decent novel or story. The interior is infinite, you know. The frontier, we have seen, it ends. Where is the centre? Where is the core? That will go on forever.

JF: Do you feel this applies to you personally as well?

OKM: I am my own country. I want to be my own country.

JF: How has your own country responded to your work, and to all your successes, like the win at the Iveys last year?

OKM: We have an expression in Sanjania: You don't have to keep crabs in a bucket down. Because every time a crab tries to escape from a bucket, the ones behind pull her back. I think you can tell what I'm trying to say. My Sanjanian reviewers often start with trying to explain why I get so much attention. It doesn't help that I haven't lived there for a decade now.

JF: The expression in New York is "cutting down the tall poppy."

OKM: I think everywhere in the world has a saying on the theme. The exact same words I just used, the crabs in the bucket, I know are used in the Southern States. I wonder if the same thing happens here in Canada? It must.

JF: All the international attention must be nice, though.

OKM: It is so wonderful, such a fantasy realized, that it's just confusing. In America, I am turned into something in between a *de facto* diplomat and a travel agent. It is quite clear that I am the introduction to Sanjania for all of my readers, and no one could be less representative of anything Sanjanian than myself. That is exactly what I don't do. I don't represent.

JF: And the English?

OKM: The English relationship to books from their previous colonies, in my experience, is, again, gargoylish. Like a performer overacting. I think most of them are just impressed we can write at all. Like dogs playing poker, it's not whether we win or lose really. My image of the English comes down to a London-born fellow I knew in Paris: he ate spaghetti on toast. I watched him do it. That was Italian food to him. I believe that that's how the British are reading Sanjanian books, if you know what I mean.

JF: Why haven't you returned to Sanjania in so long?

OKM: I love where I'm living now.

JF: Prince Edward Island?

OKM: New York. You know, I was born on Sanjania's Lower East Side, and somehow I've managed, despite trying to avoid it as much as possible, to find myself living again on the Lower East Side. [Laughs]

JF: And Manhattan is an island.

OKM: Exactly. I'm always aware of the sea there.

BIOGRAPHICAL NOTES

Wherever possible, authors have provided their own biographies. I am indebted to Goodfriday Forster and Mary Wellings for their aid in compiling the others. — S.M.

JULIAN BACK, 1863?–1921

During the 1880s and '90s, Julian Back wrote over twenty melos for various theatre companies in Port Hope, and only began to write fiction when he retired from city life in 1903 for a small village on the East shore. As is so often the case with early Sanjanian writers, he left no trace of himself other than his works. One of the few Tayler House authors who did not live in the city, Back sent his manuscripts by geevee to Samuel Tayler, who published over forty Professor Saintfrancis stories, including eight novella-length works. It was the most popular crime serial of its day, converted into dozens of plays and even an opera. Professor Saintfrancis was so popular that he survived his author by decades; at least a dozen writers stole the character for unattributed imitations or cameos.

ARCADIO COLE, 1891–1926
The twelfth son of a fishing family from the isolated North side cove of Seachain, Arcadio Cole attended King's College Secondary School on full scholarship from 1905 to 1910. He was granted a post at the Ministry of Mines after his education, and remained in that position until 1914. He was the third man to enlist for the King's Sanjanian Rifles at the outbreak of the war in Africa. He died in a fishing accident while visiting Seachain, leaving a wife and one son, Sherlock, who would later become the first Chair of the Literature Department at Port Hope University.

SHERLOCK COLE was born in Port Hope in 1920. After earning a degree from Oxford, he joined the RAF in 1943, flying over thirty-five missions as the navigator on a Lancaster bomber. He returned to London after the war and worked as a literary journalist and lecturer until his return to Sanjania in the 1950s, where he taught at King's College Secondary School and edited the *Trumpet Book Review*. After Independence, he became the first Chair of the Literature Department at Port Hope University. His ten books include *Arcadio*, a biography of his father, and *Gin and Brandy*, the first postcolonial Sanjanian criticism. A stray bullet from a party of drunken soldiers near his apartment on the Catchlands killed him during the Biddy crackdowns in 1967.

CATO "SANDY" DEKKERMAN has had a rich, colourful career (so far) dabbling in all forms of the narrative arts. Besides fiction, he has published feature articles in mainstream magazines, performed stand-up comedy based on his Sanjanian childhood, and produced plays, television programs and movies. As director of the feature film based on "A Wedding in Restitution," he won the Good Angel for Best Direction from the Sanjanian Film Institute in 1992, and was nominated for best director at six international film festivals during the following two years. Sandy's current centre of operations is Santa Monica, California.

OCTAVIA DICKENS, currently the Boggs Professor of Rhetoric at SUNY, Buffalo, has published extensively on philology and postmodernism, with particular attention to poststructuralist theory and its import on dialect studies. Her most recent book is *Tongues of Fire: Language and Displacement in Sanjanian Writing.*

F. R. FISHER, NO DATES

"The Destruction of Marlyebone, the Private King" as well as sixty-three other tales have been ascribed to F. R. Fisher (or variants like F. Fisher or F. R. Fisherman) in the rolls of authors at the Tayler House. However, as Trampasano has noted in *A Tour of the Tayler House*, "we know more about the biographies of Sophocles, Euripides and Aeschylus than we know about the lives of these men and women." Fisher mentions as an aside in his story "Killer Candel" that he once worked in a distillery, although the comment may be in jest. All else is surmise. For the majority of the Tayler House authors who, like Fisher, only wrote occasional pieces, we cannot clearly identify a Christian name, date of birth or even, sometimes, gender. Fisher was one of the more prolific writers of the group: he produced his sixty-four tales in under two and a half years.

CHARITY GURTON, one of Sanjania's leading novelists, short story writers and cultural commentators, teaches creative writing at Bard College in Annandale-on-Hudson, New York.

MARCEL HENRI is a writer, editor and broadcaster in Toronto, Canada, where he is working towards a Doctorate in English Literature at York University, applying game theory to the history of literary reception. An active fundraiser and organizer in the Sanjanian-Canadian Society, he is currently at work on an entire collection of reviews of major works of literature from the point of view of their marginal characters. The working title is *Full Disclosure.* Stories unrelated to this project have been published in *NYB*, *The Summer Quarterly*, and *Sanjancan: An Anthology*.

CAESAR HILL lives in London, England.

After receiving degrees from Port Hope University, Harvard University and the University of London, TRINITY HOPPS returned to Sanjania, where she has been employed as a civil engineer in the SIS for nearly a decade. Her short fiction has been published in *The Sanjanian Trumpet*, *International Eye*, *The Urban Commission*, *Esplanade*, and other journals in Sanjania and abroad. Her story "Under the Skin" has been previously collected in *Islands unto Ourselves: Stories from the Lives of Sanjanian Women*. Under her editorship, a collection of essays on post-Little government in Sanjania, *When the World's on Fire*, won the Prix Astral in 2002. Her first novel, *An Obsession with Indirection*, is due out in March 2008 with Yellow Ribbon Press. She is the granddaughter of George Jankin Lee.

AUGUSTUS P. JENKINS, 1904–1936
Registered as a resident of the South coast town of Sparrow Cove, Augustus Jenkins moved to Port Hope in 1919 for work hauling cargo. He quickly became involved in the Sanjan Port Union Authority (SPUA), rising eventually to vice-secretary of

information. His involvement in the destruction of the *Walker* has been hotly disputed, but we are sure at least of his presence at the ship's sinking. Charged with sedition, he died from tuberculosis in prison before the case came to trial.

LEONARD KING, 1932–

The author of six volumes of poetry, three collections of short stories and over fourteen novels, including *Melody* and the prize-winning *Nocturnal Lamentation*, Leonard King has been identified as among Sanjania's leading creators, and has been frequently nominated for the Nobel Prize for Literature. Frederick Christopher recently wrote about him: "King is the lotus flower of our reading, just as lovely in youth, maturity and old age." He spends half the year in Port Hope, and the other in London, much like the swallows.

OCTAVIA KITTEREDGE-MANN is an essayist and novelist whose works include *Apples and Oranges* and *The End of the Beach*. She currently lives and works in New York City.

GEORGE JANKIN LEE, 1896–1936

A productive, consistent and longstanding author of the Tayler House and later *The Trumpet*, Jankin Lee wrote a hundred thirty-six major and minor pieces before his death at the age of forty from complications brought on by an opium binge. Born into a prosperous middle-class family, with a father who held qualifications to practice maritime law on the colony and a mother who patronized the theatrical scene, Lee developed his lifelong love of the performing arts from an early age. He wrote in one of his voluminous letters to his mother that his only regret in life was never taking the stage. An assiduous spectator and participant in Port Hope theatrical and operatic circles nonetheless, Lee kept a diary which remains the principal record of the Scene at its height. He also produced an important monograph on the subject of "Tattoos Among Sanjan Sailors and Tavern Keepers." Many of his works were "recreations," or reworkings of popular dramatic performances, although his original titles were the only ones to which he was willing to give his own name. When working for *The Trumpet*, he signed himself as "The Beloved Janlee."

CAMDEN MAHONE, 1881–1963

From 1901 to 1923, Camden Mahone, or perhaps a group of writers working together under that name (as Trampasano argues), wrote many of the popular Christian narrative pamphlets for the Tayler House, always about redeemed thieves and prostitutes. The dates are taken from the birth and death records of the mercer Camden Mahone, whom scholars generally assumed to be the same person as the Tayler House writer. Trampasano published his incendiary article "The Scandal of Identity in Camden Mahone" in the Spring 2004 issue of *Sanjan Writing*, but a panel session at the 2005 conference of the Sanjanian English Professors Association, held in Jacks, disputed his findings. Their proceedings have yet to be published.

STEPHEN MARCHE is a novelist and scholar living in New York. His novel, *Raymond and Hannah*, was published internationally in 2005. He is currently a Pforzheimer Fellow at City College, New York.

ELIZABETH RUSHTON, 1913–1965

During her lifetime, only three of Elizabeth Rushton's works, "The Night," "Open Umbrella," and "Two Stories About the Abandon Tree," found homes, all but the last in British journals.

The political struggles of the 1930s drove her to Whitesmoke on the West shore, where she hid from the political turmoil of the struggles for Independence and where she eventually married and had children, never writing again.

IRA RUSHTON, 1913–1958
Actor, writer and revolutionary Ira Rushton's political pieces against the Colonial office earned him the status of Sanjanian hero as early as 1954. He survived to write about the Rumourstown riots, the Portlands riots and the Hope Mall Massacre. During his periodic stretches of imprisonment for sedition, unable to produce drama, he wrote fiction. Clandestinely supportive prison guards smuggled his stories out to the handbill presses when they were open, or directly to the streets when the presses were closed. He died in Simpson Street Gaol. Ira Rushton Square stands at the second intersection of the Sanjanian National Esplanade in Port Hope.

BLESSED SHIRLEY, 1897–1952, introduced the new era of the "clean style" to Sanjanian writing. He produced six novels and two short fiction collections within the first half-decade of his twenties, and founded Sanjania's first modernist journal, *The Real Story*, with the financial support of his father, who owned a chain of shoe stores. After the collapse of the journal and his failure to find a publisher for his last three books, he abandoned fiction and took a government post as tax collector along the West Coast, which he held until his death.

ARCADIO SKELTON lectures in English and Comparative Literature at the University of Sussex.

MORLEY STRAIGHTS, 1890–1964
The theorist and chief exemplar of the "clean school" or "clean style" after Shirley, Straights was almost as famous for the "coded" novels and short stories he wrote after Independence. He began writing when he retired from clerk life at the age of sixty. In 1964, the carpenter troops took him from his home in Port Hope and murdered him.

CORNELIA TRISTANOS, 1899–1986
Educated at King's College School and later Saint Magdalene's College, Cornelia Tristanos held the position of Literary Director for the Sanjanian branch of the SPCK from 1934 to 1951, overseeing the production and dissemination of Christian literature on the island. First published in the *Trumpet Cove Supplement*, "The Christbird" was the winner of the *Sanjanian Trumpet*'s annual story contest for 1953. Tristanos's *Birds and Rest*, in which "The Christbird" was collected into book form, won the Beck Prize two years later. After Independence, Tristanos moved with her daughters to London, and later New York, where she was active in a number of literary and scholarly societies. Her only other book was also a collection of short fiction, *Clever Fabulisms to Remind the Loving Heart of Home*.

RICHARD WILLIAMS, Senior Lecturer in the Humanities, Port Hope University, has authored or edited five volumes relating to Sanjanian literature during the political upheavals of the thirties, forties, fifties and sixties. He is currently at work on a biography of Blessed Shirley.

ACKNOWLEDGEMENTS

My base during the production of this volume was the National Library and Archives of Sanjania in Port Hope, where I was fortunate enough to receive a fellowship in 2000 from the Sanjanian Literary and Cultural Committee. I researched the anthology in the main circle chamber of the library, where the large iron printing press from the Tayler House is on display, and the circumference of the room is lined with the woolen binding-strings of early pamphlets. It was an ideal place to work on this material mostly because the colleagues I met there were invaluable, instantly supplying details of literary and historical fact which would have taken me weeks to research on my own, and offering gentle insight into the larger questions of the book as a whole. In particular, I would like to thank Goodfriday Forster and Mary Wellings, who helped me compile the appendix of criticism and the biographical notes, and Leonard King, who gave me extensive notes on my introduction. I also need to thank everyone at the NLAS who brought me stories and lent me books: Braithwaite Currand, Marcus Lee, Lavinia Harriston, James MacInnes, Lavinia Martin and Maxim Reich.

On a more personal and therefore necessarily more cryptic note, I have to thank Lavinia for the frangipani buttercups, which arrived at the exact moment I needed them most; Marcus and James for "slog heap work" and "cricket statistics"; and the other Lavinia for everything else that this book was missing. I would also like to thank Daniel Handler for easing my transition from Port Hope to New York, Nicole Winstanley for our fabulous conversations over beer at the Impossible Island in Toronto, Geoff Kloske for showing me the good spots along the Mall in Sanjania and introducing me to new neighbourhoods, and Sam Potts, whose images of the place have now fused with my own memories.

The editor and publisher would also like to thank the following for permission to publish copyrighted material: The Hammond Press, London, for "Sufferance Row" by Blessed Shirley, from *The Complete Stories of Blessed Shirley*, and "An Old Man Mourns for His Blind Daughter" by Morley Straights, from *Scarlet and Cash*; The Sanjanian Publishers, Port Hope, for "Flotsam and Jetsam" by Caesar Hill, from *London Road Stories*, and "The End of the Beach" by Octavia Kitteredge-Mann, from *The End of the Beach*; The Blossoming Tree Press, Port Hope, for "Two Stories About the Abandon Tree" by Elizabeth Rushton, from *The Night and Other Stories*; Fordham, Golding & Co., London, for "The Master's Dog" by Augustus P. Jenkins, from *The Master's Dog and Other Stories*, and "Men" by Charity Gurton; Leonard King for "To Be Read at the Hour of Independence" and "Histories of Aenea"; Trinity Hopps for "Under the Skin"; Cato Dekkerman for "A Wedding in Restitution"; Marcel Henri for "The Man Friday's Review of *Robinson Crusoe*."

ABOUT THE AUTHOR

Stephen Marche's first novel, *Raymond and Hannah*, was released in 2005 to critical acclaim. He is currently a Pforzheimer Fellow at City College, New York.